A Killing in Costumes

Also available by Zac Bissonnette

The Great Beanie Baby Bubble: Mass Delusion and the Dark Side of Cute

A Killing in Costumes

A HOLLYWOOD TREASURES MYSTERY

Zac Bissonnette

NEW YORK

This is a work of fiction. All of the names, characters, organizations, places and events portrayed in this novel are either products of the author's imagination or are used fictitiously. Any resemblance to real or actual events, locales, or persons, living or dead, is entirely coincidental.

Published in the United States by Crooked Lane Books, an imprint of The Quick Brown Fox & Company LLC.

Crooked Lane Books and its logo are trademarks of The Quick Brown Fox & Company LLC.

Library of Congress Catalog-in-Publication data available upon request.

ISBN (hardcover): 978-1-63910-086-6
ISBN (ebook): 978-1-63910-087-3

Cover design by Chris Andrews / Rush Agency

Printed in the United States.

www.crookedlanebooks.com

Crooked Lane Books
34 West 27th St., 10th Floor
New York, NY 10001

First Edition: August 2022

10 9 8 7 6 5 4 3 2 1

For Ryan

Cindy Cooper stared at the computer screen, wincing at the red number at the bottom of her accounting sheet: –$85,000.

Her heart pounded, pumping anxiety through her chest. Selling her Los Angeles financial planning business to move to Palm Springs was supposed to be an escape from a career spent panicking over numbers on spreadsheets. But now, too much money was going out, and not enough was coming in. She knew she'd have to cut her losses on the movie memorabilia store after the first hundred-thousand dollars. She did the math in her head: one month left before she needed to have a tough conversation about the future with her business partner, Jay Allan. Who was also her best friend. Who was also her ex-husband.

She looked up from the sea of red when she heard footsteps.

"Cindy?" Jay walked into the office, perky as ever.

She closed the laptop quickly. "Jay. What's wrong?"

He smiled. "Nothing, but I was about to ask you the same thing. You seem stressed." He crouched down on the floor next to her chair. "Tell me everything."

That was the problem, Cindy thought, with being in business with someone you had this much history with: he could read her like Farmer Hoggett could read Babe.

"Oh, I'm just . . . you know," Cindy said, stalling. "Thinking about the numbers."

"Is everything okay?"

Cindy hesitated. She loved Jay's innocence, his positive attitude. *She* was the worrier, and she didn't know what she'd do if they were both bogged down with anxiety. She and Jay had met in middle school, where they'd discovered a love of singing together. One of the best memories of Cindy's life was the forty-five-minute bus ride to a thrift shop in another county to get costumes for a talent show so their classmates wouldn't tease them for wearing hand-me-downs they recognized. Dressed in the hip outfits Jay put together at Goodwill, they'd won the show—surprising no one more than themselves. It had been the beginning of a beautiful friendship and a series of shared dreams. Now she needed to keep their latest dream alive, and Jay panicking wouldn't help.

"Yes, everything is fine," she said, clearing her throat to hide the tremble in her voice. "I'm just thinking about ways we could help boost sales."

Cindy could see Jay brighten immediately, his shoulders squaring back and his eyebrows lifting up to nearly clear his hairline. He loved marketing. He loved thinking about ways to bring people into their store—wowing them with his knowledge of Hollywood history and then convincing them they just *couldn't* go home without a lamp featured in multiple episodes of *The Golden Girls*. It worked. Just not often enough.

Jay talked excitedly about a marketing idea he'd had—local radio spots featuring a "Hollywood Treasure of the Day," with him and Cindy talking about a piece they had and how Palm Springs residents should stop by the store to make an offer. "Just think," he said. "We can do funny patter like Donny and Marie. It'll be like the old days: you and me, stars on the radio! Remember those commercials we did for the soap opera star cruise?"

He sang a few bars of the jingle, and Cindy's mind drifted back twenty years to the recording session for the commercials—back to when she and Jay were twenty-two years old. A hot, young, singing married couple playing a hot, young, singing married couple on a popular soap opera. They'd been on for two seasons, just enough to build the beginning of a fan base. Then they both came out as gay and got divorced. The press had been so cruel, and the advertisers, terrified of alienating anyone, demanded the producers remove the gay couple from the air, which they quickly did. She smiled softly despite herself. Painful as the end had been, the memories of their TV career were mostly nice now—nostalgia was a beautiful thing.

"Interesting," Cindy said, trying to sound noncommittal without letting him down. Cindy admired the blond hair that fell into his eyes boyishly as he talked about his big, creative idea—the only kind of idea he felt was worth excitement. At some point, she'd need to tell him they couldn't afford to keep spending so much on marketing. Soon. But not now. It was so hard to give Jay bad news.

"Interesting?" Jay said, popping one of the caffeine pills he seemed to go through like candy. "That's it? Come on, Cindy, do you like it? I think it would really get the word out."

Cindy touched her ear, trying to think of what to say. She was wearing her favorite earrings—a pair of emeralds once owned by Marlene Dietrich—and the reminder instantly made her feel a little better. Jay had saved for months to buy them as her wedding gift when she'd married Esther ten years ago. She saw Jay notice her touching them, felt the warmth and love in his toothy grin—it was almost enough to stave off the pangs of sorrow that came when anything reminded her of Esther. Almost.

She needed all of Jay's warmth and love now more than ever. The store had been a dream she'd had for years, first with Jay, and then with Esther. "One day," she and Esther had told each other, they'd move to Palm Springs full-time and sell movie memorabilia in an adorable little store. They'd talked about the idea during the commercial breaks on Turner Classic Movies—cuddled up with popcorn, fantasizing about one day owning a shop filled with props and costumes from the movies they loved and wanted to preserve for eternity. When Esther died, Cindy decided "one day" needed to be now—and so, a few years before her financial plan had dictated, she'd decided it was time to make the leap for a new career. Now the business wasn't working. And Esther wasn't here to help her figure out what to do.

She was saved from having to respond when the front door opened—their first visitor in hours. The stranger appeared to be in his fifties, full hair but all white, and wearing a well-cut baby-blue blazer and khakis over an ample stomach. Boat shoes and a skinny tie with whales. Very Palm Springs: conspicuous wealth, but clearly a man of leisure.

"Nice shop," the man said, running his hand along the surface of a dining room table used in a bunch of low budget, direct-to-VHS horror films in the '80s.

"Thank you," Jay said, walking toward him. "Welcome to Hooray for Hollywood Movie Memorabilia, our little slice of

Old Hollywood in a Palm Springs strip mall." He was smooth, practiced: this was why he was in charge of all their public outreach.

"What can we help you find today?" Cindy asked.

The man smiled. "Unfortunately, I'm not here to buy something." Cindy felt her heart sink. "But I may have an opportunity for you that's much more interesting."

"Color me intrigued," Cindy said, trying to keep the disappointment out of her voice. More interesting than money? Unlikely.

"It's a *chance* to make a lot of money," the man said.

Well, that was something, at least.

"Please," Jay said. "Pull up a chair."

"And not just *any* chair"—Cindy carried over a canvas director's chair—"but one that held Bette Davis's bottom on the set of *What Ever Happened to Baby Jane?*" It even said "Bette Davis" in big letters on the back, and the attached tag had a photo of Bette sitting in it, next to Joan Crawford in a similar chair. Both women were smiling, though media reports had established that their on-set rivalry was one of the most furious in Hollywood history.

"Not that I'm in the market for it, to be clear," the man said as he took a seat, "but how much is this chair?"

"Fifteen thousand dollars," Cindy said. "They made a miniseries about Bette and Joan's feud a couple years ago, which added to the legend. And, of course, increased the value."

She hoped.

The man whistled. "It's good to hear there's so much demand for this kind of stuff."

Jay ran into the office and returned with a few bottles of water from the mini fridge. The three of them sat around the horror movie table, still lightly stained with fake blood. Cindy had priced it at seven hundred and fifty dollars, but she was prepared to go lower if she didn't find a horror obsessive in the next month or two. Heck, maybe she'd even raise the price. She'd heard that sometimes worked in the antiques business: a piece no one wanted at a low price could find a whole new audience at a higher one.

"You were saying," Cindy said, "that it's good to hear there's so much demand for vintage Hollywood memorabilia. I'm curious what your interest in it is."

The man leaned back, steepling his hands over his stomach. "Are you familiar with an actress named Yana Tosh?"

"I don't think—" Jay said.

"Absolutely," Cindy said, cutting him off. She stared at Jay in disbelief. "How can you not know her?"

Jay shook his head. "You win this round."

Cindy grinned. They shared an encyclopedic knowledge of all things TV and film, and trying to "out-trivia" each other was a running game between them. "Yana Tosh played minor villains in dozens of films in the 1950s and early 1960s," Cindy said, looking at Jay. "A femme fatale. She was more sinister than your typical vixen, but, my God, she was *hot*." She rattled off a string of mostly forgotten movies from that period. "She retired by 1970, though, and nobody really knows what became of her."

"Actually," their visitor said, sounding smug, "somebody does know."

"And why do I have a feeling that somebody would be you?" asked Cindy.

"Ben Sinclair," he said, finally extending his hand for the two of them to shake in a firm, businessman-like grip. "Yana Tosh's financial advisor."

"Well, if she has a financial advisor, she's still alive," Jay said. "And I suppose she can't have done too badly with money."

"Not badly at all," Ben agreed. "She married a real estate mogul in 1969, retired from the industry, and lived a relatively quiet life. When he died fifteen years ago, she sold their other residences and has lived alone in Palm Springs ever since."

"Every day we learn about a new celebrity who has retired to Palm Springs," Cindy said. "Is she looking to buy some Hollywood treasures?"

"Quite the opposite," Ben said.

"Ah," Cindy said. "What kind of stuff does she have?"

Their 1950s phone—used in multiple episodes of *Mad Men*—rang, a shrill trilling sound, but soft enough to be endearing rather than annoying. Jay excused himself and ducked into the tiny office to answer it.

With the phone silenced, Ben continued. "I think it would be better if you come see for yourself. Yana saw a piece in the paper about your store and sent me over to see if you're any good." He looked around, eying the walls lined with movie posters and the showroom floor filled with furniture, accessories, and costumes, each piece with a tag identifying its price and connection with Hollywood history. He smiled. "You passed the test. She wants to see you."

"She saved things from her movies?"

"Oh, it's not props from movies *she* was in," Ben said. "It's memorabilia she bought—things that just scream 'Old Hollywood' and 'the star system' and 'Metro-Goldwyn-Mayer.' Think pieces of the quality and value of your Bette Davis chair. But *hundreds* of them. She put most of the collection together after she retired." He paused for effect. "With her husband's real estate fortune."

Reaching into his wallet, he extracted a business card and then retrieved from his jacket pocket an expensive-looking pen, a Montblanc that could have come straight off the set of *Poirot*. After scribbling on the back of the card, he handed it across the table to Cindy.

"Tomorrow at two PM," he said. "And be punctual. Yana goes to her aerobics class at four thirty. You'll love her, but she'll hate you for the rest of your life if you keep her waiting."

He left without waiting for a response. Cindy watched him go. The guy was arrogant, but she was too desperate to hold it against him. Twenty minutes ago, she'd been staring at numbers that promised her impending doom. Now, with one visitor, she might just have—if it was all he said it was—a chance at a deal that could save the business. And if it came together fast enough, she might never have to tell Jay how close they'd come to financial ruin.

By the time the door closed, she was already googling on her phone. Yana Tosh had been in more movies than she'd realized, from the late 1940s through the early 1960s, and then a smattering of TV appearances through the end of the decade, before disappearing into the sunset. After her husband's death in 2005, she'd come back for a few made-for-TV movies, including one Hallmark film where she'd played a mail carrier and sometime matchmaker. According to Wikipedia, tomorrow would be her ninetieth birthday.

She was still absorbed in Yana's bio when she heard Jay say her name. "Hello?" he said, sounding slightly annoyed. "Third try here."

"Sorry," she said. "What?"

"A gift," he said. "We need to bring Yana a gift. Obviously. But what does one bring to a 1950s movie vixen?" He gestured to the store.

Cindy nodded, liking the way he was thinking. She got up and walked around, picking up a vase from Barbra Streisand's *A Star is Born* before setting it down. Jay did the same thing with a rotary phone used by Raymond Burr on *Perry Mason*. After five minutes, nothing seemed quite right. The Bette Davis chair would, of course, be a showstopper, but Cindy wasn't about to let such an expensive piece leave their store without some guaranteed revenue coming in. Besides, would Yana really want a chair of such significance if she was trying to offload her collection? They wanted something to make her smile—not something she could turn around and sell if she didn't end up working with them.

Jay pecked away at his phone, then walked over and picked up an Academy Award statue—or, what looked like an Academy Award statue, but was, to the right buyer, something even more special: a *fake* Academy Award statue used in "How to Dial a Murder," a 1978 *Columbo* episode guest starring Nicol Williamson. "Yana once appeared on an episode of *Columbo*."

"I remember that episode," Cindy said.

"Yeah, it was a good one. What if we bring her the Academy Awards statue?"

Cindy furrowed her forehead. "You want to bring an actress a fake Academy Award as a gift, and you think that'll make her like us?"

Jay grinned, his face full of mischief. Cindy couldn't help but notice once again how handsome he was, as good a catch as he'd ever been. He had prominent cheekbones from regular exercise and a low-carb diet, and his slight build went well with his tailored seersucker suit, complete with silver pocket square and a turquoise bow tie. Truth was, even though they had been divorced for almost twenty years, she was still as madly in love with him now. Just in a different way.

"So, we give her the award," Jay said, excitement growing in his voice, "and tell her we think she deserved a real one for *Columbo*, but all we have is a fake one from *Columbo*."

"She'll laugh at us," Cindy said skeptically.

"Exactly!" Jay said. "We'll make her laugh. She'll like us—and realize we already have such an amazing collection that we can bring her something that special on such short notice. It'll give us instant credibility. And then, we swoop in with the sales pitch. The collection will be ours. It'll be just that simple."

"Just that simple," Cindy repeated.

Jay felt optimistic—cautiously optimistic, but optimistic nonetheless—as he and Cindy climbed into her 1992 Ford Explorer to drive over to Yana's house. A few curious passersby had stopped in to browse that morning, and he'd sold them a couple of old movie posters from their 50-dollars-each, three-for-a-hundred bin.

It was clear the bin was going to be a hit, even if sales hadn't been as great as he'd hoped so far. People were always surprised at how affordable huge old movie posters were. For the price of a restaurant meal, you could have an original poster, featuring stars like Marilyn Monroe or Cary Grant, from the 1950s onward.

He leaned back against the leather seat, bracing for dear life, as Cindy pulled out onto the busy main road. She was a good driver but drove a lot faster than Jay ever did. Normally an Explorer would be the most boring car in the world, but this one was special. It had been used in the original *Jurassic Park* movie and still had the famous green and yellow paint, along with the theme park logo on the hood. Cindy had paid $40,000 for it a year ago, but the price was worth it, as were the endless trips to the garage to fix its frequent maladies. It was the best advertising Hooray for Hollywood could ask for.

Cindy slammed her palm on the steering wheel. "I hate traffic!" she cried. Jay winced—not a good sign. They had left plenty of time left to get to Yana's house for the two o'clock meeting, and it wasn't like Cindy to complain, which meant that something else was on her mind. She'd seemed down lately. Of course, that was understandable after watching her wife, Esther, succumb to cancer a year earlier. Cindy never wanted to talk about it. So Jay focused on what he could do: make the store amazing so she could worry about the business as little as possible—which was still a lot.

Luckily, the store was in good hands in good hands in their absence, manned by their longtime friend, Mary Rawlings. Mary was eighty-five now and had been their personal assistant long ago, during their soap opera days. When Jay and Cindy had hatched the plan for Hooray for Hollywood, there was clearly only one thing for Mary to do: come out of her southern Florida retirement, move to Palm Springs, and work the register.

"I meant to tell you," Jay said. "That phone call we got yesterday when Ben Sinclair was visiting was from a guy named Dylan Redman. He runs the entertainment memorabilia department at Cypress Auctions."

"Cypress Auctions?" Cindy said. "That's big time. What'd he want?"

"He read about the store in the paper. He wanted to wish us luck, maybe see if there might be an opportunity to work together. Oh, and he happens to be in Palm Springs this week. We can go meet with him at his hotel after we find out what Yana has to offer us."

"I wonder what his angle is," Cindy said, finally moving the Explorer forward again.

"Why does everyone have to have an angle?" Jay asked.

Cindy smiled. "This is *business*, Jay. Everybody is working a scheme. It's not all about art and joy and jazz hands and leg kicks like Las Vegas."

Jay sighed, remembering how little joy there had been in his last few months in Sin City. He'd been in Vegas for nearly two decades after he and Cindy had split up, playing in cocktail lounges, using his hammy, showy piano skills and Elvis impersonations to eke out a living. It had been fun. Then, a year ago, it had become very *not* fun when his boyfriend of five years had dumped him, saying he needed to be alone. A few weeks later, Jay had found out he'd moved in with Jay's bass player and then hired the bass player to start a competing act, using the savings he'd stolen from Jay as his start-up capital. Jay had barely been able to listen to a bass line since, let alone hire a new player to keep his own act going. Cindy's call with the idea of opening a movie store had been a lifeline. He straightened his red-and-white-tablecloth-patterned bow tie, a nervous habit. "Well, I'm not sure the Cypress guy had an angle. He seemed nice."

Now Cindy was speeding along, leaning over the steering wheel like a racehorse jockey. "No one is nice," she said. "Nice people don't go into the collectibles business."

"What about us?" Jay said. "We're nice."

Cindy smiled. "We are the exception," she said. "And I can be cutthroat when I need to be. But you're nice. That's why you're handling the collectibles, and I'm handling the business." She patted him gently on the leg, just to make sure he knew she was joking. *Mostly* joking, Jay thought.

Ten minutes later, they arrived at Yana Tosh's house, right on time. It was the kind of Palm Springs getaway Jay would have expected from Barbra Streisand, not a second-tier character actress. A short driveway led to a large, flat-roofed ranch, its sprawl making up for the lack of a second floor. Jay had read that Palm Springs had ordinances that mostly banned two-floor homes, and the result was a flat paradise that didn't look quite like any other city. The modernist style reeked of martinis and mood music. Jay could almost hear the din of the half century of pool parties Yana must have hosted in the backyard.

The sun was sweltering as they walked to the door.

Cindy reached for the doorbell, but Jay stopped her. He hated doorbells—they made him feel like he was summoning someone. He rapped gently against the uber-chic, mid-century teal door. Just touching it made Jay feel like a member of the Rat Pack.

"Coming," came a man's voice. A few seconds later, the same voice said, "Who is it?" The tone was pleasant, but the door remained closed.

"Jay Allan and Cindy Cooper," Jay said. "With Hooray for Hollywood Movie Memorabilia." He smiled to himself, feeling very professional. What had been a dream for twenty years was now so very, very real.

"What are you looking for?" The voice sounded less friendly now.

"Ben Sinclair came into our store yesterday," Cindy said. "We have an appointment to look at the, uh—collection."

Just then, there was another voice, clearly a woman's, from inside, deep and husky and full of power. "Let them in, Warren, for goodness sake."

The door opened, and Jay saw an elderly woman, somehow still with ramrod straight posture, perfectly made up, with a sparkly pink top over black leggings and a full head of fluffy, coiffed white hair. It took Jay a second to realize it was a wig, and then only an instant more to know that this was Yana Tosh: the picture of Hollywood elegance, even if she hadn't been near a major movie set in half a century.

The man, half hidden by the door, younger and about six feet tall, had none of Yana's presence. He was dressed in unseasonably warm jeans and an untucked black button-down with the sleeves rolled up. It wasn't quite long enough to hide his beer gut. "You didn't tell me you were expecting visitors, Mother."

"I don't have to tell you anything," she snapped, like a cat playing with a toy—no real bite. She gazed at Jay and Cindy as if taking their measure, clearly used to sorting out who belonged and who didn't. "My apologies," she said finally, extending a hand to each of them. Apparently they'd passed that first test. "I'm Yana Tosh. And this is my son, Warren Limon." Cindy opened her mouth, but Yana cut her off. "I know who you two are," she said. "And Jay, I remember your act from Las Vegas—saw it a few times. Wonderful stuff, simply marvelous!"

"Thank you," Jay said. "You've made my day by remembering it." And it was true: she had. Playing to lounge crowds of loud-talking drunk tourists had taken its toll on his ego as a performer, and it was exciting to meet someone who actually remembered his show.

The former star waved her hand, which was thin and slightly shaky, with almost as many gemstone rings as liver spots. "Oh, the false modesty," she said. "It's quite endearing. When I read about your store in the paper, I sent Ben over right away, to see if we should meet. He was impressed, and so here we are."

"It's really a joy to meet you, Ms. Tosh," Cindy said.

"Yana," the former star said. "Please call me Yana."

Cindy smiled. "Yana, it is. And I'm so glad you saw the newspaper piece. Jay really hustled to get us that coverage. I've been such a fan—for decades. I mean, no one played evil the way you did. No one. The way you played that temptress who seduced married police officers for her mob boss lover? Iconic."

Yana batted her eyes. Still charismatic and arresting—and loving the attention. "Yes," she agreed. "It was a wonderful little run I had, wasn't it? God, it's been so long. But when I'm reminded of those days, sometimes it feels like I was just on a set with Omar Sharif, or battling it out with Janet Leigh for a part in the next Hitchcock picture." She fluffed the wig. Another mannerism of a woman who'd come of age under the lighting of a soundstage, Jay thought. He was getting serious Eartha Kitt vibes—fabulous, but more than a little scary.

"Please come in and let me show you some things," Yana continued. "Ben will be back in a few minutes. He ran out to get a bottle of champagne."

"Champagne?" Her son's expression was disapproving.

"Yes, Warren," Yana said, her voice dripping with contempt—her moods seemed to swing from flirtatious to bullying, with little in between. "Champagne. In case we make a deal here and have something to celebrate. We could toast, even. Like people do when they're happy."

Jay exchanged a knowing glance with Cindy—a look that had been developed over their decades-long relationship. *What have we gotten ourselves into?*

Yana looked back at them. "May I show you the collection?"

"It would be an honor," Jay said. "But first, we'd like to present you with a small gift—a little token of what we hope will be a long friendship." With a flourish, he pulled out the *Columbo* statue he'd been hiding in his vintage plaid summer jacket and presented it to her. He used the line he'd planned about the Academy Award.

Sure enough, Yana laughed. "I adore this," she said. "Thank you so much! And I can't believe you remember my *Columbo* episode. It was one of my favorite TV shows." She paused. "One of the last things I did before I retired. What a gem Peter Falk was—exactly like you'd hope. Brilliant and warm, and what a terrific character he created. I do wonder, if I'd stayed in the business, whether I could've done my own mystery show." She paused, as if lost in a memory. "God, you get to be my age and everything reminds you of a regret." She brightened, mercurial as the sun emerging from behind a cloud. "But what fun is that? I must be cheerful! I have a new trophy, and it's a beautiful one."

"Will you keep it with your other trophies?" Cindy asked.

Yana smiled. "Oh, I sold all of those decades ago."

"*Sold* them?" Jay asked, unable to disguise his shock.

Yana nodded. "I don't care about my own accolades and trophies—those are just gifts. But I wanted to have a connection to the movies themselves. So, before I was married, I sold the trophies and bought more costumes, and I've never once regretted it. Helped to have a husband as rich as Rockefeller. I don't need trophies to remember the ceremonies." She tapped her head. "I was there! But the costumes—*those* are part of the great art form that was mid-century cinema. Now, come, let me show you the collection."

"Smart plan," Cindy said.

With Warren trailing behind, Jay and Cindy followed Yana back through the house, which was sparsely furnished in modernist style. There were large abstract paintings on the walls, a baby grand piano in the living room, and a deep, gray, plush carpet. It was, Jay thought, the epitome of tasteful, upper-class senior citizen—no hints of the danger he associated with the characters Yana had played.

They made their way into Yana's bedroom, which was similarly tasteful, if more grandmotherly. A large seascape portrait hung over the bed, which was covered with a baby-blue comforter and floral throw pillows. A soap opera was playing on a large flat screen television.

"Days of Our Lives," Cindy said, nodding toward the TV. "You're a lady with taste."

"They'll cancel it one of these days," Yana said.

"Really?" Cindy said.

"Oh, sure. It's still popular, but I'm at the younger end of their viewership, and advertisers are wasting their time because old folks don't buy anything. We're in selling mode. They'll replace it with some cheap, unscripted dreck that kids like—probably a dating show where the people never meet or even talk to each other. And speaking of selling mode, may I introduce you to my walk-in closet?"

She pointed toward a pair of French doors. Jay watched as Cindy pushed them open and the average-sized bedroom opened into a closet the size of four bedrooms.

Cindy's eyes widened, and Yana laughed. "Years ago," she said, "I had the closet expanded. One only needs one bed, but one can never have too many costumes."

"I'm writing that down," Cindy said. "It will be a perfect line to give the press when we're promoting your sale."

"And perfect for the promotional video we'll make," Jay agreed. One of Cindy's sales tactics, she'd told him, was to always talk as though the deal were a foregone conclusion. Rather than saying *if* we make a deal to handle your collection, discuss details of how it *will* work.

The four of them walked in, and Jay imagined that it was like entering a storage area at MGM in the 1950s. That made sense because most of the collection probably had been in MGM storage in the 1950s. A gold-framed, full-length mirror and multiple large movie posters lined the walls. There were a few classics, like *The Caine Mutiny* and *Meet Me in St. Louis*, but many of the movies were so obscure even Jay hadn't heard of them.

"I chose posters I liked"—Yana shrugged, as if reading his mind—"and that were particularly interesting to me. The most famous movies, the posters were everywhere for years, so I got bored with them. But a flop with beautiful art? *That's* what I want in my sanctuary."

"Sanctuary is exactly the way I'd describe this room," Jay agreed. "As Goethe said, 'Collectors are happy people.'"

Yana looked impressed. "Very true."

"There's a sense of purpose that comes from accumulating and curating objects you love," Jay went on. "Looking at them always has a way of making your troubles go away, don't you think?"

"Oh, most definitely." Yana's tone seemed softer now, and Jay was surprised to see Cindy glaring at him.

Oops. If he wasn't careful, he might talk their prospective seller out of selling. He quickly shut up and listened in rapt attention as Yana spent the next hour showing them highlights from her collection: one-of-a-kind, six-figure costumes from some of the most important movies of all time. There was a green beret worn by John Wayne in *The Green Berets*, a cape worn by Elizabeth Taylor in *Cleopatra*, Vivien Leigh's straw hat from *Gone with the Wind*, and dozens of other pieces. Best of all, there was a filing cabinet that contained impeccable documentation for the history of each piece: photos of it in the film, a letter of authenticity from the previous owner—usually a star or studio employee—and detailed notes describing its history, from its life on the film set until the time it entered Yana's sanctuary. That filing cabinet made the collection much more valuable because it removed all doubts about authenticity.

"How did you find all these pieces?" Jay asked.

Yana laughed. "I got a reputation. I started seeking them out—buying them at estate sales, calling on lawyers when people died, that kind of thing. This was back when nobody else was buying the stuff, of course."

"Nobody wanted it?" Jay asked.

Yana shook her head. "Classic film wasn't yet a thing. It was popular entertainment—meant to be shown in a theater and enjoyed and never thought about again. They weren't special to anyone at the time—it was just used clothing. But to *me*, they were like Michelangelo paintings or first drafts of a Hemingway novel. When people found out I was buying pieces, word spread. People called me, and I bought everything they had. Didn't even spend much on it in the beginning. The closet renovation cost more than I'd spent on the whole collection, until the '80s. That's when prices started rising. And I kept buying."

She walked over to a dresser and pulled out a plastic bag with a pair of what looked to be boxer shorts with American flags on them. "Sylvester Stallone wore these in *Rocky*," she said. "I paid twenty-five thousand dollars for them."

"Still a bargain," Cindy said.

Yana nodded. "That's what I'm hoping."

"What has you deciding to sell now?" Jay asked.

Warren, quiet and seemingly uninterested until now, looked up. "I'm not necessarily opposed to getting rid of this stuff, but—"

"It is not *stuff*," Yana snapped, bristling. "It is treasure."

Warren shrugged guiltily. "I didn't mean it like that. I just know how much joy it gives you."

Why was her son trying to talk her out of selling? Usually, they dealt with the opposite dynamic.

"I am ninety years old," Yana said, cutting him off.

"Happy birthday, by the way" Jay said. He hadn't wanted to bring up a lady's birthday but since she'd already gone there, he decided it was okay.

"Who told you?" Her eyes were piercing.

"I—we—I was reading about you on the internet."

She softened. "Of course," she said. "I always forget how easily people can find things out now. It's a shame my son couldn't have looked it up! He could've gotten me a gift or at least a card, or even just extended a kind greeting."

"I'm sorry, Mother," Warren stammered. "I've just been distracted. I can't believe I forgot."

Cindy looked at Yana, trying to smooth past the hiccup. "You were saying? About why you want to sell?"

Yana's face was serious. "My health is good right now, but who knows how long that will last? Such things can deteriorate quickly, and I want all decisions made while I'm around and capable of making them. I want to know how much each piece sells for, and to meet with the people who buy them. I want to tell them how much these things meant to me, and find out how these movies have touched their lives. I need to make sure they know that those of us who hoard history aren't just collectors. We're caretakers, preserving cultural heritage for eternity. It's a sacred thing, don't you think?"

"I've never heard it expressed so well," Jay said.

Yana smiled. "I've thought about it a lot. And given that speech a few times. I'm good at delivering lines."

"I can assure you," Cindy said, "that Jay and I, and Hooray for Hollywood, feel the same way. Handling the sale of your collection would be the honor of a lifetime, and I know that we'll do you proud."

"Well," Yana said, suddenly less wistful, "Cypress Auctions was just here. They had a whole presentation. A mock catalog, complete with photos of me from my old movies—looking evil and alluring, with that long flowing hair I had back then. They had a—what did they call it?" She paused, searching for the word, and her face lit up with obvious pride when she remembered it. "A PowerPoint presentation! Some kind of new technology, I guess."

Jay felt his heart pound in his chest. Cindy had been right all along: The nice man from Cypress who'd called did have an agenda. Clearly, he was in Palm Springs competing with them for the Yana Tosh collection. His mind was still scrambling for a response when he heard Cindy say smoothly, "We didn't have time for a presentation, I'm afraid. We just found out about this yesterday. But if you need one, we can get you something quick."

Yana dismissed the offer with a wave. "Oh, it wasn't just that they'd done a presentation," she said. "It was the content. Cypress has an email list of forty thousand people who've bought costumes from them in the past. How many do you have?"

Neither Jay nor Cindy said anything. Jay had never been so conscious of silence in his life, how it could eat up the space in a room.

After a few seconds, Cindy spoke up. "We don't have that many email addresses," she admitted. "We're just starting out. But we have something more valuable: we care. Cypress

Auctions is a public company, and that means they care about only one thing—their shareholders. Their CEO spends all his time on a private jet, meeting with investors and billionaire contemporary art buyers. You give them your collection to sell, and they'll send a bunch of interns to put it in boxes."

"They sent over a vice president to meet with me," Yana said.

"Cypress has four thousand vice presidents," Cindy said. "They'll have one meet with you a couple of times to get the sale, and then you'll never hear from them again. You work with us, and you'll be getting everything we have to offer—because it will be the most important moment of our lives. No one's life at Cypress will change based on selling your collection. Ours will. So the question you have to ask yourself is this: Do you want someone who doesn't care about you and whose strategy is to spam an email list? Or do you want Jay and Cindy, two diehard movie buffs and big fans of yours, who consider getting your collection into the right hands a sacred calling?"

Yana smiled and clapped. Jay beamed with pride. He'd never seen Cindy sell like that.

"Brava, Ms. Cooper," Yana said. "Brava. What you may lack in substance, you do make up for with spirit and earnestness."

Cindy laughed, and so did Jay. "We're worth taking a chance on."

"Oh, I don't gamble. I *never* gamble." Yana's tone was suddenly very serious. "If I choose you, it will be because you're the best choice."

Before anyone could respond, the conversation was interrupted by Yana's bedroom door opening and the sound of Ben Sinclair's voice. "Yana, how were those Hooray for Hollywood people?" he called. "Have you decided yet? The clock is ticking, dear!" His voice was pushy and impatient, and Jay's high opinion of him instantly soured.

"They're still here," Yana yelled back just as Ben stepped into the closet.

And with that awkward entrance, he just stood there for a moment or two, a bottle of Veuve Clicquot champagne in a paper bag in hand. "Sorry about that," he said. "Just trying to keep everyone focused."

He chuckled, but no one else did. Jay had now seen a side to him that hadn't been apparent to him when they first met, and the guy was clearly embarrassed. He'd just gone from dutiful financial advisor helping an elderly client to pushy salesman rushing his client into a decision. The dynamic in the Yana Tosh household was strange: Yana seemed like she wanted to sell but was in no particular rush. Her son was discouraging her from selling, and her financial advisor was pushing her to hurry with the sale.

What was going on here?

"Relax, Ben," Yana said. "All in good time."

"Only trying to help," he said; then he looked at Jay. "How'd the meeting go?"

"It was a joy to see your client's collection," Jay said. "I can't thank you enough for setting this up. Whatever she decides, it has been a treat and an honor."

"Well," Yana said, "let's drink to that." She reached into a cabinet under one of the tables and pulled out champagne flutes. "These were used in *Father of the Bride.* The original one—with Spencer Tracy and Joan Bennett." She smiled. "And also at my wedding."

Jay smiled. "It is an honor to be part of that history."

Ben popped open the bottle and poured a glass each for Jay, Cindy, Yana, Warren, and himself.

"I'd like to propose a toast," Cindy said, raising her glass. "To new friends, the best damn costume collection in the world, and one of the greatest movie villains of all time."

"Hear, hear," Yana said, draining her glass.

After about half an hour of sipping and mingling, Cindy looked at Jay.

He cleared his throat. "Unfortunately, everyone, we have another appointment. But please do let us know if you'd like us to visit again for a discussion, or if there's anything else we can help you with. We know it's a big decision."

"I'll follow up tomorrow," Cindy said to Yana, who didn't seem to hear her. The former starlet was signaling Ben for a refill.

On their way out, Jay spotted a small painting on the floor by the door, propped against the wall, its back to Jay, out of place in a room that was otherwise perfectly staged. He picked it up and turned it around. From its light weight, he could tell that it had once been a prop in a movie; props were always lighter than the real thing, because they had to be moved around so much. The painting in his hands was a striking portrait of the Madonna and Child. Obviously contemporary, but with all the styling of a piece hundreds of years old.

"Interesting painting," he said. "What is this from?"

Before Yana could answer, Cindy squealed with delight.

"My God!" she said. "It's from *The Mirror Crack'd*—that 1980 Agatha Christie movie with Elizabeth Taylor and that's the painting that—" She stopped. "Well, I don't want to give away the plot, but let's just say it plays a vital role in the movie."

Yana smiled. "Smart girl."

"I'm an Agatha Christie buff. That cast! I mean, Tony Curtis, Rock Hudson, Angela Lansbury, Elizabeth Taylor? Come on!"

"The film was not a hit," Yana said.

Cindy shrugged. "It's still one of my favorites."

"I wonder what it would sell for," Ben said, obviously bored with cinema history.

Yana was flipping through a rack of clothes, but she perked to attention when Cindy said, "It's hard to say. On the one hand, the movie was a commercial and critical flop. On the other, that painting plays a pivotal role in the plot. Plus, Elizabeth Taylor is a gay icon, and so is Rock Hudson—and gay guys don't cheap out when it comes to divas. Get a few of them together in a room for a bidding war, and there's no telling what carnage they'll wreak upon their bank accounts." She paused, studying the painting. "The piece would also appeal to Agatha Christie buffs, so that might help."

"Well, then," Ben snapped, "what's your estimate?"

"I would price it at four thousand dollars," Cindy said. "But it might take a while to sell. You'd want to wait for just the right customer to come along, and then pounce." She looked at the piece again, then at Yana. "Where did you get it?"

Yana smiled. "They asked me if I was interested in auditioning for the movie. I read the script and seriously thought about it, but ultimately my husband and I decided I was done with acting for good. They tried to lure me back, but things worked out better for them in the end anyway. They got Elizabeth Taylor, a good friend of mine, and after they finished shooting, she sent me the painting as a thank-you for passing on the part. I still have the note she sent with it."

"Amazing," Jay said. "That'll add to the value, for sure."

Yana smiled. "I have lots of stories about all of my pieces."

"I can't wait to hear them," Cindy said. "Next time. Which I hope will be soon." She looked at her watch. "Jay and I really need to get a move on now for that appointment. Thank you so much for the wonderful showing, and let's talk tomorrow."

Jay and Cindy hurried back to the *Jurassic Park* SUV. He still wasn't sure why Dylan wanted to meet them—he was, after all, an adversary in an industry defined by ruthless competition. Jay focused on his breathing as Cindy backed out of the driveway, butterflies flitting around in his stomach. Only one way to find out.

Cindy felt like she was going to hurl as she made the ten-minute drive to The Parker, Palm Springs's most expensive hotel. The Yana Tosh pitch hadn't exactly boosted her confidence. Cindy wasn't used to failure, and watching Hooray for Hollywood struggle was painful—in part because it was so surprising. The car was silent; the only sound was the wind whipping past the half-open windows.

"I think I may have blown it back there," Cindy said finally.

"Absolutely not," Jay said immediately. "You were brilliant. Just perfect."

"I'm not as smooth with people as you are."

"Maybe not smooth," he agreed. "But . . . enthusiastic. And genuine. Never change that. It's part of your *considerable* charm. And it's the way our act works, just like in the old days."

Cindy shook her head. "I don't connect with people the way you do."

"That speech you gave to Yana was better than anything I could've come up with," he said. "I mean, where did that come from? She loved you."

"You think so?"

"Yep."

"Thanks for the vote of confidence," Cindy said. She still wasn't sure if Jay was just trying to make her feel good.

"So, do you think we can angle our way into the deal?"

Cindy was silent for a moment. "Well, you think it went better than I did, so I think we definitely have a chance. Hopefully we'll get a read on how Cypress's meeting with her went—and whether he thinks he'll get the collection."

"And if he does?"

"Then we schmooze a little and try to figure out a way to work with him on the sale."

They walked past the large, flat wall of the hotel's chic mid-century entrance, into The Parker's high-ceilinged reception area. Their voices echoed, prompting Cindy to end their conversation, and she looked around. She hadn't been to The Parker in years, but she remembered the storied history she'd learned during a tour there, and only felt more out of her league. Located on fourteen acres, The Parker had been a famous celebrity hangout since the 1960s, though it had a different name back then. Frank Sinatra had partied there with Keely Smith after her tabloid scandal divorce from Louis Prima, and the term the "jet set" originally referred to the group of Los Angeles and Las Vegas socialites who used Palm Springs as a desert hangout, drinking by the hotel's pool in cabanas that offered protection from the desert's blinding sun and the paparazzi.

Cindy went to the front desk and asked the clerk to call Dylan Redman.

"He wants you to meet him in his room," she said, handing them a key card with the number scrawled on it. "You'll need this for the elevator."

A few minutes later, they knocked on the door, and Dylan Redman let them into the suite. The room was as modernist as the lobby, with a four-poster bed painted all white, matching the white walls and complemented by the wood-grain ceiling. Cindy noted with some disdain the "sorry-we-couldn't-afford-Warhol-so-we-got-you-this" generic contemporary art that filled the walls—chic, she thought, but insubstantial.

And their host wasn't even chic. He appeared to be in his early thirties, younger than Cindy had expected for the head of the memorabilia department. Most major auction houses catered to buyers in their sixties or seventies, who had the resources to buy—and would be most comfortable trusting their peers for advice. Some auction houses, though, had begun a youth movement, grooming the next generation of star salesmen.

Dylan wore Adidas workout pants and a Red Sox T-shirt. He was notably thin—not an athletic thin, but a pale, inactive thin, like a nerdy, overgrown kid who'd spent all his youth in a dark room watching old movies. And yet here he was, staying at a fancy hotel, meeting with an important client. Instantly, Cindy understood what he was doing: He was dressed casually to intimidate her and Jay, to let them know how little they mattered.

Cindy decided she didn't like him.

They all shook hands.

"Sorry about my appearance," he said. "I had a meeting earlier this morning, and I don't like to stay dressed up for any longer than I have to."

Jay smiled. "We're the new kids in the biz. We're here to impress you, not the other way around."

Cindy smiled to herself. It wasn't a line she could ever hear herself saying, but it worked coming from Jay. She'd reel the eagerness back in when she needed to.

Dylan laughed and walked over to his en suite kitchen, opening the full-sized, stainless steel refrigerator. "I'm going to finish my coffee," he said. "I have a bunch of work to do this afternoon, and the flight out here from New York always makes me tired." He pulled out a large plastic Dunkin' Donuts cup, half filled with a creamy-looking liquid, and winced, shaking the liquid around. "I hate when the ice melts and it gets watery."

"Some places use coffee ice cubes to prevent that," Jay said.

"By God," Dylan said, his tone sardonic, "and they say America doesn't innovate anymore."

"What brings you to Palm Springs?" Cindy said, just to see what he'd say. She noted that he'd made a point of drawing their attention to his coffee—and then didn't offer them any.

Dylan paused, then said: "Business."

Cindy had hoped he would open by mentioning his meeting with Yana, but he was playing it tight. She tried to prompt him. "We just went to evaluate the Yana Tosh collection, and she mentioned you'd been there."

"Well," he said, drily, "we can't discuss a deal we're competing for, can we?"

"I suppose not," Cindy said.

"I want to hear about your new store. It sounds fabulous. And, you know, Cypress is always looking to connect with local dealers—especially in hot markets like Palm Springs, where we don't have an on-the-ground presence. I'm wondering whether there's a way we could work together."

"What would you envision?" Cindy asked. *Here it comes.*

"I'm not exactly sure," Dylan said. "Obviously, for valuable collections, people tend to come directly to us—and no one can compete with us, just because of how big we are." His voice was smug, and getting smugger. "The marketing muscle, the brand, the huge client database, our multimedia team—those kinds of things. But for smaller deals like you—"

Cindy cut him off. "Some people, even big collectors, opt for the personal touch, actually. They choose to sell with someone they connect with and trust. They know that all of that corporate speak is really just a lot of nonsense."

Dylan stared at her, something between amusement and anger in his eyes.

"But we're always open-minded about partnership opportunities," Jay added quickly.

Dylan shrugged. "I was thinking that in cases where you have a piece come in that's exceptional—higher value than you're used to dealing with—we could have an arrangement where those pieces are sold through Cypress at a discounted commission that's available only to Hooray for Hollywood. That'd be better for you because we'll get more money for it. Maybe we could even put your company's name in the press materials."

"We'd consider looking at a proposal," Cindy said before Jay could react. She knew that her partner's response would have been more enthusiastic, and she wanted to project a stronger negotiating position.

They talked about the memorabilia category for a few minutes. Dylan said that it wasn't as hot as it had been a few years ago, but that he was optimistic it would recover once the Turner Classic Movies–loving hipsters had the buying power to drive up prices.

That was always how it worked with collectibles, Cindy thought. You needed diehard young fans who would hopefully go on to make a lot of money in their careers. Once all the nerds who grew up playing the card game Magic: The Gathering in the cafeteria became software geniuses with billion-dollar companies, the paintings that illustrated the cards had shot up in value fiftyfold. The same thing would happen with movie memorabilia.

"So," Dylan said, clapping his hands on his thighs. "I'm going to give you a piece of advice."

Cindy arched an eyebrow as dramatically as possible. "Oh?"

"Tell Yana you don't think you're up to handling a collection as big as hers. Because, let's be honest, you're not. Tell her to go with Cypress, and I'll toss some business downstream to you. I don't want her using you to negotiate a lower commission from me. Just back off, and we'll both make more money."

Jay started to say something, but Cindy cut him off. "You're asking us to collude with you," she said. "And we can't do that. It's not ethical."

Dylan yawned. "You know," he said, "I thought this coffee would give me a jolt, but I'm just spent. Can we talk later? I need a nap."

"Sure," Jay said, tossing one of their business cards on the table, seemingly eager to end the conflict.

Cindy loved their new cards, printed on the back of vintage Pan Am luggage tags. Jay had bought a box of a thousand at a retired flight attendant's yard sale, and stamped their logo and contact information on the back.

"Cool card," Dylan said, flicking it onto his desk without glancing at it for more than half a second. "It's . . . cute."

Cindy did her best not to roll her eyes so hard they got stuck. They were on the way out when she literally bumped into an attractive woman in her early twenties, walking into the room at the same moment. "Oh!" Cindy said. "Sorry."

The woman stared at her. She was wearing a tight-fitting Lycra dress—probably from Lululemon, Cindy thought. Expensive, but meant to convey a lack of interest in fashion.

Which was somehow even more pretentious. "Who are you?" the woman asked.

Cindy extended a hand. "Cindy Cooper, Hooray for Hollywood," she said before introducing Jay. "We just opened our own memorabilia store here, and Dylan was nice enough to invite us over for a meeting."

"When did your store open?" the woman asked, her voice suspicious and unfriendly.

"Six months ago," Cindy said. Had it really only been six months? Had they really lost that much that quickly? Then she added: "It's been a real adventure. It was my late wife's dream for me to pursue this, so—here we are."

As she had hoped, the woman softened at the mention of Cindy having had a wife. She was probably Dylan's girlfriend and had been less than pleased to bump into another woman leaving his hotel room. Cindy was twenty years older, but apparently, Cindy realized with some joy, still a possible romantic threat.

"Well, it's nice to meet you," the woman said. "And I wish you a lot of luck." She nodded. "I'm Eydie Jackson, Dylan's assistant."

Dylan smiled. "Colleague," he said. "She's as important to the business as I am. But I really am tired, so if you could excuse us—I really do need a nap."

* * *

Jay loved the two-family home that he shared with Cindy. It was one of the hippest, most modernist homes in a town known for them, and on his first trip to visit in Palm Springs seven years ago, he'd felt the first unpleasant pang of jealousy. He'd quickly chastised himself for it, of course, but that did nothing to stop him from thinking of how nice it would be to have a home like that when he went back to Las Vegas on his own.

And now he did have that home . . . sort of. He didn't own it, of course, but Cindy had been so welcoming that he occasionally found himself forgetting that. Which was, he knew, exactly how Cindy wanted it. They were both at a crossroads.

Cindy was less expressive about her emotions than Jay—*then again, who wasn't?*—but he could see she was struggling. More than a few times, he'd come into the living room to chat and found her with her head in her hands, or paging through the book of inspirational quotes Esther had prepared for her during her last days. Cindy loved inspirational quotes, and had collected them herself for years in a scrapbook. Esther had taken that scrapbook and created a gift that would last a lifetime: the lines that had always inspired Cindy most, inscribed in the distinctive, elegant script of her soulmate.

It hadn't always been a two-family home, but Cindy had renovated it to create a large in-law suite for him. Jay offered to pay rent, but she wouldn't hear of it. Sometimes he found himself laughing at how bizarre the whole setup would sound to anyone else: Cindy's ex-husband, moving in with her to live rent-free—pursuing a dream at a time when they needed each other most.

When he and Cindy returned home after their meeting with Dylan, Mae West, Jay's eight-year-old tuxedo cat, was sunning herself on a windowsill. She looked like she was playing for an audience, posing in a way that would be alluring to other cats—at least, Jay assumed that's what passed for feline pinups these days. He wondered whether that was just him projecting West's character onto her, or whether he really owned a cat with all the personality of the original Mae West. The original, five-foot Mae had once shown up nude, in platform shoes and a big blonde wig, to her first meeting with a costume designer, and introduced herself by saying, "I thought you'd like to see the lovely body you're going to have the opportunity of dressing."

Cindy's German shepherd, Bob Hope, who was descended from the original Rin Tin Tin of silent film fame, was asleep on the black leather couch that faced the giant TV. The Turner Classic Movies channel was, as nearly always, playing with the sound off; the dog was dozing in front of the famous catfight scene in *Valley of the Dolls*.

"Well," Jay said, having finally had time to process the day's meetings, "how do you think we did?"

"I thought it was . . . okay," Cindy said.

"You were incredible," Jay said. "But it'll be hard for our little business to compete with Cypress for such a big collection."

"We can't think of it that way," Cindy said.

"Would we work on consignment, if we get it?" Jay said. "Or would you try to just buy the collection outright?"

Cindy flopped onto the tan-and-white-striped sofa beside her; it had been in Rock Hudson's bachelor pad in *Pillow Talk*. "It's so much stuff, and so valuable, that there's no way we could buy it outright. The only way it'll work is if we take it on consignment, sell it for her, and take a commission."

"How much of a commission are we talking about?" Jay said.

"I was thinking about asking for twenty percent, which is definitely less than that Cypress jerk will do it for."

"Yana is probably just using us as a bargaining chip to get a lower rate from them," said Jay.

"I don't think so," Cindy said. "Yana liked us, and I have a feeling she's someone who makes decisions that way—instinctively, emotionally. Dylan Redman is a snarky little troll, and I'm trying to keep the faith that Yana won't fall for his smarmy timeshare salesman shtick. He seemed desperate in his pitch to us."

Jay went into the kitchen and prepared a chicken recipe from the new Trisha Yearwood cookbook. He was an expert cook, with an ever-growing collection of hundreds of cookbooks, but he was exacting and never deviated from the recipes, measuring everything out to the eighth of the teaspoon and leveling out measuring cups with a knife. As much as he loved being creative at the piano, Jay didn't trust his own culinary skills. He preferred to copy the work of greater talents.

"Smells delicious, Jay," Cindy said. "You're such a good cook."

"Thank you," he said, sensing an opportunity to try to talk to Cindy about her feelings. "Cooking in your kitchen always reminds me of Esther. I'll never be able to cook like she did."

Cindy didn't say anything.

"You know," Jay tried again, "I remember her special chicken parm recipe—she taught it to me the weekend of your wedding. I could try it tomorrow, maybe."

"Maybe," Cindy said softly. She looked down at her phone and began scrolling, her way of signaling that the conversation was over. Jay knew Cindy wanted to talk about Esther. She needed to, or something in her would just give. But it was, as it always had been, impossible to get her to talk about feelings.

He went over to the turntable and thumbed through their communal '60s movie soundtracks. Chicken, what went well with chicken? He settled on early Barbra Streisand: *Funny Girl*. Barbra's breakout role, but also a rare example of Omar Sharif's charming vocal style.

"God, I love this album," Cindy said. "Remember singing the complete soundtrack together in the hotel room after that Tupelo County Fair show we did? That was so much fun." Jay relaxed a little. It was her way of letting him know that she appreciated him and understood he was trying to help her by bringing up Esther—even if she wasn't ready to talk.

He was just pouring each of them a glass of pinot noir when the doorbell rang.

"One of your gentlemen callers, Jay?" Cindy teased.

Jay laughed. "Your lips to Eva Gabor's ears."

He opened the door to find an unusually handsome man. Late forties, lean and sinewy, tall, and bald—Jay's type, though really, most people's type. What was more alluring—and more concerning—was that he wore a police uniform.

"Hello, Officer," Jay said. "Can I help you?'

"It's detective," the man said. "Detective Simon Fletcher, Palm Springs Police Department. Can I come in?"

Jay hesitated. "Sure," he said. "What's wrong?"

Fletcher didn't answer, but instead walked to the dinner table, where Cindy had just started eating. Introductions were made.

"Mind if I have a seat?" Fletcher said.

"Okay," Cindy said, notably less friendly than Jay had been. Jay noticed that Cindy was channeling Esther and her slightly paranoid, lawyerly protectiveness concerning law enforcement. He loved the reminder that even though Esther had passed, Cindy kept her alive in so many quiet, little ways.

"I don't think I've met you," Fletcher said. "New in town?"

"We've had this place for years," Cindy said, "but yes, we just moved here full-time to open our store." She paused, as if wondering how much information to offer up voluntarily, before adding, "Hooray for Hollywood Movie Memorabilia."

"Yes," Fletcher said. "I know of it."

"Well, that's good," Jay said.

"Is it?"

"Depends," Cindy said evenly. "Have you bought anything?"

"I haven't been in yet," Fletcher said.

"I just meant it's good that word is already spreading a bit," Jay interrupted, instantly feeling awkward. This guy made him nervous. But then again, a detective had mysteriously shown up at their door and hadn't yet told them why he was there. Wasn't nervous the correct thing to feel? "However, that's not really a surprise, right? It's a wonderful store. Stuff for all price ranges. Just last weekend, I bought some great '60s police movie posters—hero cops who were locking up gangsters back when Bobby Kennedy was taking down the mob. I was going to price them at five hundred dollars each, but for a local public servant, I'm sure—"

Fletcher raised an eyebrow. "Are you trying to bribe a police detective?"

"Of course not," Jay said quickly, embarrassed again. *Was this guy just a complete jerk?*

Fletcher cracked a smile. "I know. Just making a joke."

Cindy spoke up. "I don't mean to be rude, Detective, but our dinner is getting cold. I'm assuming there's a reason you stopped by this evening?"

Fletcher nodded once, slowly. "I understand you went to see Dylan Redman at The Parker earlier today."

"Yes," Cindy said. "We did. Why?"

Fletcher ignored the question. "Tell me about that meeting."

"Detective," Cindy said, "I think you need to tell us what this is about before we talk more about it."

"Why? Something to hide?"

"No," Jay snapped. He looked at Cindy. "It's okay. We have nothing to hide."

This time, Fletcher turned to Jay. "Tell me about the meeting, please. Just the facts."

Jay walked him through the encounter with Dylan Redman—what had precipitated it, how it had gone, and how they'd left things.

"So basically, the two of you were competing for a consignment, and he made it very clear that he didn't want to work with you on it and that he felt he had the upper hand?"

"No," Cindy said. "He wanted this deal, yes, but he offered us favorable terms if we partnered with him long term."

Jay felt his chest tighten as he listened to Cindy and the detective volley back and forth about the meeting with Dylan. *What in the world was going on?*

"But he made it clear," Fletcher said, "that he was feeling optimistic about his prospects for winning the Yana Tosh collection."

Cindy shrugged. "He's a salesman. So are we. Salesmen always project confidence. He'll be certain he's going to win the Yana Tosh consignment until the day he finds out he didn't."

"And when would he find that out?" Fletcher said.

"You'd have to ask Yana Tosh," Cindy said.

"How was Dylan Redman when you left?" Fletcher asked.

"Fine," Cindy said. She paused. "Tired, but fine."

"Even though he'd just had an iced coffee?"

Jay felt his throat sink into his chest. How did Fletcher know that Dylan had been drinking iced coffee?

"Yes," Cindy said smoothly, unruffled. "He commented, in fact, that it hadn't given him the caffeine boost he'd hoped for."

Jay interrupted now, his voice suddenly louder than Cindy and Fletcher's. "What is this about, Detective?"

"Dylan Redman was found dead a couple of hours ago," Fletcher said simply.

Jay went silent, his throat suddenly dry. He grabbed a glass from the table and chugged it before realizing, from Fletcher's arched eyebrow, that he'd just gulped down a glass of pinot noir in just about one swallow. He looked at Cindy, whose expression was similarly still and stricken. After what felt to Jay like an hour, he cleared his throat. "How did he die?"

"We'll know more after the autopsy." Fletcher dropped three business cards on the table. "I'll be in touch. I'm sure we'll be talking a lot more. Don't leave town."

"Who found him?" Jay asked, as Fletcher stood up to leave.

Fletcher stopped and turned, as if deciding whether to answer. Finally, he said, "His assistant, Eydie. You know her?"

"We met her briefly," Jay said, "right as we were leaving."

"You didn't mention that."

"I didn't think of it," Jay said, now more than nervous. "It didn't seem important. I wasn't trying to hide anything."

Fletcher nodded, then saw himself to the door. As he walked away, Jay wondered how he'd ever seen the detective as attractive. He'd gone from Montgomery Clift handsome to Ernest Borgnine terrifying in the span of five minutes.

"Well," Cindy said, "that's a wrinkle."

"Yes," Jay agreed, too distracted to say much more. Dylan Redman's death had him rattled and unexpectedly sad, his thoughts ricocheting around in his head more than usual—and Jay's thoughts usually ricocheted, what with his regular caffeine pills. As he met Cindy's stony face across the table, he could tell that they were thinking the same thing: if this went any further, if they actually became suspects in a murder investigation, what would it mean for the store?

Without a word, Cindy grabbed the bottle and poured him another glass of wine.

In less than twenty-four hours, Hooray for Hollywood had gone from an exciting new business to a high-stakes battle for a make-or-break consignment, with a competing vice president dead under suspicious circumstances and a cop who viewed Jay and Cindy as suspects. The next morning, Mary joined them in the store for moral support, and Jay didn't see how he could keep going. After Fletcher left, they'd spent three hours drinking too much wine and discussing the murder, and then, when Cindy finally went to bed, he'd tried to as well. But it hadn't worked. He was exhausted from a sleepless night spent staring at the ceiling, with his stomach flipping somersaults. He said as much to Cindy.

"We'll get through it," Cindy said simply, with a shrug of her shoulders so casual it had to be forced. "We've been through worse."

"If you need more money to keep going," Mary said, "I could put in a little. I don't want to stand in the way of your dream." She laughed. "I'm so old, I don't need to have much in savings."

"We aren't running out of money," Jay said. But when both women remained silent, he paused, with the same sinking feeling that he'd had in his stomach the night before. "Are we?"

Cindy and Mary looked at him, and Jay felt something boiling his blood that he so rarely felt: anger at the two people he loved most.

"Does no one tell me *anything*?" he snapped. "I'm a partner here. You just tell me everything is fine, and then you tell Mary all about problems—"

"Jay—" Cindy said, but Mary interrupted her.

"I'm sorry," she said. "I didn't realize you hadn't talked to him about it."

With a long sigh, Cindy explained the situation—she had committed to putting one hundred thousand dollars into covering the business's operating losses, and they were rapidly approaching that mark. She had more in savings, but with Esther's income gone and Cindy having given up the financial planning business, she needed to be careful. She had enough to commit all her time to Hooray for Hollywood after she sold her investment business—but not enough to subsidize indefinite losses.

"I have twenty thousand dollars in an IRA," Jay said, his voice rushing out before his mind could catch up. Maybe it wasn't the smartest idea, but who cared? The store made him happy, and money sitting in a bank account didn't, and as far as he was concerned, that was the end of it. It wasn't like he needed to worry about making rent anyway. What did he need it for? "I can take it out. I know it's not as much you have, but I'm all in on this business. I believe in it, and I care about it more than anything. I'll give everything I—"

Cindy waved a hand. "The taxes on taking it out would be a disaster, Jay. I would never ask you to touch that money. The plan was that I would fund this." She paused, thinking. "I'm the one who did the financial projections. If things are going slower than we thought they would, it's my fault for being too optimistic in my financial model. You two have been amazing. You're killing it. It just takes time to build a business, that's all. We just have to keep working, staying passionate."

"Well, I'm passionate," Mary said. "I'm passionate about anything you and Jay want to do."

"Let's worry about it later," Cindy said. "And we may not run out of money, anyway. If this Yana Tosh thing breaks our way, then—" She sang a few bars of "Happy Days Are Here Again," doing a wickedly nasal Barbra Streisand impersonation to lighten the mood.

A few minutes later, Mary left, and Jay tried not to be mad at Cindy. She was only trying to help him and protect his feelings, and being upset with her wouldn't do any good. They had enough trouble as it was. Still, he was annoyed. He wanted their relationship to be transparent, and it sure didn't feel that way.

The radio was, as usual, playing KWXY, a local station so steeped in mid-century nostalgia that they were still spinning—literally—the same vinyl records they'd had since they went on air in 1964. Henry Mancini's theme from *The Pink Panther* had just finished, and now Andy Williams was singing "Moon River."

Jay wandered the store, cleaning what was already clean, organizing what was already compulsive. When he felt stressed out or upset, he channeled all that nervous energy into perfecting his environment. He was, as always, dressed to sell vintage memorabilia. He had a wardrobe full of bow ties—some originally owned by Groucho Marx—and today he sported a money-green one over a white shirt with a blue suede blazer. His accent piece was a gaudy, rhinestone-encrusted watch that had been pawned in Las Vegas by Wayne Newton during one of his numerous financial valleys. Wayne had probably thought the watch was classy, but Jay loved it for what it was: tacky and over-the-top, lowbrow fun.

Today Hooray for Hollywood was getting its first national press coverage, and everything had to be perfect. Worrying could wait—it would have to.

As if reading his mind, Cindy spoke. "Put all thoughts of Dylan and Yana and money and fear out of your mind," she said.

Jay laughed, darker and harsher than he'd intended for it to come out. "Easier said than done."

"Do it anyway," Cindy said. "We can't fix that problem right now. All we can do is run the store as well as we can—and when Lenae gets here, give her everything she needs to hand us a press clipping that will bring in customers."

Lenae Randolph, America's star celebrity columnist, was coming in to do a profile of the store. Her huge audience, combined with her frequently acerbic pen, which she reserved for people she didn't like, made the prospect of their meeting extremely exciting—and terrifying. Jay would have to be in peak charming salesman mode, and that was the opposite of how he was feeling.

He and Cindy opened the store at nine, and a smattering of foot traffic came in and bought a little of everything: a lamp used on the set of the '90s sitcom *Full House* went for seven hundred and fifty dollars. A *Seinfeld* lamp would have gone for a lot more, but *Full House*, popular as it was, just didn't have an especially rabid collector base. Aunt Becky did okay—especially after Lori Loughlin spiked in notoriety after the Varsity Blues scandal—but Kramer would have done a lot better.

At eleven AM, right on time, a 1990s Wagoneer with wood trim pulled into the parking lot, past Kohl's and the Olive Garden, until it parked right in front of Hooray for Hollywood, its hood jutting out over the barrier and onto the sidewalk. Several minutes later, a woman, so bent over she definitely should have been using a walker, walked in and sat down on a grandfather chair from an early Nero Wolfe movie.

"Just give me a minute to catch my breath," she gasped.

Since Jay knew he was going to spend a sleepless night after Fletcher's visit anyway, he'd spent hours in bed reading everything he could find about Lenae Randolph. She was rumored to be in her nineties, but her age was a closely guarded secret; she'd been telling people she was "almost eighty" for at least fifteen years. She'd written a society column for Palm Springs papers since the late 1950s, switching among them as mergers and her imperious attitude necessitated, before striking out on her own. She was short and plump, with rounded shoulders, as if she'd spent a life cramped over typewriters. Her fashion sense veered toward tragic: sweatpants and socks with sandals. In a way, though, Jay thought, her style was a statement, a declaration that she was above the vanity of the beautiful people she reported on, there to observe them almost as a sociologist.

Three years ago, she'd quit in a spat over expense accounts with the editor-in-chief of Palm Springs's last remaining independent newspaper, and had shortly thereafter started her own blog and social media accounts. She now had over half a million Twitter followers and was a regular on the talk show circuit, comparing the lives of current stars to people she'd known a half century ago.

Once Lenae had caught her breath, Jay brought her a bottle of water. She sipped it slowly, then rose, signaling that she was ready for the tour. She took notes, using a pen on a pad of paper, and then spoke a few more thoughts into a bulky cassette recorder she pulled from her battered—but somehow more fabulous for it—Chanel purse.

After half an hour of wandering the store with Jay and Cindy, discussing their vision for the store and their biographical details, Lenae sat down at the horror movie table, turned the microphone off, put down her pen, and stared at Jay.

"So," she said, "tell me about that meeting with the Cypress guy."

Jay was shocked. He started speaking before it even registered that it might be smartest to say nothing at all. "How—"

Lenae cut him off. "I'm Lenae Randolph," she said. "I know everything that happens in Palm Springs. If I like you, I can make you. And if I don't like you, I can destroy you. As it happens, I like both of you. For now. But I am doing some reporting on that case, and I'm hoping you can help me. We'll trade. I'll say glowing things about your store; you help me with the Dylan Redman death. I won't mention you. You'll be anonymous sources 'close to the investigation.'"

Jay glanced over at Cindy, who stayed silent.

"You two may need me," Lenae said. "You're the prime suspects, after all." From the wickedly calculating gleam in her eyes, she was well aware that bit of information was new to them.

"Suspects?" Cindy said. Given how surprised she sounded in comparison to her normally calculated tone, Jay knew how taken aback she must be. "What are you talking about?"

Lenae laughed easily. "Well, of course. You're the last ones who saw him alive, and you were competing with him for a consignment. You had motive and opportunity." She paused, playing a little with the strands of her thinning hair. "Look, I don't think you did it—though even if I did think you did it, I probably wouldn't tell you. But even if I agree that you *didn't* do it, you have two things to worry about: one, mounting a defense; and two, preserving your reputation so it isn't destroyed before your business has even begun. You tell me what you know, and maybe I tell you something I know. I would never mention you in my column, other than in a glowing puff piece about your new store. But the off-the-record information you give me helps me piece together my homicide reporting."

Jay and Cindy exchanged glances, and Cindy nodded slightly. Jay told Lenae about the conversation with Redman and the iced coffee. Once he was done, Cindy told her a little more about their meeting with Redman. She mentioned that they'd been over to meet with Yana before that, and that their understanding was that Yana had met with Redman that morning, as well. Jay filled in some gaps as Cindy spoke, but when Cindy left out any mention of Warren or Ben Sinclair, Jay didn't add it in. He figured Cindy was saving all of that, for whatever reason.

Finally done weaving the tale, Cindy leaned in. "Okay, we've spilled. Your turn."

Lenae smiled. "I know these characters quite well."

"Including Redman?"

She paused. "Yes. We met for breakfast. He was hoping I'd put out a story about his huge success as a rising star in entertainment memorabilia, thinking that would impress Yana."

"What'd you tell him?"

"I told him that, alas, there was no story until he won the consignment."

"Ah," Jay said. "A Catch-22."

Lenae shrugged. "He wasn't pleased. But then, people who want publicity never are. The only other little thing I can tell you, which I'd appreciate you keeping confidential, is that Dylan Redman's coffee was likely poisoned and ultimately his cause of death. And they found another set of fingerprints on the coffee cup in question."

"So that's why Fletcher brought up the coffee," Jay muttered. Then, to Lenae, "Do they know who the other set of fingerprints belonged to?"

"Yes," Lenae said. "It was a person in the system."

"Who?"

"Warren Limon, Yana's loser son."

"Loser?"

"Hollywood offspring, my dears," she said, "they're all the same: train wrecks and idiots, nitwits and schemers. Though Warren's rather boring, for whatever he's worth. Just a couple of DUIs some years ago. No big deal, but enough for the local constabulary to match his prints."

"Do they know for sure it was poison?"

"That'll take longer. But based on what my source tells me, there's no way he dropped dead of natural causes." She stood up and gathered her bag. "Let's catch up again soon, shall we?"

And with that, she walked out—slowly, but with an expression that indicated the conversation was over. Whatever else Lenae knew about the death of Dylan Redman, they would have to wait to find out. A few minutes later she was back in the car. Jay watched her drive away.

"Should that woman really be on the road?" Cindy asked.

"I doubt it," Jay said. He headed back to the vinyl section, his partner trailing behind him. The records didn't really need much more organizing. It was mostly a way for him to try to avoid unproductive worrying.

Cindy picked up a copy of the *La Dolce Vita* soundtrack recording and shelved it next to *Lawrence of Arabia*. "So what do you think?"

Jay tapped his head twice. "She's more together than we are."

"Well," Cindy said. "Now we know that she met with Dylan for breakfast."

"Are you saying—?"

"Sure, why not? She could've killed him. That's the thing about poison: Anyone who encountered him could've done it. That means Lenae, Yana, her ne'er-do-well son, her jerk financial advisor, Redman's assistant."

"Five people," Jay said.

"Seven."

"Seven?"

"Us. You and me against the world, babe."

"Well, obviously we didn't do anything."

"I know," Cindy said. "But we have to approach this as the police will."

Jay suddenly remembered the phone. During Lenae's visit, he'd heard it ring twice, but he hadn't wanted to interrupt her. He went over to the counter and saw that the message light was blinking. He logged into the store's voicemail and, since they didn't have any customers, put it on speakerphone for Cindy.

"Hi, Jay and Cindy," the caller said. "It's Ben Sinclair. Obviously, the circumstances right now are terrible, and I hope you guys are hanging in there. But in any case, Yana and I have discussed it more and decided we'd like for you to come over again. Our thinking is that we might give you a few pieces to sell, kind of a trial run, and maybe have Cypress sell a few too. Then, depending on how that goes, we'll see where we're at. Anyway, give me a ring and we'll figure it out."

"Well," Jay said, "that's good news. At least we're getting something."

"Yes. And obviously, Ben Sinclair is not interested in delays. It looked like he was in more of a rush than Yana was yesterday. In fact, it looked like he'd step over a corpse to get her collection sold."

Cindy hoped that the death of Dylan Redman wouldn't make their meeting with Yana somber or awkward. She wanted the consignment—needed it, really; and for selfish reasons, she was glad that Yana wasn't delaying the sale—but she knew Jay was put off by the speed with which they were back to negotiating. Cindy was always ready to get down to business, but even she could see Jay's point. Yana had seemed carefree the day before, but Cindy was certain Ben Sinclair had been applying pressure. Sure, it had only been one stray remark—but it was the only time they'd heard Ben Sinclair talk without knowing he had an audience of strangers, and he'd made a bad impression.

She didn't want to read too much into that—but she didn't want to forget it either.

They were back in the walk-in closet, Yana and Ben, and Jay and Cindy. Warren was both absent and unmentioned.

"Should we wait for Warren?" Cindy asked as delicately as possible.

Yana gave the briefest hint of a smile. "No. He couldn't make it today."

Cindy started to say something, but Yana stopped her. "My son is awful, dear. There's no need to say anything more." She paused, looking around the room that housed the collection. Cindy could tell, just from the way that Yana's gaze softened, her jaw going just a bit slack, that what was in this room was everything to her. "It's a terrible thing that happened with Mr. Redman. But, you know, you get to be my age, and you've outlived virtually everyone you know. Death loses its power over you somewhere down the line." She tried out a laugh, attempting to lighten the mood. "Besides, I got killed off in so many of my movies, I feel like I've already died. Doesn't bother me anymore."

Cindy nodded. Who was she to judge the way a ninety-year-old Hollywood icon reacted to the death of someone she'd only met once? "What was your meeting with Mr. Redman like?"

Yana shrugged. "All three of us met with him—Ben, Warren, and I," she said. "It was pleasant enough, I suppose. Showed him the collection, and then each of us talked to him privately to learn a bit more about the services."

"Privately?" Jay said.

"Yeah," Ben interrupted. "Dylan explained that when they're handling collections like this, they always like to talk to everyone involved separately—in this case, the heir; the financial advisor; and, of course, Yana. Just to see how everyone's thinking about it and to make sure there isn't some angle they're missing or a conflict that could blow up the whole deal."

"Is that typical?" Cindy said. "Why would he want to talk to the heir if the consignor is still alive? What business is it of his?"

Ben was silent for a moment. "I didn't think of that. I really don't know. It is strange, now that you mention it. But he wanted private meetings with everyone, and so that's what happened."

Cindy nodded. "Were you leaning toward giving him the consignment?"

"I hadn't made up my mind," Yana said airily. "And my sense was that he wasn't pleased with that. I think he came in looking to close a deal right then and there. It's one of the things I appreciated about the two of you: the soft sale, no pressure."

"Thank you," Jay said.

"As Ben probably mentioned, I'd like to start by having you take a few things from me and see if you can find buyers. Whatever you sell them for, you can keep twenty percent, and I'll need receipts to make sure you're giving me the full amount." She winked. "You know how some people can be."

Cindy sensed Jay open his mouth more than she saw or heard him, and she jumped in before he could agree to anything foolish. "We were thinking more like thirty," she said quickly.

Yana and Ben conferred briefly. "Twenty-five percent," Ben said. "On these first few pieces. If we give you the whole collection, we'll expect fifteen percent."

"And we can get started today?" Cindy asked. "There's no complication because of . . ." She let her voice trail off, unsure of how to reference the homicide that hung over everything.

"The costumes aren't murder weapons, dear," Yana said. "The police came here, did all those crime scene things they like to do, and cleared it. Everything that's here is mine to do with as I please."

Cindy and Jay spent some time sorting through the collection, selecting a dozen pieces they thought they might have potential buyers for. Cindy knew they needed to handle this first batch efficiently and at top dollar. Unsold pieces or heavy discounting might mean missing out on the rest of the collection. They chose a pair of Marilyn Monroe costumes and a pair of tap shoes worn by Fred Astaire. Then Cindy picked up a red ribbon given to Shirley Temple, honoring her as the grand marshal of the 1939 Rose Parade.

"Ah, Shirley," Yana said. "A magnificent star, and a magnificent piece—one of a kind!"

"It is," Cindy agreed. "I loved Shirley Temple. Her movies were my favorite when I was a kid, and I admire how she grew up to be such a positive force, even after her acting career ended."

Yana nodded. "Not many kid stars you can say that about. Those movies give me an ice cream headache, but some people need that, with everything in the world the way it is." She paused briefly. "Take it," she said. "I'm sure you'll find a buyer."

"I'm not sure this one will be easy," Cindy said. "Thirty years ago, sure. But the truth is, people don't really watch Shirley Temple anymore. Her biggest fans are mostly dead."

Ben spoke. "She never showed enough leg to be a grown-up movie star, I suppose. Should have followed Marilyn's lead."

"There was a lot more to Marilyn Monroe than leg," Yana snapped, ice running through her voice. "She was a great actress, an underrated singer, and a wonderful human. Do you know the story about her and Ella Fitzgerald?"

Ben shrugged. "No."

"There was a club in Los Angeles—Mocambo," Yana said. "Beautiful room. Ella Fitzgerald wanted to play there, but the owner thought she wasn't 'quite right' for the space—meaning, she was Black. So Marilyn said she would go every night and sit in the front row if he booked her. The owner relented, and Marilyn kept her promise. Ella was a big success, and the show helped bring Ella's career to a new level, paving the way for other African Americans to play those high-end clubs. That's who Marilyn was: a tortured soul, but a beautiful one."

Cindy made a mental note to listen to Ella when she got home—and to watch a Marilyn Monroe movie. Probably *How to Marry a Millionaire*. Bad people could create great music and movies, but Cindy always enjoyed it more when she could experience the art knowing that the person behind it was someone she admired.

They talked a little more, and Cindy and Jay wandered the closet, looking for one last piece to take.

"I know," Jay said, excitement peppering his voice. "I've been thinking about that Madonna and Child painting from *The Mirror Crack'd* you showed us last time. Is there any chance you'd allow us to handle that? I have a fun thought about how to promote it on social media."

"Of course," Yana said, walking over to the spot by the door where the painting had been. She started flipping through a few other pieces that were there, but gave up quickly. "That's funny. I know it was here. I . . . must have misplaced it." Her voice trailed off, and she reached up to touch her headpiece, as if reassuring herself that it, at least, was still there.

Cindy and Jay helped her search the room with increasing urgency. No luck.

"I must have moved it," Yana said finally. "I'm mostly all here, but, you know, even Yana Tosh has senior moments now and then." She tried to smile, but Cindy could see that she didn't really think this was a senior moment. There was anxiety in her face: The Madonna and Child painting wasn't especially valuable, but it was a piece of film history with a personal connection. Losing it must be traumatic.

"It's okay," Ben said. "I'm sure it'll turn up. You and I can look for it later. It has to be here. No one's been in here except us."

"That Cypress man was here," Yana said. Cindy noted how quickly he turned from Dylan Redman to "that Cypress man," depending on how Yana's mood swung. She wondered if they'd ever been "those Hooray for Hollywood people."

"Yes," Ben said, "but Jay and Cindy saw it after him, and then he died, so I really don't think he would've had time to come back and steal it."

"Fact is," Yana said, "anyone could have. This house isn't the most secure place. I lock the doors, but it's Palm Springs. I've never thought I needed a security system." She paused. "That awful assistant of his could have. Eydie Jackson." She spat out the name like a hairball.

"Oh," Jay said, "you met her?"

Yana snorted. "Only on the phone, but that was enough for me. She called to confirm Dylan's appointment and find out more about my plans. I found her pushy and intrusive. A secretary's role is to book the appointment and wish me a nice day."

"Well, I think she might be a junior person in the department, more than Dylan's assistant," Jay said. "If they flew her out here with Dylan, she's probably the one you'd be dealing with on Cypress's end." Cindy smiled to herself, pleased that Jay couldn't resist adding a dig. He was getting better at being a businessman—slowly, but also surely.

"Well, I found her impertinent," Yana said. Her expression grew dour as she continued: "I wish I could find that painting. It's driving me crazy. I live in absolute terror of becoming an old lady who misplaces things. That will *never* be me. I won't let it. Yana Tosh *cannot* be batty and confused!"

"When Warren gets home, the three of us will find it," Ben said, soothingly. "I promise."

"Thank you, darling," Yana said. "I do believe we will. I'm sure it's just a little mistake."

Cindy pulled up a consignment contract on her phone and emailed it to Ben, who printed it out so everyone could sign it. Then he made photocopies of each piece's provenance file from Yana's filing cabinet. Jay took photos on his phone of each piece they were taking, and they loaded them into a few large Rubbermaid containers they'd brought with them.

"I wonder what the deal is with that painting," Jay said on the drive back to the store.

"She probably just misplaced it," Cindy said. It was the most likely option, after all. Sure, Yana Tosh didn't seem like the type of old woman to be losing her mind. But she was old, and what was more likely? That one of the few people who knew exactly where it was had broken in and stolen it on the same day that Dylan Redman had been murdered? Going down that road made things sound like a conspiracy theory.

Jay laughed. "You, Cynical Cindy, think that?"

She shrugged. "It's possible. What do you think?"

"That someone took it, obviously. It's just too big of a coincidence otherwise. The Cypress guy gets killed, and then Yana misplaces a painting? It just makes more sense to assume there's a connection—doesn't it?" Leave it to Jay to vocalize the thoughts she was trying to hide, even from herself.

"Out of everything she had?" Cindy asked. "Why would someone steal that? It wasn't worth much relative to her other stuff."

"Weirdly," Jay said, "the fact that the painting probably isn't especially valuable makes its disappearance seem more important. It means it wasn't just stolen for money. It had to have been taken for some other, very specific reason."

"Or whoever stole it *thought* it must be valuable."

"Yeah. There's that too."

Cindy hummed along quietly with Bruce Springsteen on the radio as she drove, trying to distract herself from the spider's web they found themselves in. "I don't think it does us much good to speculate about it right now." Bruce Springsteen gave way to Bertie Higgins's "Key Largo," the worst song inspired by the best movie. She turned down the volume. "What are we going to do about you?"

"About me?"

"Yes," Cindy said. "About your love life."

"Oh, wow." Jay laughed, and not happily. "You really don't want to talk about that painting, do you? Man, Cindy, we just got a bunch of stuff from Yana Tosh's personal collection to sell at a twenty-five percent commission. Can we not just take a few *minutes* to celebrate?"

"Of course we can," Cindy snapped. "We can bask once we've sold the darn things." She realized her tone and snapped her mouth shut. No sense in fighting with Jay over what was really nothing. He must have been right: Cindy worked with numbers—with things that were definite and real. A murder and a burglary happening within twenty-four hours of each other, with no clear motive or answer? Yeah, that put her on edge.

Jay, for his part, must have sensed that she needed the distraction, because, after a moment of silence, he finally said quietly, "There's really not much to talk about. With my love life."

"And why not?" she asked, grateful for the gesture.

"I just . . . I can't deal with *men* anymore," he said, throwing his hands up in the air. "They're all terrible. I just want to be alone with Mae West and Bob Hope and you."

"Someone who overheard you saying that and didn't know those were our pets would think you'd lost your mind."

"They'd be right. Just for the wrong reasons."

They were silent for a few moments, and then Cindy spoke. "I think that police detective likes you."

"Fletcher?" Jay asked. "I think I'd have more luck with *Jessica* Fletcher."

"Okay, Eeyore. Drop the long-suffering shtick. You're a catch. The best fresh meat Palm Springs has seen in decades."

"Palm Springs hasn't seen much fresh meat in decades."

"Well, you're it, and he digs it. I could tell by the way he looked at you while we were talking."

"Cindy, he was probably trying to figure out if I'm a murderer."

"That's not what that look is," she said. "He's trying to figure out if I'm a killer too, and he doesn't look at me the way he looks at you."

"Well, then, he must be a homicide detective with a possible kink for murderers, so I'm not sure that speaks highly to his own qualifications as Palm Springs's most eligible bachelor." Jay shook his head. "I don't even think he's gay. And you know I hate speculating about that."

He had a point, but Cindy couldn't help it. Jay always pointed out that lots of people talked about the idea of "gaydar"—the ability to instantly identify whether or not someone was gay—like it was a science. He said that it wasn't like that and that people who claimed to be able to tell were either lying or relying on often inaccurate stereotypes. Cindy didn't see it that way, but she respected Jay's view. Except when it got in the way of her matchmaking.

"With a guy as hot as Fletcher," Cindy said, "can we make an exception and speculate anyway?"

Jay tried to suppress a smile, but she caught just the faintest hint of lip curling.

"Putting aside whether he's gay—because he is: Did you think he was hot?"

"Of course," Jay said. "I have two eyes and a pulse."

She made a tsking sound with her tongue. "So shallow, Jay. Muscles and height and charisma and a shiny handsome head aren't everything, you know."

Jay threw his head back dramatically. "If there was any more, I couldn't stand it!"

They rode in comfortable silence for a few more minutes.

"I want something like you and Esther had," Jay said finally.

"Not as much as I want what Esther and I had," Cindy said, her heart sinking.

"Oh, Cindy. I know. Believe me, I know. You're working so hard and functioning so well, but I know your heart's broken. I know you're in pain all day, every day. I just wish there was something I—"

Cindy cut him off. "There's nothing you can do for me. And I hate talking about me, so let's talk about you. There's no way I can consider dating again soon, but you? I know how painful what happened with he-who-shall-not-be-named was, but you got off lucky finding out five years in, not twenty-five. And you're as hot as ever, by the way."

"Am I?"

"Of course," she said. "Your energy has only grown."

"Energy? You sure you don't mean the caffeine pills?"

"Magnetism. That thing you have where people like you and want to be with you. The reason we were stars."

"Your voice had a lot to do with that."

Cindy shook her head, but a wistful smile curled her lips. "You were the one people watched every show. Their eyes were always on you."

"I never noticed."

"That's part of the allure, part of your charm. So unaware of your own specialness. It's the same reason you have no idea that Detective Fletcher was into you last night. But my point is, it's still there, now more than ever, and you should use it."

Jay cackled. "Even if we did go on a date, he'd just use it to interrogate me for his investigation."

"Well, that's even more reason to ask him out, then," Cindy said. "The deck is stacked in your favor. And an interrogation could be fun foreplay."

Jay ignored that. "It seems risky."

"Love is always risky," Cindy said softly. She reached out and touched his arm. "Fortune favors the bold."

When they arrived back at Hooray for Hollywood, Mary was behind the counter, ringing up a book of Lennon Sisters paper dolls for an older woman. *The Lennon Sisters,* Cindy thought with joy. They'd been famous on the Lawrence Welk Show in the 1950s and 1960s, but now they'd been mostly forgotten. But this lady remembered, and their store had something that would, for ten dollars, provide a spark of joy in her day. Without the store, the book would've been in a landfill. A win–win.

After the woman left, Mary helped Cindy and Jay stack the consignments from Yana in the back room. Cindy admired Mary's upright posture and personal style, which consisted mostly of pieces she'd made herself or found at thrift shops. Today, she had on white turtleneck under a turquoise cardigan she'd crocheted, along with a big gold cross necklace she'd bought at a flea market. At first, Cindy had thought the flashy necklace was more suited to a hip-hop star, but she'd come to see that, like everything about Mary, it suited her perfectly because she liked it so much. It was *her*. Cindy loved Mary's enthusiasm for life, never too set in her ways to try something new. An accomplished knitter, Mary had scoured old movie magazines for fun sweaters and blankets and hats. Then she began furiously crafting replicas to be sold online and in-store. She was already doing a brisk business on Etsy, receiving frequent special requests, and the display by the counter represented the only new merchandise featured at Hooray for Hollywood. Each piece came with a photo of the star wearing the piece it was based on, along with a note clearly explaining that, unlike everything else in the store, Mary's pieces were replicas to be worn and enjoyed. She took her little business as seriously as Jay and Cindy took theirs, and her late-blooming entrepreneurial instincts were inspiring. And so far, Cindy thought, with a little jealousy but mostly just joy, Mary was actually in the black on her knitting.

Right now, though, Mary's knitting needles were in her tote bag, and she was helping Cindy and Jay organize. It was five o'clock by the time they were finished, so they locked up and Jay made a pot of tea, and they sat at the horror movie table, drinking and laughing and talking about the store, its future, and the twenty-plus years they'd known each other.

"When y'all split up," Mary said, "I was so sad. This was before I understood what being gay meant and all, and I am just so sorry I was judgmental about it." Mary had apologized to them a hundred times, and they'd forgiven her each time, but it filled them with love for her that she still felt a need to keep saying it. "But when I see what you and Esther had, and I see the way you and Jay are still such friends, I think—there are so many ways a relationship can be loving. And that's all that counts, no matter what, you know?"

Cindy put her hand on Mary's. It was liver spotted and wrinkled from her eighty-five years on earth, but her friend had never stopped growing and improving. Mary wasn't conventionally sophisticated, Cindy thought. She'd never been to college, never read anything that wasn't from the inspirational section, and she'd never traveled outside the United States. Still, more people should be as willing to learn as she was. Cindy realized she needed Mary's calm, wonderful spirit now more than ever. Cindy was usually hyper-confident when it came to business, but a sinking feeling came over her: What if the Dylan Redman murder case sank their store before they'd even had a chance to launch it?

As if reading her mind, Mary spoke. "Please don't worry about all the drama," she said. "The store is going to be a big success. I just know it."

Just then, Cindy's phone beeped. It was an email alert she'd set up to notify her whenever there was a news story mentioning the store. She read it quickly, her heart sinking fast into her shoes with each new word. "Oh, crap."

Jay looked over. "What?"

She read it aloud, a story from a local television news station. It quickly recounted the death of Dylan Redman and then cited police sources saying that it was being considered a probable poisoning. It was the end that was the problem:

> *According to a police report obtained by this network, Dylan Redman's last meeting prior to his death was with Jay Allan and Cindy Cooper, the owners of Hooray for Hollywood Movie Memorabilia, a local memorabilia store that was competing with Mr. Redman for a consignment. Allan and Cooper are best known for their infamous divorce following a career as soap opera stars decades ago. The two are considered likely suspects, sources say.*

"*Decades* ago?" Jay said. "It was only twenty years, and they make it sound like it might as well have been ninety. Somehow, when they put it like that, it makes me feel really old—like I'm the gay Rudy Vallee or something. I get that they're accusing us of murder, but do they have to be so rude about it? And why did they have to bring up our divorce?"

"And since when is coming to terms with being gay something that makes you *infamous*?" Mary said, spitting out the words. "Those sons of beestings!"

Cindy didn't want to—because none of this was funny—but she had to laugh. No matter how angry she was, no matter how bad the situation, Mary could *never* swear. *"Sons of beestings"* was the equivalent of anyone else hurling the worst curse words they could think of.

"This story is going to destroy our business," Cindy said.

"You never know," Jay said optimistically. "A lot of people are into the serial killer stuff these days. We might even draw in a bigger crowd now. Just . . . a different crowd, is all."

Cindy sighed. "I didn't want to tell you, but a minute ago we got an email canceling an appointment to look at Old Hollywood furniture for some guy's living room. The timing is too perfect. It has to be because of the story. So if you know any true crime fanatics, now's the time to send them our newsletter, because it doesn't look like our usual customers think it's all that cool."

"But you're innocent!" Mary yelled. "People will realize that. You didn't do it, and people will figure that out."

"The police move so slowly, though," Cindy said. "They'll wait nine months to clear us, and by then we'll have lost what few customers we have, and we won't have gotten any new ones—because who wants to buy a movie poster from a pair of washed-up, gay, divorced Bonnie and Clyde types who were stars, to quote the media, *decades ago*?"

"Look," Jay said, "we can't wait for the police, then. We're going to have to solve this ourselves."

"While we try to save the store?" Cindy said.

"We have to solve it *to* save the store," he said, reaching into his pocket and popping another caffeine pill. "And think of it this way: saving the store means getting the Yana Tosh consignment. And getting the Yana Tosh consignment means clearing ourselves. It's all one thing. We do both, or neither will succeed."

Cindy thought about that. Jay was crazy—that's what she loved about him—but there was a certain amount of logic to it, she had to admit. "You're right," she said finally. "Singing stars turned memorabilia dealers turned amateur detectives."

Jay grinned in return. "Should I print new business cards?"

Jay was fixated on getting every detail of his photo shoot right. Somehow, it relaxed him. He knew that he needed to be thinking about the murder and clearing his name and saving the store. Eventually. For now, he was going to focus on photographing Yana's items perfectly so they could sell the pieces for top dollar—so the business would have a chance if they ever did get that murder case cleared up.

He had a complicated lighting rig along with a wide assortment of backgrounds, and he was using those to create the perfect shots for the consignments. He had the Rocky Balboa trunks on a mannequin, and then, behind those, a projection screen displaying a scene with Sly Stallone wearing them just as he landed a crushing blow to the head of Apollo Creed. Selling memorabilia was all about romance, Jay knew. It wasn't about selling people a product they needed, or even one they knew they wanted. It was about creating an experience—a feeling, really, almost a combination of nostalgia and envy—that would leave them thinking their life would never be as good as it could be if they owned this object they just found out about five seconds ago.

He worked for hours, only stopping to change the record on the phonograph. Inspired by Yana's story, he listened to the album *Ella Fitzgerald Sings the Jerome Kern Songbook*, start to finish, marveling at the joy that Ella brought to her singing, to say nothing of the rich, syrupy voice that seemed to contain so many notes in each word.

"Jay!" he heard Cindy shout over the music. "Jay!"

"Coming!" He put down the camera and rushed to the front of the store, heart pounding. "What is it? What happened? Everything okay?"

"Oh, it's fine," she said. "I just wanted to show you something."

He sagged with relief. "I thought we had an intruder and you were calling on me for muscle."

"I love you, Jay," Cindy said, "but we both know you're not the muscle in this relationship."

"True," he admitted. "What did you want to show me, then?"

"Come look at the laptop with me."

He joined her behind the desk and saw that the tab on the screen was open to a site called FINRA. "What is FINRA?"

"Financial Industry Regulatory Authority—it's the agency that regulates financial advisors," she said. "Keeps track of complaints, makes sure licenses are up to date, that kind of thing."

"Uh-huh."

"I just started surfing around on it because the more I think about Ben Sinclair, the less I like him. He put on a good front with us, but then the way he spoke with Yana was not the way someone should be talking to the person they have a fiduciary duty to look out for."

"And?" Jay asked. "What did you find?"

"That Ben Sinclair is not a licensed financial advisor."

"Wow," Jay said. "But maybe he doesn't have to be—if he's not actually selling her products and is just helping her with things?"

"Right," Cindy said. "But he *used* to be one."

"*Used* to be?"

"He was, and now he isn't. His license got revoked."

Jay felt that sinking feeling of doom that starts in the head and then consumes the whole body. The only reason financial advisors got their licenses revoked was that they'd acted improperly. Financial elder abuse had been a major concern of Cindy's for years. Sleazy, greedy money guys—and, yes, they were almost always guys—found rich old people who were isolated and perhaps infirm and bullied them into financial moves that benefited the advisor at the expense of the client. Cindy had done hundreds of free lectures at senior centers over the years, warning people of the dangers conmen posed.

"Does it say why?" Jay said.

"The notes from the hearing show that he was churning client accounts," Cindy said. "And then—"

"Hold up, Suze Orman. What does 'churning client accounts' mean?"

"Basically, he was trading things more frequently than necessary so that he could generate excess commissions for himself."

"I see."

Cindy was still looking at the monitor. "It got worse."

"Oh?"

"In 2005, he just started dipping into client accounts and taking money. The only reason there was never a criminal case was that when his mother died, he was able to pay everybody back. But by then, the regulators were onto him, so they launched an investigation and revoked his license. In 2010, he was barred from being a financial advisor for life."

"Did he have any response to the allegations?"

"No," Cindy said. "He declined to contest the charges. So, basically, there was a hearing, and he was found guilty, and he agreed to never be a financial advisor again, and that was the end of it."

"Except that now he's a financial advisor again."

"Yes," Cindy said. "That's the problem."

"Do you think Yana knows?"

Cindy didn't answer because a young couple came into the store. They were dressed head-to-toe in Ralph Lauren, Jay noticed, except for their sunglasses, which were Prada. The woman looked at the horror movie table.

"What are those stains?" she asked.

"Fake blood smears," Jay said. "It was used in a bunch of horror movies."

"Which ones?"

Jay walked over and showed her the tag. "Bunch of B movies, to be perfectly honest, but if you're a fan—"

"Oh, my God!" the woman said. "I know all those movies. And I can picture the scene in *Chopping Mall* where this table was used."

"Chopping Mall?" her husband asked.

"It's not my fault you can't appreciate art." She turned back toward Jay. "Seven hundred and fifty dollars?"

"Yes, ma'am."

She reached into her wallet and handed him an American Express card, ignoring her husband's pleas. "I'll put it in my workshop," she said. "You'll never have to see it." She turned to Jay and they arranged a delivery time. Jay sent a text message to the moving company they'd contracted with. And with that, the happily married couple left.

"I think," Cindy said, "that she'll have the table longer than the guy."

"I don't know about that," Jay said. "There was a certain joy about the argument—like, he made his view clear, she overruled him, but then she compromised by saying it wouldn't be in a common area."

"True," Cindy said.

"So where are we with Ben Sinclair?"

"Well, we know he's not a registered financial advisor, which means he could be taking advantage of Yana."

"Does it also mean he'd have a motive for killing Dylan Redman?" Jay ran his hand along the horror movie table for what would be one of the last times.

Cindy didn't say anything for a moment. "I want to think it does," she admitted, "but I don't really see how."

"I do."

"Tell me."

"Dylan Redman was a conniving little schemer," Jay said. "He did his research on us before we even met with him, and I'm sure he did the same on Yana. Learned all about her career so he could suck up to her. And he probably did some research on Ben Sinclair too."

Cindy nodded. "FINRA's not behind some locked door that only financial advisors can get through. Dylan could have had access."

"Would it have come up just by googling him?"

"No," Cindy said. "Because it wasn't a news story, and it's a regulatory website, so they don't have the best search engine options. You have to type his name into the directory, then open the file with his record, and scroll down to page thirteen to find the complaint. It would take some doing, but an enterprising researcher could find it."

"Well, that would make it even more valuable for someone like Dylan—he could've done the work to find that little nugget, and known it was hard enough to find that it wouldn't be common knowledge. That he could have weaponized it. Which he might well have done. Ben told us, with Yana right there, that Dylan insisted on meeting with everyone separately to discuss the consignment."

Cindy nodded. "In which case, he could've told Ben that he was on to him—that he knew that he didn't have a license because he'd stolen from clients."

"And he could've threatened to tell Yana about that—*unless* Ben used his position of trust to talk Yana into giving the consignment to Cypress." Jay felt a surge of energy, and it wasn't *just* the caffeine pills, even if it was *also* the caffeine pills. They were talking like real sleuths, putting together the puzzle, trying to figure out what happened. The stakes were high, but—and he chided himself for thinking this—it was also, in its own way, kind of fun. Exhilarating.

"For someone who's such a nice guy," Cindy said, "you're good at imagining what bad people might do, Jay Allan. But it goes deeper than that. Practicing as a financial advisor with a revoked license could get Ben arrested and sent to jail—with extra penalties for elder abuse."

"Wow," Jay said. "Now that would be a motive."

"But then how would the missing painting play into it?"

"Oh, that's easy," Jay said. "Ben saw the walls closing in on him. Figured with Dylan knowing about the license issue, it was likely he'd told someone else. Maybe his assistant, maybe even Yana and her son. With his honeypot nearing an end, he swiped something."

"And sold it."

"Or he's keeping it in a safe place to sell it later, once the heat's off."

"Either or," Cindy said. She paused before speaking again. "But he could've taken something much more valuable."

"Maybe he thought no one would notice," Jay said. "I should tell Detective Fletcher about this."

"*You* should? Why shouldn't *we* tell him?"

Jay flushed. He could feel the heat rising to his cheeks. "Well, I—that's what I meant."

"I'm just messing with you," Cindy said. "You can tell him, if we decide to go that route. I want you two to fall in love so you can live happily ever after with a handsome police detective." The phone rang, but she ignored it. "I think, though, that we should tell Yana first. And that we should tell her ourselves."

"Why?"

"Because if we tell Fletcher, he may need to keep the info secret for his investigation. But I'm worried about Yana here. I don't want her to be with Ben one minute longer than she needs to."

"Maybe we could tell Fletcher and then tell Yana?"

"Except that he'll probably direct us to keep it to ourselves. And then where will Yana be? If we override Fletcher and tell Yana anyway, after he tells us not to, you'll have to disobey your future husband before you've even been on a date. I'm telling Yana."

Before Jay could respond—even though he had no idea how to respond to that—she picked up the phone and dialed.

Jay walked out of the office to help a customer find a piece of costume jewelry once worn by her favorite actress—Debbie Reynolds. He sold it to her and then returned to find Cindy hanging up.

"That was Warren," Cindy said. "I told him we needed to meet with Yana. He said she's at the gym but will be finished up with her aerobics class in thirty minutes. He's texting her to meet me at the juice bar there."

"And suddenly," Jay said, "I feel like I'm lazy."

"Driving to meet a ninety-year-old after her aerobics class will do that."

"Should we walk?"

"Nope. And I don't think you should come."

That stung. Jay tried not to show it, but he could tell that Cindy sensed it. It was always hard to hide his emotions from her.

"I think it's better if it's just me," Cindy said, her hand on his arm. "This is what I did for a living, and I've had these professional conversations more times than I can count. Telling someone they've trusted the wrong person isn't easy, and it's better one-on-one. It'll be miserable enough for me, so no need to inflict it on you too. You'll have more fun working on your photo shoot anyway."

Jay trusted her, but that didn't mean he wasn't going to worry. People rarely liked to be told uncomfortable truths, and while he'd never tell her this himself because he loved her too much to hurt her feelings, he wasn't sure Cindy could deliver the news as delicately as it needed to be with someone like Yana Tosh, a client they desperately needed to stay friendly with.

But as he stared into Cindy's eyes, he could see that same, familiar determination he'd known for years, and he knew that there was no talking her out of this one. Best to get back to his photo shoot and occupy himself—that way, he might not think about all the ways their store could be pulled out from under them.

Yana's health club was everything Cindy had expected a nonagenarian movie star's Palm Springs gym to be. A sign out front advertised a special: ninety-nine dollars for the first month, three hundred and forty dollars per month thereafter, with a one-year commitment. The price staggered Cindy. She'd made enough money to afford it, and she valued exercise, and the facility did look nice, but she was too practical and wary of affectation. Where she and Jay had grown up in small-town Oklahoma, working out usually meant manual labor, and if you were a competitive athlete, it meant joining the YMCA. Personally, Planet Fitness was the perfect gym for her—clean and fresh, nice people, plenty of equipment. Running on the treadmill next to Esther, watching whatever cooking show Esther had turned the channel to, had been one of the highlights of every weekend they had together. She willed the memory out of her mind, desperate to focus on the task.

Trainers carrying clipboards wandered the lobby, backslapping each other and greeting visitors. The forced social energy of fitness people always annoyed Cindy. She preferred a gym rather than a social scene.

A trainer in his mid-forties, tall and muscular in a chemically enhanced sort of way, immediately approached her. "Welcome to Tinseltown Fitness. How can I help you get started with your fitness goals today?"

Cindy shuddered. The scripted sales pitch of gym workers was the last vestige of 1980s multilevel marketing culture. "I'm just going to meet a friend in your juice bar."

"It's a lovely juice bar," the man said. "A perfect place to cool down after a workout. I doubt your current gym has anything like it."

"Look," Cindy said, "you seem like a nice guy, and I know how hard sales is. But I have a gym I like, and I'm never going to pay three hundred dollars a month to run and lift pieces of metal. So if you could just direct me to the juice bar, I promise I'll tip the server well, and you'll have better luck selling a membership to literally anyone else who comes in here." She smiled as she spoke, and the guy smiled back.

"I do appreciate your directness, ma'am," he said. "Right upstairs and to your left." He pointed, veins popping out of his sleeves.

"Thank you." Cindy hurried up the stairs.

Yana was sitting at a table alone, reading an issue of *Closer* magazine, a gossip rag with a laser focus on the fifty-plus set, a readership more interested in a cover with Marie Osmond than Justin Bieber.

Cindy sat down next to her. "*Closer* magazine," she observed.

"Yes," Yana said, without looking up. Clearly she intended to finish her article. "Old celebrities. And I'm so old that I recognize fewer and fewer of them every year. When you get to be my age, things that happened forty years ago seem like the hot new thing. I've just been too damn old for too damn long."

Cindy smiled, waiting patiently and in silence until Yana dog-eared the corner of the page she was on, closed the magazine, and slid it into her bag.

"Why did you want to meet?" Yana asked. "Any issue with the consignment? I still haven't found the *Mirror Crack'd* painting, if that's what you're wondering about."

"I'm sorry to hear that," Cindy said.

Yana grimaced, as if she was in physical pain. "I just don't know where it could be. It's only one piece, I know. But it is a nice one."

"Is anything else missing?"

"No," Yana said. "Ben and I spot-checked the inventory today. Got through a hundred or so pieces. Took damned near all morning."

"Hopefully it will turn up," Cindy said.

"Yes," Yana said. "So, what can I help you with?"

"Well, actually, it's something I'm hoping to help *you* with. A delicate matter, Yana, something that's awkward but I think important—"

"Cindy," she said, "I just turned ninety. If you subtracted all the time I've wasted listening to people meander around with niceties, I'd still be in my seventies. Just tell me what you want to talk about."

"It's about Ben Sinclair," Cindy said.

"A lovely man. He looks out for me. Takes care of things, cares about me. Sometimes I feel like he's the only one who does."

"He seemed a little pushy about selling your collection."

Yana waved. "He's just trying to balance out my moron son."

"Warren doesn't want you to sell." Cindy noticed, not for the first time, that Yana danced around saying Warren's name whenever possible.

"No. His fantasy is that when I die, I'll donate the collection to establish a museum, and he can obtain a sinecure managing it. Then maybe, for the first time in his life, he can draw an honest paycheck that doesn't have his mother's name on it. But that's never going to happen. I don't want a museum. I want to sell."

"Well—" Cindy stopped. "Forgive me for prying, but couldn't he just help you sell the collection and inherit the money when the time comes?"

Yana laughed. "I'm not leaving him a cent, and Warren knows that. If I sell those costumes, I'll have a pile of money, and a lot of causes a lot more deserving than him."

"You wouldn't leave him *anything*?" As soon as Cindy said it, she worried she'd overstepped.

Yana either didn't care or didn't seem to notice the incredulity in Cindy's voice. "Maybe I'll leave him a hundred grand so he can buy a little house and live off Social Security. Though how much he'll get from that, I have no idea. Don't you have to have worked to get Social Security?"

Cindy wanted to steer the conversation back to the reason for her visit. "Yana," she said slowly, cautiously, "how much do you know about Ben?"

Yana stared at her blankly. "Enough to know that I trust him unequivocally."

"And how long has he worked with you?"

"Fifteen years. Why?"

Cindy did the math in her head. He'd lost his license in 2010, which meant that Yana had employed him five years before that. "What was he doing when you met him?" Cindy asked.

Yana suddenly tensed, and she looked downright nasty. Scary, even. Her face was more of a mask than anything soft and human. "Let me ask you, Cindy," Yana said, leaning forward, her hands clenched, "what is it that you know, or think you know, about Ben? I've already asked you once to be direct, and I won't ask you again. Out with it, or you can see yourself out."

Cindy hesitated briefly, then told her what she'd found on the FINRA website.

Yana sat in silence, betraying no reaction. At last, she said, "Since when does your client services offering include snooping into the private affairs of your consignors?"

The waitress stopped by again, and Cindy took advantage of the opportunity to let the tension float out of the conversation. She ordered a fourteen-dollar carrot juice and a gluten-free, fat-free, sugar-free ice cream sandwich—free of everything, including taste, Cindy assumed. She offered to buy Yana one, but Yana demurred, saying that she never ate desserts of any kind, even tasteless, odorless ones. MGM bosses had banished them from their starlets' diets in the 1940s, and she'd avoided them out of habit ever since. Instead, she ordered a glass of celery juice.

The server brought over the fake ice cream right away, and Cindy sucked on it while she waited for the juice. It was like inhaling a freezer. "Yana, I'm sorry if you were offended by what I just told you."

"I am offended, so I appreciate your apology, although I don't accept it yet. Continue."

Cindy tried not to smile. Yana was ninety, but she was far from tender and docile. Her attitude was inspiring—even when it was directed at you. "I used to be a financial advisor myself, and I'm always concerned about people getting taken advantage of. I saw it all the time. I could spend the next hour telling you stories that would make you cry."

"You can skip that. Do I look like somebody who allows herself to be taken advantage of? How about I tell you a story that might make *you* cry?"

Cindy raised her eyebrows, knowing better than to protest or push things further. "Oh?"

"I already know all about Ben's past."

"You do?"

She grinned with pride and fluffed her big white hair. "Of course."

"Then why did you still hire him?"

"Because I adore him and trust him. Ben Sinclair has been a movie buff his entire life. Back in the 1980s, when there were enough people still alive who'd heard of me, he was the president of my fan club. He must've been in high school. We had probably fifty members paying ten dollars a year in dues, and for that, Ben sent them a full-color newsletter twice a year, with trivia about me and old photos he'd found in magazines. Then he went to college and became a financial advisor."

"Your financial advisor?"

"Eventually, but he had other clients back then too."

"The fan club is gone?"

"Ben would be our last surviving member, I'm afraid."

"So how did he go from successful financial advisor to—" Cindy paused, wanting to word it carefully to avoid causing further offense. "To financially troubled and barred from the industry?"

"What I'm about to tell you," Yana said, "stays strictly between us."

Cindy nodded.

"Ben had a gambling addiction."

Cindy felt her stomach tighten, and it wasn't due to the ice cream. "He did?"

"Yes. It was bad enough that he started dipping into clients' funds. That's the nature of addiction. It gets progressively worse until the person hits rock bottom. When it did, he lost everything. I'd known him so long, and he never took that much money from anyone, including me. So I forgave him. I even paid for him to get treatment when he lost his health insurance. All of his clients were compensated, and everything turned out just fine. The only lasting consequence of the whole affair was that he lost his license. So I keep him on my payroll, at a modest salary, and he helps me with just about everything, including my money."

"I understand," Cindy said, meaning it. "You're a wonderful person to have maintained that connection through it all."

"He's the most loyal man you could ever hope to meet. But he's not a broker, and he doesn't have custody over my assets or anything like that. So, you see, there's no issue in terms of his standing in the industry."

"But you still refer to him as your financial advisor."

"Pride, Cindy," she said, as if explaining shapes to a baby. "*Pride.* If I can make him feel a little better by still calling him that, what's the harm?"

Cindy wasn't sure what to say. "So that's it?"

"Yes," Yana said. "That's it."

After an awkward end to the conversation, Cindy picked up the check—Yana didn't even bother with a perfunctory protest, her way of showing she still didn't fully forgive Cindy's prying—and left feeling like a conspiratorial moron.

Or was she? Yana's story made perfect sense, and it seemed to shut down Ben Sinclair's regulatory run-ins as an avenue of investigation. On the other hand, people with addictions did relapse, and who knew what he was capable of?

Cindy sighed as she swung into the SUV and roared out of the fitness center parking lot. She hadn't really learned anything at all from talking to Yana, other than that the woman trusted her "financial advisor" absolutely.

When she reached Hooray for Hollywood, there was a police cruiser parked out front, and through the window she saw Jay and Detective Fletcher sitting at the horror movie table, engaged in animated conversation. Hopefully Jay's afternoon had gone better than hers.

But by the looks on the faces of the two men as they talked over a bloody kitchen table, she doubted it.

Jay was almost disappointed when Simon turned his attention from him to Cindy after she walked into the store. *Almost*—he was still too smart to let himself get swept up in Cindy's romantic nonsense. Simon—*Detective Fletcher*—was investigating a homicide that Jay was involved in. Nothing more than that.

"How's the parallel investigation going, Ms. Cooper?"

"Who told you?" she said. Jay noticed how immediately Cindy stiffened when she started talking to Fletcher, hackles up and on guard.

"We were just talking, and the subject happened to come up," Jay said.

"Jay, you are the *worst* at keeping secrets." Cindy pulled up a chair and joined them at the table. "Is this the part where you're going to tell me to leave police business to the police, Detective?"

"Nah," Fletcher said. "That would be such a cliché, and you haven't done anything illegal. Yet. But I *will* tell you to be careful. And while I understand you have a business to run, and know a lot about money and want to help people . . . it wouldn't be a bad idea to give us a heads-up on anything you learn."

"Fair enough," Cindy said. "Are we suspects?"

Simon's expression gave away nothing. "I can't answer that. What did you learn meeting with Yana?"

Cindy hesitated briefly.

"Look," Simon said, "you're in a bad spot here—I'm not gonna lie. You were the last people to see Dylan alive, and you were competing with him for a big deal. You had motive, means, and opportunity. If you're innocent, telling me what you know can only help you prove that. Otherwise, this investigation is going to take a lot longer, and I'm not sure if you'll be able to save your business. Fair enough?"

Cindy nodded, though she glared at Jay. Apparently she didn't think he needed to mention their dire financial straits too. Whoops.

"So what did you find out from Yana?"

"Not much, sadly." Cindy walked them through her conversation with Yana at the juice bar. Jay wasn't sure what to make of it—of what Cindy was telling him or of Fletcher's response. It sounded like a dead end, and a perfectly innocent explanation for Sinclair's role in Yana's life, but who really knew? Sinclair's regulatory rap sheet was what it was—and Yana's affection for him and knowledge of his crimes didn't make him any more trustworthy. If anything, it suggested that Yana, as much as she seemed like a tough old bird, might be too trusting and vulnerable. But then, Jay thought, the people who put on the toughest acts often had the softest hearts.

When Cindy was finished, Fletcher spoke. "Huh," he said.

"That's it?" Cindy said. "That's your response?"

Fletcher nodded.

"He's like the detective in a silent film," Jay said. "Doesn't talk."

"Nah," Fletcher said. He didn't say anything else for a moment, then gave the hint of a smile. "Sorry, but I can't just give you information about ongoing police investigations, for about a hundred reasons. Most of which you're probably already aware of. But I can tell you, on behalf of the entire Palm Springs Police Department, that we do appreciate the public's assistance in all cases."

Jay knew, in the back of his mind, that Fletcher had been working him during their conversation, probably just sounding friendly to get information out of him. But there was still something hurtful about being referred to as "the public."

"So let me ask you a question," Cindy said.

"I can't promise I'll answer, but fire away."

"Guys or girls?"

Jay stepped in before Simon could. "Don't mind my business partner, Detective," he said. Then, eyeing Cindy: "She has no filter and says a lot of inappropriate things."

Simon laughed, and so did Cindy. "Let the man answer the question," she said.

"I didn't stop by to tell you about my personal life," Simon said. "But since it seems like you'll google me as soon as I walk out this door, you'd find out one way or another that you're speaking to the first openly gay homicide detective in the history of the Palm Springs Police Department."

"Told you!" Cindy practically shouted.

Jay winced with embarrassment.

"Is it hard, being an openly gay cop?" Cindy asked.

Fletcher's expression turned serious. "I don't really think about it."

Jay liked that—liked how quiet he was about it. Someone who was making social progress by being who he was, not through speeches and grand gestures. His thoughts of admiration were interrupted by Cindy's voice.

"Are you single?" Cindy said.

"Something like that," Fletcher said.

"Oh," she said. "Complicated. I like that."

Jay was starting to feel uncomfortable. Cindy had already crossed the boundaries of appropriateness. He felt like she was on the verge of playing matchmaker at any moment, and he really didn't want to put Fletcher on the spot like that. He also wasn't in the mood to get turned down today. "Let's get back to the case, shall we?"

"I was hoping you two could answer some more questions," Fletcher said. "Just to tie up a few loose ends."

"Happy to," Jay said.

"Great," Fletcher said. "Unfortunately, this will work better if I talk with you each separately. Can we use your office?"

Jay and Cindy agreed, and Jay volunteered to go first, even though he was starting to feel nervous again. Casual banter aside, the detective's desire to interview them separately suggested that he was concerned about them colluding on their answers. That meant he viewed them as suspects or possible suspects—or at least persons of interest. Of course, they could have just said no, and by the relaxed way Fletcher had asked, he didn't think that it would have been a huge deal.

Jay didn't hate the idea of being alone with Simon again, in any case. He liked the idea of being Simon's person of interest—just not the criminal kind.

The office was mostly Cindy's space, and it looked like the workspace of a nutty finance professor. She'd set up a computer with three monitors, and each one had a spreadsheet open on it. Budgets, marketing plans, and a document tab titled "Burn

Rate" that he caught out of the corner of his eye. Jay made a mental note to ask her about those spreadsheets later. She'd told him a little, but he needed to know everything there was to know about the business so he could be a good partner.

Jay saw Simon glance at the monitor before he sat down in the office chair, which annoyed Jay. He was definitely looking for clues. Maybe another reason he'd asked to speak to him alone—hoping that he could see more of the store, scope out the office. A reminder that Fletcher was here on business, and that Jay should treat it as such.

He sat down on the daybed tucked against the wall, removing a stack of Cypress Auctions memorabilia catalogs and setting them on the floor.

"Where'd you get those?" Simon asked.

"We subscribed to them when we started planning this business," Jay said. "We also bought a lot of old ones online, just for research."

Simon nodded. "You know the Cypress people well?"

"Not at all, Detective."

"You can call me Simon, and I'll call you Jay. How does that sound?"

He could get through this by channeling Cindy. How would she react? "It sounds a little like you're trying to put me at ease so that I'll spill some information, Detective."

"Simon," he insisted, but there was the slight hint of a smile as he said it. "So you're saying you don't know anyone from Cypress?"

"Yes, Simon," Jay said. "The first interaction we had with anyone there was the phone call from Dylan Redman that he wanted to meet. Then we had our meeting. And you know what happened after that."

"I do," Simon said. "How about Mr. Redman's assistant?"

"Eydie Jackson?"

"So you do know her."

"No. I mean, we met her once, briefly, like I told you. Yana complained about her too—said Eydie had called her to confirm an appointment and offended her. So I'd say we know *of* Eydie more than we *know* her."

"You said Ms. Jackson offended Ms. Tosh?"

"I mean, she just struck Yana as impertinent. But Yana is probably old-fashioned that way—very big on roles and seniority and that kind of thing. I didn't make anything of it. She's gotten prickly with us a few times too, but we're still on good terms as far as I'm aware."

"Did they argue?"

"I really don't know. All I heard was what Yana told me, which was that Eydie had annoyed her. She didn't give me a transcript of the conversation."

"Okay," Simon said. That hint of a smile was back. Was he enjoying Jay standing his ground? Was this a game to him? "So, Jay, tell me again about your meeting with Dylan Redman. Everything that you remember."

Again? But Jay did. The faster he got through it, the faster he could leave. Was it just him, or was the room hot? How could it be this hot with only two people sitting in it?

"You're aware," Simon said, "that Eydie Jackson was staying in the room adjacent to Dylan's at the hotel?"

"I was not aware of that, no," Jay said.

Simon was silent for a moment, flipping through the pad of notes he'd been taking. There was, Jay thought, a performative quality to the action. Like he wasn't really looking at notes, just creating a few moments of awkward silence to rattle Jay.

The detective seemed practiced and measured, like everything he did was on purpose. Somehow, the lack of spontaneity was alluring.

"If I told you that Eydie Jackson was in her hotel room during your meeting with Dylan Redman, would that change anything in your story?"

"Why would that change anything?"

"The walls at The Parker are famously thin, much to the chagrin of celebrity guests, and the joy of three generations of gossip columnists."

"Ah," Jay said. "Well, I didn't hear anything next door. But you're suggesting Eydie overheard the conversation between us and Dylan."

"Yes."

"And I'm guessing her recollection of it is not the same as mine and Cindy's?"

"No," Simon said. "It sure isn't. So you can see the problem I'm having."

"I sure can."

Jay heard the door open, and hoped it was a big-spending customer for Cindy to close. That gave him something nice to hope for, and distracted him from this interview that seemed likely to be the source of many future problems.

"Good," Simon said. "So is there anything you want to change in your version of the conversation you had with Dylan?"

That was it. The detective had, at last, gotten him angry. "No, Simon, I don't want to change my story, because you can't change the truth. And if Eydie told you she heard something different, she's either mistaken, which seems impossible, or lying. And that means you should be focusing your little investigation on her, not on me."

"*Little* investigation?" Simon's lip turned up in a smirk.

"I just meant that she's lying, so she's the one who's suspicious here. Didn't you say she was unusually upset when she found the body—like more than you would've expected?"

"I might have. But as you rightly pointed out, people react to trauma differently. And finding the corpse of someone you worked for would certainly be traumatic."

"Most people who travel together for work don't book adjoining rooms," Jay pointed out. "Maybe that's a better angle for you to explore than Cindy and me."

"Perhaps they didn't book adjoining rooms, and the hotel just assigned them together because they were booked at the same time," Simon suggested. Jay got the distinct sense that he was enjoying this back-and-forth, whether it was banter or an actual argument. That was a nice change for Simon; the cop of few words had been replaced by someone more fun. Simon started flipping through his notepad again.

Jay pressed on. "Look, Simon, we want to help you," he said. "We aren't hiding anything. But we can't help you unless you're giving us some information too."

Simon was silent for a moment, as though, Jay thought, he already regretted that he was about to tell them more than he had originally planned. Unless that was all calculated, to get on Jay's good side, and he'd gone into this conversation knowing exactly what he would and would not say. Simon spoke, "Eydie said that she overheard the whole conversation, and that it was cordial enough. *Until* Cindy started pressing Dylan about giving Hooray for Hollywood a role in the Yana Tosh collection sale."

"What?" Anyone who'd spoken to Cindy for longer than five minutes knew that she would never beg like that.

"She said that Dylan was polite about it but emphatic that he was highly confident that Ms. Tosh would choose Cypress to handle the collection."

"Well, you already know that's not true because Yana has begun consigning pieces to us to sell."

"Possibly because your primary competition is dead."

"Are you saying Cindy or I killed Dylan to get the consignment?" Jay knew he sounded indignant, but still. He was maybe being accused of murder. If you weren't allowed to be indignant in the face of a false murder charge, then when?

"Not necessarily. And neither is Eydie Jackson. But she mentioned that Cindy became angry, and then despondent when Dylan rebuffed her efforts to cut her way in. Eydie also said Cindy begged him for a piece of the action, until he finally got angry and told you both to leave."

"She's lying," Jay said. "Cindy doesn't beg. And if you can't see that already, then you're the wrong detective for this case."

Fletcher was silent for a moment, and Jay heard the cash register ring out in the store. Maybe business was starting to pick up. If they could avoid a murder indictment, there might just be some hope here.

"Look," Simon said, "I'm just trying to figure out what happened."

With that, he stood and opened the door. The sounds of the Ray Conniff Singers doing "You're the Cream in My Coffee" wafted into the office, along with a few conversations among customers. It felt jarring and out of place, given how poorly the conversation with Simon had gone. One minute they'd been sitting around the horror movie table, with Jay even flirting a little bit despite his reservations. And the next, that detective was outlining a strong murder motive for Cindy and him.

Had Simon been stringing him along earlier, to build rapport between them? Maybe he'd even lied about being gay so that Jay would let down his guard.

Paranoia, Jay thought, *is a terrible feedback loop.* He tried to dismiss it from his mind. "Good luck," he told Cindy as he exited the office.

* * *

Half an hour later, Cindy left the office, fuming with rage, and Fletcher drove away in his cruiser. "Good riddance," she cursed under her breath.

"How'd it go?" Jay asked. As if it wasn't obvious.

"Don't ask," Cindy snapped. "Let's get out of here."

It was five o'clock, so they closed up the store, and Cindy checked Twitter for the first time in hours. She scrolled quickly through depressing political news, then saw Lenae's latest Tweet. She called out to Jay: "News from Lenae!"

"Oh?"

"She's reporting that a police source says Dylan's cause of death was sodium fluoride poisoning."

"So if that's true, it really was murder," Jay said.

"Yep." Sometimes Cindy had to wonder about him: they'd just spent an hour with a homicide detective. Of course it was murder. But she didn't want to snap at Jay; she knew that would just be unfairly venting her anger at Fletcher. And to think she'd been trying to play matchmaker with him earlier! If she never saw Fletcher again in her life, so much the better.

"Any mention of us or Yana Tosh?"

"No," Cindy said. "Lenae seems to be keeping her word."

Cindy navigated away from Lenae's Twitter and opened Google's browser, where she typed in "sodium fluoride." She read about the effects of oral ingestion, which was the most likely way it would kill. That meant it probably had been something in Dylan's coffee—unless there was something else he'd eaten. Death could occur within thirty minutes of ingestion, but it might take longer. Symptoms might include pain, excess salivation, and fatigue. Death would likely be by respiratory failure. She told Jay about it.

"How easy would it have been for whoever killed him to get that?" Jay said. "Would it have required a lot of planning? What kind of killer are we dealing with here?"

Cindy searched a little more. "It's used in a lot of pharmaceuticals and in rat poison," she said. She kept reading. "Oh, this is kind of interesting. It can last forever if you store it in a cool, dry place."

"No expiration date?"

"None," Cindy said. "Apparently it's unusual in that way."

"Interesting," Jay said. "That will make the investigation harder, won't it? The poison could have been purchased anytime, going back forever. It's not like they can call up all the local chemical companies and see who's been buying it lately."

"It's probably something we should leave to the police."

Jay nodded. "What did Simon tell you?"

Cindy told Jay about her conversation with Simon and listened as Jay told her about his.

"It seems like Eydie's relationship with Dylan was more than professional."

"Agreed. Let's talk to her."

"Would Simon be okay with that?"

Jay grinned. "He didn't say not to!"

Cindy rolled her eyes. "Probably because he didn't think it needed to be said."

Jay shrugged. "Doesn't change the fact that he didn't say it. I'll do it alone."

"Don't you need me?"

"No," he said. "I think it's better if I handle it. We don't want her to feel like people are ganging up on her."

"I could handle it alone, then," Cindy said. "Why you?"

Jay paused. "If Eydie and Dylan were involved romantically and she killed him, then maybe Dylan betrayed Eydie—and I'm the one who has experience with romantic betrayal, so maybe I can relate to her, connect with her better based on what I've been through."

"Good thinking," she said.

"Thank you. I thought of it all by myself."

They were silent for a moment, then Cindy spoke. "You think it'll be safe for you, if she is the killer?"

"Yes. I'll make sure I meet with her in public. What would point the finger toward her being the murderer more than having me turn up dead right after I go talk to her?"

Cindy hated to give up control, but Jay did have a point. "Okay." She watched as Jay picked up the store phone and looked up the number for Cypress Auctions's entertainment department on his cell phone. He dialed it, asked for Eydie, listened briefly, and hung up.

"Interesting," he said. "She's still in Palm Springs. And presumably still staying at The Parker."

Cindy smiled. "Take my car. I'll stay here and go back to those spreadsheets."

"Speaking of which, sometime soon I'd like to go over them with you. I don't know as much as you do about money, of course, but it's not like I'm Gomer Pyle on Valium. I want to learn. You can teach me."

Cindy inhaled, uncomfortable with the conversation's direction. "I like you as Gomer Pyle," she said. "Pure, incorruptible. Why don't you let me do the worrying?"

Jay gently put his hand on her arm. "If we're going to be partners," he said, "I need to know how it all works. And I don't like you keeping stuff from me. The business is in trouble—you and Mary told me that, but I want to know the details. It'll help me help us."

She nodded. In a way, it might be good to have him in on everything—aware of the numbers and how little room they had. It made her feel less alone. Perhaps, she thought, she should let herself lean on Jay more for emotional support—and let go of her need for him to be carefree. He was stronger than she gave him credit for, and he could help her with all the miseries on her mind. "Okay. I'll show you." Cindy pulled up her laptop and started showing him the budget she'd worked out. She suspected that Jay was bored within thirty seconds.

When she was finished, Jay said, "This isn't good."

"No," she said. "It isn't."

"You should have told me sooner."

Cindy had been waiting for that, and she didn't have a good answer. "I didn't want you to worry."

"It wasn't your choice to make for me, Cindy. I have a right to know about my future."

"You were working so hard. All it would've done was stress you out. I couldn't have both of us stressed. Besides, we get the Yana Tosh collection, and all of this is solved."

Jay shook his head. "It would help to have the murder overhang removed quickly so we can just worry about the business—and focus on finding consignments, not lawyers."

"Absolutely," Cindy said. "Maybe your little chat with Eydie will help us get to the bottom of Dylan's murder—and the rest of that consignment."

"Isn't that what you business types call synergy?" Jay smiled. She could see that he was trying to let her off the hook—but just a little bit.

Cindy winked. "You're learning."

She watched as Jay wandered the costume section of the store and returned a few minutes later in a ridiculous get up: large sunglasses worn by Elton John in *Tommy* and a bowler hat used in a string of forgotten 1960s cop shows. He looked ridiculous and nothing like Jay, which, she quickly realized, was the point. Her dear partner was going to confront Eydie wearing a disguise. Most people couldn't pull it off, but Jay had supported himself for two decades doing impersonations in Vegas cocktail lounges. She liked his chances. Her only regret was she wouldn't be there to see it.

Jay got in the *Jurassic Park* Explorer and drove faster than he usually did, hurt and angry about more things than he could count. He loved Cindy endlessly, but there was a condescension about her that hurt his feelings. It was true: she was the numbers whiz and knew infinitely more about money and business than he did. She had the bank account to prove it. But at the same time, they were business partners, and that meant he needed to know what was going on with the money and what she was planning. He wondered whether she wasn't thinking clearly because of her grief. He reminded himself to extend grace to Cindy. Still, he also had to be practical. If the business was about to fail, he needed to know so that he could make other plans. He couldn't imagine what he would do. Go back to Las Vegas and put his trio back together? Nothing sounded more horrifying. He understood why Cindy didn't want him to worry, but it was his life at stake too.

Cindy was just trying to protect him, he knew. And in any case, it didn't matter. He was obsessed with the business, loved working with Cindy, and they were going to make it work. He hooked his phone into the music streaming service and put on his favorite singer: Barry Manilow. It was the only thing that could get him out of any funk, no matter the cause. He'd been seven years old the first time he saw Manilow on TV, and he'd instantly felt a connection—before he knew he was gay or that Manilow was gay. But the connection went beyond that. Manilow's style was so his own—unique, profoundly unhip, and yet it worked. It made people happy, and his unwillingness to conform to trends made him cool in a way no one more conventionally cool could ever be. Manilow's music had been his lifeline during his and Cindy's scandal twenty years ago, and he'd seen him in concert at least a dozen times since.

With Barry belting out "Looks Like We Made It," Jay was able to center himself—to calm his nerves, put aside his anger, and focus on the task at hand: trying to meet with Eydie and make the most of it. That meant not blowing up at her and just trying to find out what she was up to: why she was lying about them, who exactly she was, and what she wanted.

As Jay looked out the window, he was reminded of everything he would lose if he had to move back to Las Vegas. Not just Cindy's companionship and company, but . . . man, he was reminded every time he looked around why he'd been so willing to pack everything up and move to Palm Springs. The view was exquisite: palm trees, yes, but also mountains in the background, and vast, uninhabited stretches of meadows, along with deserts. And then there was the wildlife: Palm Springs had enough land that was undeveloped to be a haven for endangered species. Whatever Jay missed of the Las Vegas burlesque scene was more than offset by the chance to see nature up close.

A few minutes later, he pulled back into the parking lot at The Parker. It was funny, he thought, how quickly normalcy had returned. The room where Dylan Redman died was probably still cordoned off, maybe even that whole wing of the floor, but the rest of the hotel was back to Palm Springs paradise. Most of the hotel's guests probably didn't even know what had happened, thanks to the staff's famous discretion.

Jay walked up to the reservation desk, then stopped, thinking better of it. If he strolled up to the desk and asked to speak with a murder-involved guest, he might be shown the door. Or they'd call up to her, and she'd refuse to see him. Maybe better to go through unofficial channels.

Walk around like you own the place, Cindy's dad had taught him when he was a kid, *and no one will question you.*

He headed through the lobby, out onto the patio, and through to one of the pools. There was a lifeguard there, a guy in his late sixties, hairy and with a gut. Social progress, Jay thought: Lifeguards shouldn't be hired for their abs.

"Hey there," Jay said.

"What's up, dude?" the lifeguard said.

"I'm hoping you can help me with something," Jay said. "There's a lady from Cypress Auctions here. I heard she has some hot merchandise for sale, and I'm hoping to see if I can make a deal with her, but I don't know where she is." He pulled out a photo of Eydie from the company's website on his phone. "She look familiar?"

The lifeguard hesitated.

"Listen, I know you need to be discreet," Jay said, lowering his voice to a deep, conspiratorial whisper, "but, well, I represent a big client, and there's a lot of money in it for her. I'm sure she'd be grateful if you could help me."

The guy looked at the picture and smiled at Jay. Jay reached into his pocket and handed him a crisp hundred dollar bill, forking it over before he could think better of it. He wasn't going to ask Cindy to reimburse him, and his own savings weren't exactly hefty. Still, talking to Eydie was his best option for a next step on clearing him and Cindy of a murder allegation, and a hundred dollars was a small price to pay.

"I'd appreciate your help too," he said.

The lifeguard laughed. "That lady," he said, "is nuts. Every time I see her, she's either at the bar or walking like she's on her way back from it."

"Which bar? This place has, like, five bars."

"And she's been to all five of them. You can wander around and look, but I wouldn't go around showing her picture to any of the bartenders. They're trained on privacy here, and they might kick you out. I'm too old to care about that, and you seemed desperate." He paused. "And very generous. Just walk around, check the bars. If she isn't passed out in her room, you'll find her here somewhere, eventually."

"Do you know what room she's in?" Jay said, looking at the company iPad the guy had on the stand next to him

"Sorry, pal. Even I draw the line there."

Jay nodded and walked away. The pool was mostly empty, but the handful of kids in it, splashing and screaming as they played Marco Polo, had provided enough noise cover for their conversation.

He meandered around the resort, checking out the bars, each of which seemed to represent a different side of Palm Springs—though only the wealthy sides. There was Norma's, a cozy hangout catering to the senior set that probably also patronized Norma's sister restaurant in New York City. Then there was Mister Parker's, which billed itself as "Dark. Discreet. Decadent." and "A guy's guy sort of place." Jay rolled his eyes at the desperate machismo—as though there were anything inherently manly about cigars and brown leather. With three more bars to go, Jay wandered, or at least tried to look like he was wandering, into The Mini-Bar. Designed to look like a jewel box, it boasted a dark emerald bar top, mirrors everywhere, and contemporary art: giant sculptures shaped like oversized pill capsules. Jay smiled. It wasn't a coincidence that the word "contemporary" was what you got when you combined the words "con" and "temporary."

His rumination on the commercialism of creativity was interrupted by the sight of Eydie at the bar, sitting alone. No one else was at the bar yet, and the bartender, a young guy, was facing the opposite direction, polishing glasses—or perhaps pretending to, so he could avoid interacting with his only customer. Eydie wore an all-red power suit, a gold Cartier panther necklace, and a lot of makeup—some of which was running, along with the tears that had collected in the pile of tissues by her side. The scene reminded him of Tammy Faye Bakker.

Jay walked over, sat on the stool next to her, ordered a screwdriver, and debated whether to tell her who he was. He could see that the disguise had worked, and so far there was no hint of recognition from their previous meeting. It was either his disguise, her state of inebriation, or the fact that they'd only been face-to-face for a minute, maybe less. Or even a combination of all of those things, Jay thought. He always liked to be honest and straightforward with people, and she might be more willing to open up to him if she knew who he was. If she figured out who he was without him telling, it would backfire, and she'd shut down completely. On the other hand, she was intoxicated enough that strategizing the best course of action was like predicting the direction of a staggering drunk's next step in an open field. He did a mental coin flip and decided to stay incognito.

The screwdriver arrived right away, and the bartender went back to his previous position.

"Rough day?" Jay asked Eydie.

She nodded.

"I'm a good listener," Jay said. He almost felt bad. Eydie was too drunk to know what she was doing, and in most settings, he wouldn't have wanted to take advantage of that. He would never, for instance, negotiate a price for a piece of movie memorabilia with someone in this state. But Eydie had lied about him and lied about his best friend, and he needed to find out why. His life and Cindy's were riding on it.

When Eydie didn't respond to his prompt, he spoke again. "Guy trouble?"

She nodded. "And then some."

"Been there, done that, kiddo," he said. "I'm probably twenty years older than you, and I'm here to tell you: there's nothing that can happen with a guy that's so bad it's worth getting depressed over. When I look back, my biggest regrets aren't the things that happened with guys. The thing that always hurt me was how much I let guy trouble get me down on myself. You can't let your self-image and self-worth be tied up in that." Jay smiled to himself. Here he was, pumping Eydie for information and at the same time giving himself the pep talk he needed to hear.

She thought about that, then took another sip of her drink. "The problem here is more complicated."

"Try me."

She nodded, mustering what judgment she had to decide how much to tell him. "The guy I lost," she said, "we worked together. He was my mentor. But it became more than that."

"Ah," Jay said. "A workplace romance. A setup for guaranteed, reality TV–style drama." Like his own Las Vegas situation, he realized. Who was he giving advice to here?

Eydie scowled. "It wasn't creepy like that. It was an immediate connection. Both of us felt it. But our romance wasn't good for my career."

"Why not?"

"He took credit for everything," she said. "Every deal we landed was *his* deal, which meant I didn't get the commissions I should've gotten, and the higher-ups didn't notice me. He made me invisible—all for his own benefit."

"Did you ever complain?

She nodded.

"What did he say?"

"Oh, he'd just blow it off. He'd get really condescending and say, 'Eedles, don't worry.'"

Jay had to force his face still so that it wouldn't pucker and betray his distaste. "He called you 'Eedles'?"

She smiled. "My name is Eydie, but guys always call me that—if we're tight."

Jay forced a smile of his own. "Gotcha. And what would he say about it?"

She made her voice unnaturally deep and sultry. "He'd say, 'We're a unit, babe. What makes me look good will make you look good.' And then he'd make a move on me. And I believed him." Eydie sighed, far more heavily than a woman her age should ever sigh. "But it never did. The credit just kept going to him, and I stayed right where I was while he kept getting bigger bonus checks."

"So what are you going to do about that?"

"He's out," she said, apparently not wanting to mention the death specifically. "And now I'm in charge of this big deal he was about to close. Except the seller appears to be getting cold feet."

The bartender stopped by and asked Jay if he wanted another drink. He didn't really, but he accepted in the spirit of making friends. And, really, to celebrate. He shouldn't feel elated over all of this, but if Yana was giving Eydie the sense that she had "cold feet," that could only mean that she was leaning more toward Hooray for Hollywood.

"You think he had the deal for sure?" Jay said.

Eydie gave a short, bitter laugh. "Well, he seemed really cocky about it. Said the bumpkins he was up against had nothing to offer and that it was ours—the biggest Hollywood memorabilia deal Cypress had ever seen."

Jay felt more than a twinge of anger. He was tempted to break character and tell her off, but he restrained himself. One thing he'd been learning from Cindy: in business, emotion had to be harnessed. If it wasn't going to help your cause, you stifled it. "What are you going to do about it?" he asked instead.

"All I can say is, people shouldn't underestimate me." The grandiosity of the threat was undermined by her slurring speech.

Again, Jay contemplated telling her who he really was, to see how she reacted, but thought better of it. He could confront her about that later. Until then, he'd probably gotten all he could out of her for now.

He paid for his drinks, including the second one he'd left untouched, and wished Eydie well with whatever it was she was up to. As he turned away from the bar, he spotted an out-of-uniform Detective Fletcher watching from a booth directly behind Eydie, perhaps twenty feet away. He'd been so focused on Eydie when he walked up to the bar that he'd completely missed Fletcher. Had he been listening to their conversation just now? Had he overheard everything? Jay started to say something as he passed, but Fletcher locked eyes with him and put a finger up to his lips.

Jay exited the bar and immediately noticed Simon tailing behind him.

"What are you doing?" the detective snapped.

"The same thing you are. Trying to find out what Eydie is up to."

"The difference is, I'm a professional, and this is my case. My advice to you would be to leave this case to the Palm Springs PD. Unless you're worried about your own legal risk, which you probably should be, in which case you should hire an attorney instead of you and your partner going all Bobbsey Twins here."

"Bobbsey Twins?" Jay said. "Really? You couldn't have just said The Hardy Boys?"

Simon looked momentarily hurt. "The Bobbsey Twins books were my favorite ones as a kid. They got me into the idea of being a detective."

"Are you joking?"

"No."

Jay patted him on the shoulder. "Look at you," he said. "Shaved head, muscle-bound tough guy, but really just a little nerd. Funny." He didn't mean it as an insult, but when he realized it could have been taken as one, he decided to cut the conversation short and turn away. He could keep Simon guessing just as well as the other way around.

He started to walk away, but Simon called after him. "Jay," he said. His voice was firm and professional. But was there just a hint of gentleness in it? Jay didn't want to turn around and see Simon's face. "Just be careful, okay? And the best way to do that is to stay out of my case."

Cindy generally liked a bit of excitement in her life, but she was delighted when three days passed by without incident or news—how things changed when you were under investigation for murder. By the time Wednesday rolled around, she was profoundly grateful that she and Jay had chosen it as the one day a week Hooray for Hollywood was closed during morning hours. Instead, the store would be open from three to five or by appointment. They needed a morning off each week for local travel to look at collections or help brainstorm decorating ideas for clients, and midweek was perfect because that way they hopefully wouldn't miss out on any of the high-income, weekend-getaway shoppers. The problem was that the home visits weren't happening. That one canceled appointment had been just the beginning. A flood of cancellations had followed—with no new appointments to fill in the gaps.

She felt like a leper—a leper whose business was going to be destroyed by the smell of scandal if she and Jay and Simon couldn't hurry up and get to the bottom of this.

And Simon didn't appear to be in any rush.

For now, though, she and Jay wanted to take a morning with Mary to boost morale.

Cindy drove them to the Sunny Dunes Antique Mall, a multi-dealer store not far from their own. It was a route she and Esther had driven together frequently—always looking for little tchotchkes to make their Palm Springs dream home more personal. *Will there ever be a time when I can do anything without being reminded of Esther?* Cindy wondered. But maybe she was making progress in her own way. For the first time she could remember, the memories of Esther weren't making her miserable exactly. Just wistful. She said as much to Jay.

"I hope," he said, "that you'll have more moments like that. Just remember that Esther is always with you. Always. That's why this is going to work. Hooray for Hollywood was her dream just as much as it was yours."

Cindy nodded. "Hopefully, Esther is leading us to some underpriced treasures at Sunny Dunes—something we can flip quickly to get some cash coming in."

They wandered the aisles in search of treasures for themselves, but mostly for inventory. The dealers at Sunny Dunes were sophisticated and knowledgeable, so it was unlikely they'd find huge bargains, but Cindy's thinking was that they might find things that had been marked down because Sunny Dunes didn't typically draw buyers focused on movie memorabilia. One of Cindy's friends was an antique dealer who'd made a living doing what she called "antique arbitrage"—buying a piece at one flea market that didn't cater to that particular item's fans, and then selling it at a different one where it would be more appreciated.

The pickings were slim that day. Cindy bought a handful of '80s movie magazines for fifty cents each—not her favorite era, but one that was increasingly nostalgic for Gen-Xers. Jay one-upped her by finding a set of glasses from a charity golf tournament hosted by Bing Crosby—a bargain at ten dollars and a perfect item for Christmas, which was only four months away. Cindy always marveled at the fact that Jay could find better deals than she could. Now all they needed to do was keep the business afloat long enough to make it to the holidays, when those ten-dollar glasses would sell for a few hundred with the right *White Christmas* signage. Cindy smiled. Esther had loved Christmas.

Mary didn't know enough about entertainment or antiques to be much help, but Cindy loved her enthusiasm for indulging her own highly specific tastes, which struck most people as corny. For a dollar each, she bought three Precious Moments figurines, including one featuring Miss Piggy, her favorite Muppet.

They'd just gotten back in Cindy's SUV, put on a smooth jazz station, and started to drive toward a nature preserve for a picnic brunch when Mary said, voice grave and crackling with concern, "Okay, Cindy and Jay, I'm as much a part of this business as you two are, and I've cared about you for a long time. So it's time to tell Auntie Mary everything about everything."

Cindy looked at Jay, who was riding shotgun, and nodded.

"Okay," Jay agreed, "we'll tell you."

Jumping in when the other left something out, Cindy and Jay spent the rest of the ride and most of their picnic explaining everything they knew about the death of Dylan Redman. They told her about the missing painting and Ben Sinclair's financial foibles, and Yana's response to them.

"How could anyone, let alone a professional detective, think you two had anything to do with it?" Mary said.

"Well, they don't know us the way you do," Cindy said.

"I can be a character reference!" Mary said.

Cindy laughed. "It's not like renting an apartment or applying for a job," she said. "You don't just send them the names of three people who tell them you're not a murderer and then they cross you off the list."

Mary frowned. "No, I suppose it isn't. So how will we get them to stop thinking about you as suspects?"

"Well," Cindy said, "alibis would help, but we don't have that. So our best bet is to hope they find the real killer." She thought about adding that they were working on that, but didn't feel like a stern lecture from Mary about the need to be careful and stay out of police business. She already knew that's what they should do, but had no intention of listening. Too much was at stake.

"Everything about everything" didn't have to include *everything*.

They parked at the nature preserve, got out, and set up their picnic. They were sitting in the calming shade of the feathery foliage of a huge mimosa tree, tea sandwiches and fruit salad spread before them. When Cindy and Jay were finally done explaining the case, Mary spoke. "You talked to Yana about Ben Sinclair," she said.

"Yes," Jay said.

"And you also told that detective about him."

Cindy nodded.

"But you never spoke to Ben Sinclair about it directly?"

"No," Jay said.

"Matthew 18:15," Mary said.

Cindy and Jay both knew that verse by heart, but Mary recited it anyway. "'*If someone sins against you, go privately and point out the offense.*'"

"But this isn't about a conflict we have with him," Jay said. "It's about a murder investigation. I'm not sure that applies."

"Perhaps not," Mary said. "But you did speak negatively about him to his employer, and I think he deserves a chance to explain things to you, since you've taken enough of an interest in him to investigate him." She cracked an almost imperceptible smile, but Cindy spotted it. "Plus, it might help with your sleuthing."

"Okay," Jay said, pulling out his cell phone. "I'll call him and see if he can meet with us—assuming Yana hasn't already told him what we said, in which case he'll be in no mood to talk to me."

"I doubt she told him," Cindy said. "She wouldn't have wanted to hurt his feelings. And it wasn't anything new to her. Plus, it could hurt our relationship with him if we ended up working together and he knew we knew. Yana wouldn't want the drama."

"Sometimes I think Yana likes the drama," Jay said.

Cindy called Yana and asked for Ben, telling her there was a minor item related to the contract she wanted to discuss. A lie, but a harmless one. Yana said that it was his day off and hung up. Not rude, exactly. But definitely terse.

Cindy pulled up Ben's address on Google. It was an apartment complex just a few minutes away, and from what she could see on the map, each unit had a separate entrance. Cindy suggested she drop Jay and Mary back at the store in time to open up, leaving her to drive over to have a word with Ben Sinclair.

"Are you sure it's a good idea?" Jay said. "For you to go alone?"

Cindy waved. "It's a big complex, and there will be a lot of people around. Besides, I think I can take him." At the look of worry that still lingered on his face, she added, "I let you go talk to Eydie. Trust me with this one, okay?"

Twenty minutes later, Cindy pulled into Ben's apartment complex. It was nice enough, but nothing like the opulence Yana lived in. Most financial advisors weren't rich, Cindy knew, and it wasn't uncommon for even successful advisors to work for a lot of clients with vastly greater sums of money than they had. That dynamic could sometimes breed resentment and entitlement in certain people. A life spent serving rich people and knowing every detail of the extent of their wealth could lead to bad behavior in the wrong person.

She parked in a guest spot not far from Unit 147 and walked down the cracked sidewalk, passing a few children playing in the yard. She smiled at them. Cindy loved children, even though she and Esther had never had any desire to have their own.

There was no answer when she knocked on Sinclair's door. She tried again, but still nothing. Cupping her hand above her eyes, she looked in through the front window and saw, even through the curtains, that there were no lights on.

She noticed the mailbox by the door was still full, unlike the ones nearby. Today's mail hadn't arrived yet, so that probably meant Ben hadn't been home in a day. Cindy looked at one of the kids, a boy, probably five years old, riding a tricycle.

"Excuse me!" she called.

The boy stopped. "Hello!" he said. Friendly. They must not tell kids not to talk to strangers anymore, Cindy thought.

"Do you know Mr. Sinclair?" she said, pointing toward the door to his apartment.

"Yeah, he's nice," the boy said.

"Have you seen him today?"

He shook his head.

"How about yesterday?

The boy nodded.

"What was he doing?"

"Putting boxes in his car," the boy said.

"Do you know what was in them?"

Another headshake.

"How many boxes?"

He shrugged and held up five fingers, keeping one hand on the handlebar to steady himself, and flashing the other twice.

"Ten boxes?" Cindy said.

The boy nodded.

"Anything other than boxes?"

The boy thought about it. "Clothes," he said. "Hung up, like grown-ups wear to work."

"What kind of clothes?"

He looked confused.

"Boy clothes? Girl clothes?"

"Both," he said.

"Were they fancy?" Cindy said.

"Some," he said.

"And others?"

He thought about it. "Funny clothes," he said. "Like on TV—or *Star Wars*!" he said, excited at the memory of a film he obviously liked.

"Anything else he had with him?"

"A picture," he said. "Like the kind you hang on a wall."

"What was it a picture of?"

"I only saw the back," he said.

"Do you remember how big it was?"

More thinking. "No."

Cindy thanked him profusely, shuffled through her purse until she found a pack of stickers she'd bought to send her nephew, and handed them to him. The boy smiled. They were stickers for different Pokémon characters, which, she was happy to see, were apparently still popular. Some things never went out of style. She'd have to buy another pack to send her nephew.

She bolted to her car to call Detective Fletcher. Thinking better of that idea, she called Jay instead. She told him what she'd learned, then hung up and sat for a minute, thinking. Could Ben Sinclair have skipped town? It had only been a day—too soon to know for sure—but the pattern was concerning: He'd loaded up boxes of things, including a lot of clothing, at least some of which sounded like costumes, and hightailed it. She'd know more soon, when he either showed up at Yana's or didn't. But for now, it was suspicious.

And she wondered if the picture he'd taken with him happened to be that missing portrait.

"Enough drama," Cindy declared as she parked the *Jurassic Park* SUV in Yana's driveway, excited to be back to work. She and Jay had talked about Sinclair the whole drive over, but now it was time to focus. Nailing this meeting with Yana was the most important thing they could do right now. "Time to work on the sale."

"Yes," Jay crowed. "Business! I love business!"

Cindy rolled her eyes. He was a sarcastic little thing, but he was right. They could now, after much distraction, start to work on the details of the pieces they'd be selling for Yana. But when they walked in, Yana wasn't in any mood, and neither was her son—though Warren seemed decidedly less agitated than his mother. Ben hadn't shown up, Yana explained, which wasn't like him.

"He's an idiot," she said, "but he's reliable. If he says he'll be somewhere, he's there. And he said he'd be here. And he isn't."

"Did you call him?" Cindy said.

"Did I call him?" Yana snapped, her voice suddenly louder. "Do I look like a fool? Of course, I called him. His phone was off. And he isn't answering emails either."

It took her some time, but finally Cindy mustered the courage to pitch her idea—risking incurring Yana's wrath and possibly losing the consignment along with the chance at the rest of the collection. Plus, it would annoy Jay because they'd come here to work on the sale—they'd made that deal in the car. But the idea she had now might just be the key to figuring out who killed Dylan Redman.

"Would it help," Cindy said, "if I look at your finances with you? I could see what Ben's been up to. I know you trust him, but I think recent events may have given a reason to cast some doubt."

"I'm too tired to get into all that," Yana said.

"Your son could help me," Cindy pressed.

Cindy noticed Jay standing silently, carefully examining the sleeve of a leather bomber jacket from *Grease 2*.

"My son doesn't have a hand in my finances," Yana snapped. Warren looked at his mother with something like sadness in his eyes. *Or was that resentment?*

Cindy dropped the matter, planning to revisit it later. "Have you informed Detective Fletcher that Ben is missing?" she said.

"Yes," Yana said. "I called first thing this morning."

"That seems a little hasty," Warren said, sounding anxious. "He's only been gone a day."

"Someone is already dead, Warren," Yana said. "*Murdered.* And a painting given to me by Elizabeth Taylor is missing. Strange things are happening. I hope Ben just decided to take a few days off and get away—I wouldn't blame him if he did; it's been stressful. This was supposed to be a low-key job for all of us and a fun project for me. So far, it's proving to be anything but."

"I'm so sorry, Yana," Jay said, putting his hand on her arm.

"It's not your fault, dear," Yana said, softly. Good on Jay for stepping in, Cindy thought. If Yana liked one of them, at least, it was important to use that affection. "Or maybe it is. And if so, you'll rot in hell for it." She paused. "But I really don't think it's either of you. At least, I desperately hope it isn't."

Cindy listened patiently while Jay told Yana about his promotional plans. He'd made YouTube videos for some of the pieces, featuring just enough archival footage to highlight their importance while staying under the thresholds for copyright violations. An entertainment lawyer friend had helped him with that, he said. The plan was to start sending the videos to top news outlets in two weeks. The videos would end with a bit about Yana Tosh and how she'd assembled the collection. At some point, they'd need to schedule a sit-down interview for that part, but this wasn't the time to ask Yana about that.

Jay showed Yana some clips, and at last her mood improved. She squealed with delight. "They're wonderful! You were able to do all of that, just on your computer?"

Jay nodded.

"Things *have* changed," she marveled. "So the plan is to just post the videos, hope lots of people watch them, and people will send you offers?"

"Yes," Cindy said, "that's exactly what we want to do. We think we'll get thousands of views on these. We know how to make sure they get to all the right social media accounts. We will find the people who want this stuff desperately, and we'll see how much they'll pay for it."

"Why is that preferable to having an auction?"

"Because," Jay said, "with an auction, you might not get the highest price. Let's say you have one person who's willing to spend a million dollars for something, and the second highest bidder is only willing to spend five thousand dollars. How much will the item sell for?"

"A million?" Yana asked.

"No," Jay said, perfectly reciting the argument Cindy had given him. She was proud, watching him work with Yana like this. Much as he claimed to need her as the business end of things, seeing him interact with a client like this, with a manner Cindy just didn't have, it was so clear that she needed him too. "It will sell for five thousand five hundred dollars—one bidding increment over the second highest bidder. And you, my dear, will have left nine hundred and ninety-four thousand five hundred dollars on the table—or in the delighted owner's pocket."

Yana's groomed eyebrows rose. "We can't have that!"

"No, we can't," Jay agreed. "But this way, we'll get emails from people who are interested. Cindy will talk to them on the phone, research them a little, and figure out what their pain point is—the absolute most they'll pay. And we'll get it."

Yana smiled. "I like that plan."

"And that is why you should forget that Eydie Jackson at Cypress even exists," Cindy said. Jay shot her a glance, chiding her for taking the risk of overstepping.

Yana laughed, but her mood darkened, and her mouth twisted into more of a scowl. It was almost like she'd forgotten Cindy was in the room. "Now, now," she said. "Eydie doesn't speak so kindly about you either. Just do your best, and we'll see what happens."

She stopped for a second to examine her reflection in a dressing room–style mirror surrounded by lightbulbs. Cindy had a flash of realization: the former star enjoyed the attention that came with people competing for her objects and money.

"And let me know when you're ready to shoot the interviews," Yana added. "It will be a delight telling people the stories behind how I got the pieces."

"It will make the sale," Jay said. "With you in the video, the prices will double."

"That would be wonderful," Yana said.

Warren was watching this exchange, from beginning to end, not saying anything, but Cindy could tell he didn't share the excitement of the rest of the room. His face was impassive, like he was holding in an emotion he didn't want to express.

Cindy and Jay left. They called Mary to make sure everything was in order at the store, and then Jay pitched Cindy on the idea of a long run together, like they used to do. Even better, a run that would take them on a tour of movie stars' Palm Springs getaways. Cindy agreed, to Jay's obvious delight. They made a plan to meet Mary back at Cindy's house for dinner.

The two of them got in the car, stopped home to change into shorts and T-shirts, and made the five-minute drive to their starting point.

As they started to jog, Cindy recalled she'd once heard a TV doctor say that the healthiest run was a pace at which you could still carry on a conversation. That was exactly what she had in mind. Twenty years ago, she recalled, she and Jay would've challenged each other to races and wind sprints, but they'd mellowed now into a less competitive vision of exercise. As long as it raised their heart rates, she really didn't care.

They made a detour off the route and headed up Via Las Palmas, where they caught a glimpse of Elvis and Priscilla's Honeymoon Hideaway, at which the couple had arrived via private jet after a tiny wedding. Jay, somehow reading from his phone as he jogged, explained that the small guest list, Elvis's manager knew, would maximize publicity by making the whole event seem mysterious. "There's a lesson in that for selling memorabilia," Jay said, puffing a little. "Market the mystique. People want what seems elusive."

"You holding up okay?" Cindy said as they jogged back down the hill, back onto the route.

Jay smiled, but she could see that he was struggling to keep pace. He stayed thin by exercising a little and watching what he ate, but Cindy was the gym rat. She slowed the pace a bit, hoping that Jay wouldn't notice she was taking it easy on him.

"I'm okay," Jay said once he caught his breath. He brightened. "We're doing really well with Yana. She's excited about our ideas, and she likes us."

"We're a great team," Cindy agreed.

"And you're teaching me the business part," he said. "It's like *The Godfather*."

A car was rolling behind them, passive-aggressively braking rather than just decelerating, so Cindy and Jay dipped closer to the side to let him pass. Cindy lightened the pace even more, and Jay followed. She put her arm around his shoulder.

"One of the things I've always admired about you," she said, "is that you're willing and eager to learn new things and try new things."

"Even if I'm not good at them."

"Exactly," she said. "I could never do that. If I'm not good at something, I don't want to even think about it."

"The only way to get good at things is to start bad and work through it."

"Your advantage," she said, "is that you usually start out pretty darn good."

"I do?"

She smiled. "Do you remember what happened on November thirtieth, 2001?"

"I don't think so."

"Third night of our Christmas tour," she said. "We were about to play the Westbury Music Fair—a sold-out crowd, two thousand people plus standing in the back—biggest crowd we'd ever played to. We'd been doing 'It Could Happen to You' for our encore, and you decided it wasn't working."

Jay's face lit up at the memory. "It wasn't," he said.

"I know. But you didn't bring it up to me until an hour before showtime."

Jay laughed.

"Our musical director told you not to worry about it, and Mary told you to relax, but you didn't listen."

"Nobody in the history of the world has ever relaxed just because someone told them to."

"And it was a good thing you didn't! You came up with an arrangement of 'You'll Never Walk Alone'—just me on voice, you at the piano, the rest of the band quiet. You taught it to me in twenty minutes, and we went on with it."

Jay smiled. "And after the way the crowd reacted, we had no choice but to close with it, exactly the way we did that night, for every show we ever did again together."

They stopped to catch their breath in front of a mansion with a sprinkler system, and Cindy leaned over the water to wet her face, getting water in her hair and down the rest of her body in the process. They laughed like kids, splashing each other and pushing, until they were soaked and praying no one would come out from the house to yell at them. Having fun with him had always been so natural, so easy—she'd never had another friend like him and couldn't imagine ever having one.

"It's a beautiful song," Jay said.

"I love it because it can be about so many things. It can be about a good friend or about love, or maybe even spiritual—whichever you choose."

"For me, it'll always be about all those things," Jay said, and Cindy nodded her agreement.

Soaked, they started to walk back toward the car. Luckily, it was close by, as they'd nearly completed the route before they got distracted. Suddenly, Cindy saw that Jay's eyes were tearing up.

"What's wrong?" she said.

"That version of 'You'll Never Walk Alone' we did," he said. "We didn't get to do it many times—I think twelve shows—before it all ended."

Cindy nodded. Midway through that Christmas tour, she and Jay had had a long discussion about their marriage—Cindy had told Jay she thought she was gay, and Jay had shocked her by saying he thought he was too. They'd decided they needed to end their marriage; their managers, the production company for the soap opera, the network executives, and their record label begged them to stay together just for show, but Jay and Cindy could never have lied to their fans like that. They came out and then watched as the network was bombarded with "fan letters" from the older, more conservative soap opera base demanding they be fired. The most painful had been the editorials calling them "bad role models." The ticket sales had dried up. It was the last tour they'd ever done together before Jay had gone to Vegas and Cindy had returned to school to study finance.

Jay continued, "Do you ever think about how, if all that had happened a few years later, we would've been able to keep performing together? People have become much more open-minded since then. We could've gotten divorced and stayed together as performers, doing the soap and singing the songs we loved, entertaining and inspiring the people we cared about."

"I do think about that," Cindy admitted, "and it makes me happy, in a way. Because it means society is progressing. And sure, the music career was fun. But I never would've met Esther if I hadn't become a financial advisor—and look how much fun you had in Las Vegas!"

Jay nodded. "And this business is going to work too," he said. "It has to. We're going to get to the bottom of Dylan's death, and we're gonna get everything in the Yana Tosh collection. I just know it. And if both of those things happen, we'll be back in the chips."

They got in the car and drove, singing along together, a cappella, harmonizing just as well as they ever had. Cindy loved Jay's voice because it reminded her of Perry Como's—perfectly in tune, mellow, and all about the song, not the singer's ego. They made it through "The Way You Look Tonight" and "It's Only a Paper Moon" before they arrived home.

They pulled into the driveway. Four police cars and a crime scene van were there, and yellow tape in front of the mailbox cordoned off the entire property. Mary's car was in the driveway—she'd arrived a bit early for their dinner, and they hadn't heard from her. And now the police were there in force. Cindy started to cry, then began screaming. Her heart was racing, like she was about to die.

Cindy looked at Jay and noticed him looking at her. She felt briefly embarrassed, which was insane, but there it was. She counted on herself to stay calm and collected. Now her usual demeanor was replaced by anguish and fear. *Not again,* she thought. Cindy's capacity for trauma and tragedy had reached its limit. As if reading her mind, Jay spoke.

"It's going to be okay," he said. "Whatever it is, we're going to deal with it. I promise. Together."

Somehow, she believed him, even though she knew he had no idea if what he was saying was true. She felt Jay's hand on her back as they ran toward the house.

Simon greeted them at the door.

"No one is hurt," were the first words out of his mouth. Cindy felt the thudding in her chest slow—just a little—and then quickly reaccelerate. "Everyone is fine," Simon added. "Try to relax and stay calm, okay? We're here to find out what's going on."

"Tell me everything," Cindy said. When Simon didn't respond immediately, she said, more loudly, "This is my house, Simon. Jay's too."

Simon stood in front of them on the lawn, behind the police tape but far out of range of the other cops on the scene. He continued to hesitate, so Cindy intensified her stare. "Ordinarily, we wouldn't have this much of a presence for something like this," he said, haltingly. "It's just that, given the circumstances, we're acting with an abundance of caution—"

"What circumstances?" Jay said. Cindy appreciated him taking control of the situation—she felt lightheaded and faint. "Just tell us what happened, Simon."

"There was a suspicious item in your mailbox, an envelope that looked like it had been damaged in delivery. Mary didn't see a return address, and her curiosity got the best of her. She started to open it, realized there was something wrong, and called us. There was poison in it. We roped everything off in case it was a larger crime scene, but that doesn't appear to be the case."

"What made Mary suspicious?"

"We're not done talking with her," Simon said.

"Well, tell me what you do know," Cindy snapped. "Is Mary in danger? That woman has been in our lives for twenty-five years. She's old and frail. We're responsible for her."

Simon didn't respond.

"What is your problem, Simon?" Jay asked. "You're talking to the two best friends of somebody who's been the victim of an attempted crime."

"It's lucky Mary acted quickly," Simon said. "Before anyone got hurt." He let slip a little smile, and Cindy stepped back to avoid doing something she'd regret. Apparently realizing he'd gone too far, Simon added, "Look, I'm sorry if this seems officious, but that's what this job is. There are protocols to be followed. We'll have the house cleared in an hour, and Mary will be done talking with us by then. Why don't you two go for a ride and come back? Then, if I need to talk to you, we can set something up for tomorrow."

Cindy nodded and thanked him, and she and Jay walked back to her still-running car. She fishtailed out and drove, not even realizing where she was headed until she parked in front of a Domino's Pizza. Clearly her body wanted carb-laden, greasy comfort food—she remembered the three blackout drives she'd made to Domino's in her life: once when Esther was diagnosed, then when the cancer came back, and finally when Esther passed. And now, things had deteriorated to the point where she was back.

They were the only people in the restaurant when they walked in, which she was profoundly grateful for. She just wanted to be alone with Jay, at least until she could be home and hug Mary. Domino's was the kind of food both of them hardly ever touched, but it was exactly what they needed now.

Jay ordered cheesy breadsticks, and Cindy could see in his face how much he enjoyed them as he ate. She sawed at a piece of greasy pizza with a thin plastic fork and knife. The cutlery obviously wasn't up to the task—but then, few people other than Cindy would try to eat pizza with a knife and fork.

"I'm scared," Jay said.

"Me too," Cindy admitted. There was only one word for what she felt clawing and scrabbling in her stomach: fear. It was becoming all too recognizable these days, and Cindy was getting sick and tired of it.

Jay frowned. "You're *never* scared. You've always been the tough one, between the two of us."

Cindy shrugged. "Only way to be."

"We just had a poisoned letter mailed to your house," Jay said. "Where I live too. This isn't worth it. It's *insane*, Cindy. Either of us could've died. Mary could've died." Cindy heard his voice getting higher and higher, spiraling out of control, but she also knew from their long relationship that the only way out was through. She had to let him spin until he exhausted himself.

"We have to just give up on Yana Tosh," Jay continued. "I know that means giving up on the store too, but we can consign our inventory to an auction house and get most of your money back. I'm sorry this didn't work out—I really am. But we have to cut our losses. None of this is worth more lives."

Cindy stared at him evenly, waiting until she was sure he was done talking. When he was finally silent—and cramming another breadstick into his mouth—she said, simply, "We're not giving up."

Jay spoke around the mouthful of dough. "Why not?"

"Because good people giving in to evil is how evil triumphs. It's how all bad things happen. Every terrible tragedy is about good people not standing up to bad people. Esther believed in this store and wanted it to happen. Therefore, it's going to happen."

"We're talking about a Hollywood memorabilia store," Jay said. "Your retirement project. It's not some grand principle—"

"But that's *exactly* what it is, Jay." Cindy could hear her own voice getting louder, gearing up for a pep talk that was probably as much for her as it was for him. "A grand principle. No one is going to push me around, and it's time for you to stop letting people push you around too. I'm not giving up on our dream because some jabroni mailed us a scary note."

"It wasn't just scary—it was poisoned! Evil! And not just a jabroni. It was a vicious killer!"

"It was a jabroni."

"What is a jabroni?"

Cindy pulled out her phone and did a quick search. "It was added to Dictionary.com in September 2020. Made popular by the wrestler The Rock."

"God, he's hot."

"Focus, Jay."

"So, what does jabroni mean?"

"I don't know. It says it's what The Rock calls the people he faces in the ring, right before he crushes them."

"Well, we will defeat the jabroni. Because in this analogy, we are The Rock."

"Yes," Cindy said. "They're a minor nuisance—a minor pebble in the path to our success!"

"If Domino's sold liquor, we could drink to that."

Cindy smiled. "Now you're talking. See? You've gone from 'Let's shut down the store and give up' to 'Let's get hammered at Domino's and celebrate the looming demise of the jabroni who tried to kill us.' But we don't need to get drunk. Here's what we're going to do. We're going to find out who killed Dylan Redman, and we're going to find out who tried to kill us. And we're going to get Yana Tosh's collection—the whole freakin' thing—and we're going to sell it for a lot of money. And we're going to be the successes we deserve to be."

Jay smiled. "I haven't seen you this optimistic and energized in a long time."

"I'm mad," Cindy said. "I'm just so mad. And when I get mad, things don't get in my way."

"I'm with you," Jay said. "Also, Taco Bell has liquor. Should we go to Taco Bell?"

"I won't always be so optimistic," Cindy said, ignoring Jay's Taco Bell suggestion. It was for the best. "And neither will you. But that's why we have each other. If I'm ready to give up, you'll talk me back. And vice versa. Just have to make sure we don't both give up at once."

They toasted with Diet Coke and resumed their meal. Cindy was reminded of the late nights on their first tour together, playing to half-empty dinner theaters and then meeting up at bad fast-food joints, the only ones they could afford, to go over what was working in the act and what wasn't. That made her optimistic—those late-night conversations always led to good ideas and new successes.

* * *

They pulled back into their home exactly an hour later, and just as Simon had promised, the police had cleared out. Mary was sitting on the couch, completely composed—serene, even. That was what made her such a good assistant: she was utterly unflappable. Cindy sat down next to her, and Jay took a chair opposite the couch.

"Tell us what happened," Cindy said. Then, noticing Mary's hesitation, she added, "Leave nothing out. Please. We need to know."

Mary nodded. "I'm fine. But when I pulled in, your mailbox was overflowing—mostly just magazines, so I brought everything in. I was here early, so I decided to sift through the mail, maybe see if there was a magazine I might want. I'm sorry if that's—"

Cindy laughed. "Mary, you're allowed to sort through our mail. We have no secrets from you."

Mary nodded. "There was an envelope with no return address and a Las Vegas postmark from two days ago."

"Two days?" Jay said. "That means it could've been sent by Ben Sinclair. Las Vegas would make sense, given he's a gambling addict."

"Could also have been Eydie," Cindy said. Jay looked at her. "I called the hotel this morning, pretending to be from the payables department at Cypress, to ask when she checked out. Three days ago, the morning after you met up with her. I meant to tell you."

"No worries," Jay said. "It still could've been anyone, though. Las Vegas is only a four-hour drive away. Less if you go at night and a lot less if you fly."

"Anyway, the envelope didn't look right," Mary continued, "and given everything that was going on, I was worried. So I felt it a little bit, and it had kind of an inconsistent feel—like there was sand inside, or something." Cindy felt queasy, imagining their friend testing this suspicious envelope while she and Jay were out. Or maybe it was just the pizza. "I called Detective Fletcher, and he sent a bomb squad over right away. They roped everything off and opened the package, then ran some on-location tests on it."

"Did they tell you what it was?"

"It's only preliminary, and they have to do a bunch of lab work still. But Simon said it looked like sodium fluoride."

"Sodium fluoride?" Jay said. "That's the same stuff that killed Dylan."

"Yes," Mary said. "It's most dangerous if ingested orally, Simon told me, but if you got a few grains of it on your hands and then touched your face—well, you could definitely die from that."

Adrenaline jolted through Cindy's body. "And you didn't touch any of it, right, Mary?"

She shook her head. "I'm fine. The paramedics already checked me out. If I were in any trouble, I'd be in the hospital right now."

Cindy took a deep breath, slowly in and out, like she did in yoga. "I'm guessing there was a lot of it in the envelope?"

Mary nodded. "Definitely more than enough to be fatal, the paramedics said."

"Who was it addressed to?"

Mary paused, then spoke in a whisper. "It was addressed to you, Jay."

The pounding in Cindy's chest accelerated, but she willed herself to be calm. She needed to be strong, to show the two most important people in her life that they could get through anything together—just as long as they stayed powerful and confident.

"Well, Mary," Jay said, "you may have saved my life. Thank you."

She smiled. "I just hope they find out who did it."

"There won't be fingerprints on the envelope, I'm sure," Cindy said.

"No, there won't," Jay agreed. "Why would anyone want to kill me, though? Why not you, Cindy?"

"We're one unit as far as this goes," Cindy said. "But you're right; it doesn't make any sense. Maybe there'll be a poisoned letter for me, waiting at the store."

They were all silent for a moment before Mary looked up, wringing her hands. Her eyes were red, as if she were trying hard to hold back tears. "I'm scared," she admitted.

"I know you are," Cindy said, and pulled her into a tight hug. Mary smelled like the same coconut shampoo she'd been using when they'd first met her twenty-five years ago. A comforting scent.

"But we'll keep going," Jay said. He looked at Cindy. "What's that line our pastor used to always tell us? Bravery doesn't mean you aren't scared. It means you *are* scared, but you keep going anyway."

Cindy buried her head in her hands. They could do this. She knew they could. But damned if her resolve wasn't already fading, thinking about what could happen between now and whenever this was all wrapped up.

Jay scooted toward Mary on the couch and put his hand on her knee. "You don't want us to give up," he said, "do you?"

Mary looked taken aback. "Of course not! I just don't want to be scared. Any of us. We don't deserve this."

"We've been scared together before, Cindy," Jay said. "We've been through stuff. Remember when the paparazzi camped outside our house after we came out, like we were having wild gay parties or something? And inside we were just freaking out, trying to figure out who we were and afraid that opening up and accepting ourselves would be the end of everything. We survived that. We'll survive this too."

"No one was trying to kill us then," Cindy said. "Just our careers."

"Well, we helped them with that," Jay said. "That was real teamwork."

Cindy could see that Mary was struggling not to laugh, but after a few seconds, their friend couldn't help but let a giggle escape. It was contagious: the situation was *ridiculous*. They owned a Hollywood memorabilia shop, for God's sake, and now they were in the middle of a murder investigation. Cindy felt the laughter bubble up her own throat too. The second it escaped her lips, she let loose, until a few moments later she was howling, clutching her stomach, with tears streaming down her face. "I'm so sorry," she gasped—but now Mary and Jay were cackling too.

"We're going to get through this," Mary said when their laughter wound down. "We should call the police and have them make sure everything is okay at Hooray for Hollywood."

They were silent for a few moments, and then Jay spoke. "Simon thinks we sent the package to ourselves."

"What?" Mary snapped.

"I could tell from the way he talked to us," Jay said. "He smirked when he said how lucky it was that Mary noticed the package was suspicious right away. He thinks we mailed it to ourselves to make it look like someone else is trying to kill us, to deflect attention from us being the ones who killed Dylan Redman."

Cindy shook her head. That was something too farfetched for even a Hollywood film. "He's a cop. It's his job to be suspicious. He was probably saying that partly to flirt with you."

"Flirting by . . . accusing me of trying to poison myself to help myself get away with murder? I know you've been off the market for a while, Cindy, but c'mon."

"Pickup artists have lots of weird tricks," Cindy said.

They were silent for a few minutes, Cindy and Mary holding each other while Jay made tea.

"I think we're overlooking something," Mary said when Jay returned with the steaming cups.

"What if Eydie Jackson figured out that you were the one who pumped her for information at the bar?" Cindy asked.

"She didn't know it was me," Jay said.

"Or maybe she did," Cindy said.

"She was drunk out of her mind."

"Or maybe she was pretending to be drunk."

Jay took the bag out of his tea and set it on the napkin, rolling his eyes the whole time. "Simon was there, watching her like a hawk. I think he would have noticed if she was sober as the warden in *The Shawshank Redemption* and then started hamming up inebriation, Dean Martin style, the second I walked up."

"My point is, if Eydie knew it was you, or figured it out later, she would've been either mad at you or worried she'd told you something incriminating. Or both."

They were interrupted from further discussion by Jay's cell phone. He said he didn't recognize the number, but after he answered, he held the phone away from his face and mouthed, "Lenae Randolph."

"Sorry, I'm a bit busy right now," Jay told her, putting the gossip columnist on speaker.

"Yes, that's why I'm calling," Lenae said.

"What's that supposed to mean?"

"Come on, Jay—I'm a reporter. Somebody sent you a poisoned letter."

"How'd you hear that?"

There was a slight pause. "I listen to the police scanner."

Cindy suppressed a sigh. She didn't want to inflict any more misery on Jay and Mary, but what Lenae was saying meant that every other reporter with a police scanner knew about the letter too. Their private business would soon become public fodder. Other reporters would be calling about the incident. The last thing they needed was more publicity right now. Even if it was publicity that portrayed them as victims in a positive light, Cindy just didn't want to see any more press clippings that tied Hooray for Hollywood to crime and murder.

Jay started to say something, then stopped. Cindy reached for the phone, but he waved her away with a frown. Cindy knew what that meant—she pulled her hand back and listened. When he spoke, Jay's voice was calm but strong.

"Look, Lenae," he said. "You've been a friend to us so far, and I hope we've been friends to you. As things stand now, there honestly isn't much of a story. The police don't even definitively know yet what the substance was. If you can hold off on writing about this, I promise we'll give you a big exclusive on the most interesting angles in the Yana Tosh collection. And we'll tell you everything we know so you can have the most in-depth story whenever they do find out who killed Dylan Redman. But if you publish anything now, we'll cut you off. It won't be a very interesting story, and all it'll do is wreck our lives."

Cindy gave him a thumb's-up, then began clapping silently but enthusiastically.

"Okay," Lenae said finally. "You got yourself a deal." They hung up.

"Man," Cindy said, "where did that come from? I have never heard you negotiate like that."

He smiled. "I've been learning from the best." Then he paused. "But that only holds off one reporter. Others will be calling."

Cindy rubbed his back. "One reporter at a time, Jay. We'll burn those bridges when we get to them."

When Jay checked his phone the next day, there were no stories on the incident, nor were there any calls from reporters seeking comment. There was a message from Simon, giving them the all clear to reenter the store, which was welcome news. But Jay couldn't stop thinking about the lack of media coverage of the poisoned letter. It was strange. If Lenae had heard about the sodium fluoride letter on the police scanner, why hadn't any other reporters?

He struggled to put it out of his mind so he could focus on what he could control: the business. Mary was dusting around him as Jay continued to work in the back, taking more photos of Yana's pieces, creating videos, and loading them onto his computer, to edit later. Occasionally he watched as Cindy wandered the store, helping shoppers. He noted that she was doing a little haggling with buyers who were rich enough not to care but needed to know they'd gotten a great deal that wouldn't have been available to people who weren't as smart and special as they were.

After two hours of photographs and videos, Jay set aside his camera and did some research on Yana Tosh and her movies, printing out her Wikipedia and IMDb pages. Cindy could stare at screens all day, but this was the first job he'd ever had that required regular computer work.

Jay flipped through Yana's résumé with a highlighter, choosing all the things he wanted to ask her about during their interview. There were a few movies he hadn't even realized she was in, including *The Mysterious Affair at Styles*, the completely forgotten, low-budget 1947 adaptation of Agatha Christie's first novel that had introduced Hercule Poirot to the world. Cindy was a big Christie fan, so Jay thought it might be a good one for them to watch together. He was disappointed to see that there were no surviving prints—a not uncommon thing for movies from the 1940s. The studio was long gone, its archives probably tossed in a dumpster or destroyed in a fire. Without careful stewardship, Jay thought, so much of history was lost. It was people like Yana Tosh, and hopefully Cindy and himself, who preserved history.

He was interrupted from his musings by the ringing of the store's phone.

"Hooray for Hollywood Movie Memorabilia. Jay speaking."

"Jay," the man's voice said. Jay didn't recognize it. "It's Warren Limon, Yana's son."

"Oh," Jay said. "Warren. Good to hear from you. How are you?"

"A little stressed out." A pause. "Listen, is there a chance you're around to meet?"

Jay thought about it. He knew from Yana that Warren was opposed to selling the collection, which put him at cross-purposes with Hooray for Hollywood. Still, Jay figured there was no harm in talking. Maybe he could even convince him to make peace with selling.

"Of course," Jay said. "Do you need Cindy too?"

Silence for a moment. "No, that's okay—I don't need to bother both of you. I can tell you what I have in mind, and then we can bring her in later."

"Alright then. When would you like to meet?"

"Right now."

"Where?" Jay asked.

"Come to my house." Warren gave him an address, and Jay said it would take him fifteen minutes to get there. He told Cindy where he was going—but she was too busy with a customer to be distracted. He got into the *Jurassic Park* car and typed the address into the GPS. But when he pulled up at the curb, he was surprised. It was a nicer house than he'd have expected, given that Warren had—at least according to Yana—never made an honest living other than by working for his mother. On the other hand, maybe he'd made a lucrative dishonest living doing something else.

The house was two floors and looked to be set on at least an acre. It wasn't in one of the classic neighborhoods with movie star homes, but based on real estate listings Jay had browsed, it still had to be worth close to a million dollars. There was that mid-century modern style again: flat roofs, an old-fashioned carport, and stone steps that made their way up the grassy hill from the sidewalk to the front door. The orange door was made of some sort of plastic, and the whole place was surrounded by elaborate stonework—a blend of nature and human innovation. That mix was the reason people loved Palm Springs.

Closer inspection, however, revealed that the house wasn't as nice as it could've been. The grass was overgrown and browning, and the door, modernist though it was, had chipping paint.

When Warren opened the door, Jay was greeted by a floor that looked worn and dirty. Not that disheveled Warren seemed like the cleaning-pro type, but usually people who'd grown up with his privilege had at least a biweekly maid. If that was the case with Yana's son, Jay thought, he needed to find a new one.

"Thanks for coming," Warren said. His tone seemed more chipper than it had been on the phone.

"My pleasure," Jay said, just to say something.

Warren wore the same heavy jeans and black button-down he'd had on when they first met, but this time the shirt was unbuttoned, revealing a once-white—but now off-white—undershirt. He smelled like Brut cologne—Elvis's favorite, famed more for its strength than its nuance, perfect for lathering over the effects of a missed shower. He also had on a Los Angeles Dodgers baseball hat.

Warren motioned for Jay to have a seat at the dining room table, which was stacked with envelopes, open and unopened, and scattered papers and Post-it Notes. Warren offered him a drink, and Jay settled on a glass of iced tea, which proved to be too sweet and artificial tasting. Jay always brewed his own, but apparently Warren opted for the bottles—or worse, the powders, loaded with chemicals. Jay stirred it slowly, waiting for the ice to melt and dilute the fake sugar, while Warren talked in circles about whatever exactly it was that he'd invited Jay over to discuss.

"I can tell you care about my mother," Warren said, "but you also care about her collection."

"I do and I do," Jay said.

"My mother isn't thinking clearly."

Jay stiffened at that. "I've seen no evidence of that," he said, layering ice in his voice.

"She's ninety years old."

"A young ninety."

"Still ninety."

Warren took a sip of his iced tea and used his phone to turn on the radio. It was a classical station, and Jay recognized the piece: Edvard Grieg's *Peer Gynt* suite. He'd played it on piano when he was nine years old, winning a standing ovation at a school talent show.

"She cares about that collection a lot," Warren went on, "and she always wanted to keep everything together. We talked about creating a museum one day, and she wanted me to help her with it—you know, to actually run it, help raise money, set up educational exhibitions—things that would keep the history of the golden age of film alive, the way it had been alive for her back in the day."

"It's her collection," Jay said. "And her choice about whether to sell it."

"She's been under pressure from Ben Sinclair," Warren said bitterly. "Her now missing financial advisor. He wanted to sell all the stuff so he could get his hands on that cash she had tied up in it."

"Cindy was suspicious of Sinclair immediately," Jay said.

"And now we all are," Warren agreed. "Especially now that he's skipped town with some of her costumes."

They sat in silence for a few moments before Jay spoke. What he wanted to say wasn't nice, but he felt he owed it to Warren to be straight with him, even if it was uncomfortable. "I understand how you feel. But the fact is, it's your mother's choice to sell, and my understanding, just from what she's told me and Cindy, is that you want her to keep the collection so that you can draw a salary by setting up a museum. Otherwise, you won't have an income, because she isn't planning on leaving you much money—if any."

A crazy idea came to Jay—one that might not even work and could be catastrophic if it didn't. But there was only one way to find out. He pretended to feel his phone vibrating in his pocket, and then put his thumb on the ringer as he pulled it out, so it would start beeping. "Do you mind if I take this?" he said, pretending to look at the caller ID. "Privately? It's about another possible show in Vegas." He smiled. "In case, you know, this business doesn't work out."

Warren nodded. "Of course. I want to check my email anyway." He went upstairs.

Jay had a loud conversation about doing a Barry Manilow tribute residency with an imaginary friend from Vegas, and waited until Warren was upstairs before he executed a plan he had some qualms about. But he had no choice: his and Cindy's lives were on the line. He walked over to one of the stacks of opened mail, reached into the middle, and pulled out four or five of the envelopes. They'd been torn open crookedly, as though in a rage or a frenzy. Without looking at them, he crumpled them up and stuffed them in his pocket. He ended his fake call and was back in chair by the time Warren made it back downstairs.

"Back to our discussion," Warren said. "You can see what I'm upset about."

"I can," Jay said. "Though I'm not totally sure whether it's out of self-interest or genuine concern about your mother and the long-term impact of the collection she built."

Warren nodded. "Let's say it's a little of both."

Jay could hear the coughing of an engine and the sound of bins being thrown: a trash truck had stopped out front. He looked out the window and noticed for the first time the large stack of bags sitting in front of Warren's curb. He'd been too focused on the house itself when he'd arrived. Whatever Warren was throwing out, it was more than a usual week's trash, unless he was running a catering service out of his kitchen. And that seemed unlikely given that he appeared to be using the stove to store cereal boxes.

Jay turned back to Warren. "You invited me here, so I'm assuming you must have some kind of idea or plan you want to pitch me."

"I do."

"I can't promise anything except to say that I'm happy to listen." Jay couldn't see how Warren's agenda would line up with his and Cindy's goals, much less their obligations to their client.

"Despite her insistence on selling the collection over my objections," Warren said, "I have my mother's ear." Jay bit his cheek to stop from laughing. That didn't seem likely. "I can tell her to give you the whole collection to sell. But in exchange, all I ask is that you move slowly with some of the more expensive pieces. My mother won't be around forever, and it would be nice to have *something* left for a museum."

Now Jay was angry. It wasn't his style to get offended or to blow up at people, but questioning his and Cindy's integrity, or assuming, as Warren was, that it was for sale, was one way to get him hot. "We will continue to act in Yana's best interests," Jay snapped. "*Whatever* they may be. And if we take something to sell for her, we will take exactly as long as we need to get the best price for her, and not a moment longer."

"I'm sorry you feel that way," Warren said. And then, chillingly, he grinned. "Perhaps Eedles will feel differently."

Jay stood up. "I think this meeting is over."

By five thirty, Cindy was in the office with Jay, hunched over the desk, going through Warren's mail together. Not a jackpot, exactly—no personal letters, no threats made from letters cut out of magazine articles, like in a slasher movie.

Cindy looked up. "Looks like Warren was in what we certified financial planners call 'a pickle.'"

"That's the technical term?" Jay said.

The record player had just finished with side one of Stephen Sondheim's *Merrily We Roll Along*. He ran over, flipped it to the B side, and came back to look over Cindy's shoulder.

"He wasn't even making minimum payments on his credit cards," she pointed out, "and they'd just been turned over to a third-party collection agency."

"Ouch," Jay said. "So his mom's got all this money and a seven-figure costume collection, and he's falling behind on the grocery bills?"

"Yep." Cindy flipped through to another one of the letters. "And his mortgage, apparently."

She felt Jay's breath over her shoulder as she opened her laptop and logged onto the Palm Springs property records site.

Glancing at one of the envelopes Jay had pilfered, she typed in the address, then clicked and scrolled, and clicked and scrolled some more, before looking up.

"The plot," she said, "becomes thicker. He bought that house ten years ago for four hundred thousand dollars, with a good down payment. Everything was fine—paid as agreed every month, always kept up with the taxes, no muss, no fuss, no liens—until nine months ago, when he fell behind. He caught up two months later, then fell behind again."

"Where is he now?" Jay asked.

"He hasn't made a mortgage payment in five months. But before that, he did. Every month, without fail."

"And then, suddenly, he stopped," Jay said.

"Something must have happened." Cindy tapped her chin. "Maybe his mother cut him off?"

"But then he'd be mad. Why would he still be at her house all the time?"

Jay thought about it. "Because it's his only chance at working his way back into her good graces. Warren's given up on any chance of making a living on his own, so the best use of his time—he thinks—is to hang around his mother, hoping she'll cut him back in again."

"And maybe he hedged his bets by pilfering the painting."

"Except it sounds more like Ben Sinclair took it and disappeared."

Cindy sighed. "So many sketchy people, so little time."

"I still don't understand the role of the painting in all this," Jay said. "It's worth maybe five thousand dollars, and that's after someone markets it carefully and finds the right buyer. You take that thing into a pawn shop and they'll give you a couple hundred bucks for it, if they take it at all."

They were interrupted by a knock at the door, and Mary entered, trailed by a group of three people Cindy didn't recognize.

"Welcome, welcome," Jay said. "Thank you so much for coming." He dipped into the refrigerator in the office and laid out a few bottles of wine, along with a cheese platter, some paper plates, and wineglasses. Mary put out some baked goods she'd brought with her, the smell of chocolatey, fudgy brownies wafting up from beneath the aluminum foil.

Cindy stared. "Jay?" she whispered, making sure she was out of earshot. "What in the world is this?"

Jay smiled. "Ah," he said. "I forgot to tell you. I thought our store needed more ideas and more creativity, so Mary invited some local artisans she knows to come check out the store and see if they have any ideas for how to help us."

Cindy was impressed—even if she was still rattled. "How do you know these people, Mary?"

"I'm part of a little group of crafters and people who make things," she said. "I joined it when I moved here, to learn about business."

"You never told us about it!" Cindy protested.

Mary laughed. "I have a life outside of you two, you know. I knew you were struggling a little with business, and I figured, I know some great people with ideas, so why not bring them over? I had lunch with them and told them all about the store, and they were excited to come see it and talk about how they might help!"

Mary made brief introductions—there was a winemaker, an interior designer, and the owner of a local bakery. Cindy watched as the three guests—two men and a woman, ranging in age from early twenties to mid-fifties, wandered the store, sipped wine, and asked questions about the pieces.

The winemaker, a woman in her twenties named Stephanie, stepped forward, and handed Cindy a piece of paper with mock-ups of two wine bottles. She had a tongue piercing, and her arms were covered in tattoos. Not the vibe Cindy associated with the wine world, but she liked it.

"California wines from 2012, a red and a white," Stephanie said. "This is my idea for you guys. One named Baby Jane Hudson and the other named Blanche Hudson. Jay told me about the chair you have—and, of course, I know the movie. A classic feud, on- and off-screen. You have Blanche as the white—classy and unthreatening, hints of cedar, and then Baby Jane is, of course, the red—fiery and more than a little crazy. Maybe a tinge of cinnamon or something—you know, spicy. Could even give it pepper overtones. It's Baby Jane, baby. Make it *nuts*. Maybe even literally make it nuts with some flavor infusion."

"I like the way you're thinking," Jay said. He looked at Cindy. "Cindy?"

"Well," Cindy said, "it's an idea." It seemed so gimmicky—and maybe even a little disrespectful to a cinematic classic. Esther would have hated it, certainly.

Stephanie laid out her plan: she'd make the wines, and they could offer them for sale in her store as well as advertise them at Hooray for Hollywood. "We'll split the profits," she said. "And maybe we could do a new vintage Hollywood-themed wine every year. Cross-promote. You tell your clients about me, I tell mine about you."

Cindy thought about it. "We should definitely talk about that." She hoped it came off more diplomatically than what she was really thinking: *A Baby Jane wine? Have you lost your mind?*

Jay put his hand on her shoulder. "Cindy," he said, "we have to get creative here. This is an aspirational store—a creative store, a fun store—a way to buy something to try to capture a life you never imagined you could have. Partnerships with other creatives are the way to go. Plus, we won't have to put up any money to make it happen. It's good publicity and all upside."

Cindy nodded. "Okay," she said. Maybe Jay was right, and any marketing ideas he had needed to be considered. *Especially* if they didn't require any money from their end.

They talked with the designer, a gay guy in his fifties named Kevin, who had an idea to offer vintage Hollywood-themed children's bedrooms as a package—decorating services provided by him, with props from Hooray for Hollywood. He could market themes based on whatever they had in inventory.

"I love that," Cindy said. "We should get one of the local papers to do a story on that offering."

Kevin looked a little nervous. "There might be a problem there."

"Oh?"

"So I talked with Jay about this idea—and he was excited about it, and so I called a reporter I know at the *Palm Springs Post*, and, well . . ." He trailed off.

"Well, what?" Cindy said.

"It needs to stay between us."

Jay and Cindy excused themselves from the others in the group and went into the office with Kevin. Kevin put his glass of wine down on the printer.

"Well?" Cindy said. "What happened when you talked to the *Palm Springs Post*?"

He thought about it. "My friend, a guy I've known for ten years, always writes about projects I worked on. And he told me he'd been warned off by Lenae Randolph not to cover you guys."

Cindy felt her stomach clench. "What? Did she say why?"

"She didn't."

Jay stared at him. "And this reporter is going to listen to her?"

He laughed joylessly. "Lenae has a lot of power. She knows everyone. If she tells someone not to do a story, well, look—he's not going to mess with her just to do a nice little human interest piece about Hollywood-themed children's bedrooms."

Cindy nodded. "I get that. This is a problem for me and Jay, not for you. But I appreciate your telling us. And I'm really excited about working with you."

The rest of Jay's party went along nicely—Cindy loved how enthusiastic Jay was in showing off the treasures they'd accumulated, loved watching him pull out his phone to show their guests scenes of the pieces in movies. Whatever doubts she'd had about the business vanished when she watched them gathered around Jay to see a scene from the iconic *Seinfeld* episode featuring George Costanza's exploding wallet—and then admiring the wallet itself in their display case. People *love* this stuff, Cindy thought. This business *will* work. It *has* to.

* * *

After everyone had left—dinner plans with Mary, the social butterfly, apparently—Cindy and Jay were alone in the store.

"I hope you're not mad at me," Jay said.

"Why would I be mad?" Cindy said.

"I forgot to tell you about the open house—"

Cindy waved a hand and laughed. "It *was* a bit of an ambush, I guess, but it's probably good for me to try to get used to being less rigid. We're dealing with a lot, and you're trying to come up with ideas. And you *are* coming up with ideas. And it's sweet of Mary to help."

"I think she's making enough money with her little knitting business that she needs us to stay in business."

Cindy nodded. "Maybe we should start charging her rent?"

Jay laughed. "We could never."

"No," Cindy said, "I suppose not." She paused. "Anyway, I'm glad we got to meet those artisans. We definitely need more ideas—and if these are the people who are helping Mary come up with her ideas, we should listen to them because Mary's apparently a lot better at business than we are."

Jay smiled. "The Baby Jane dueling wines idea is a little silly."

Cindy pointed around the store. "Jay, I don't know if you noticed, but *all* of this is a little silly. No one *needs* any of this. It's all just silly fun. But it makes people feel good. And maybe the wines will too—maybe they'll help sell those chairs. It'd be nice to get our money back on those."

"Well, in that case, maybe I'll tell you about the baker's idea: Rosebud-themed Christmas cookies. You know, based on *Citizen Kane*?"

"That's dumbest idea I've ever heard. It's the darkest movie in the history of movies. You can't do Christmas cookies based on that. It's like doing Saint Valentine's Day Massacre–themed candy hearts."

Jay smiled. "I thought so too."

"Well, they can't all be winners. The interior designer guy is really good. Partnering with him on children's bedrooms could be a big get."

Jay nodded. "It would help if Lenae wasn't blocking us from getting more publicity."

Cindy sucked on her teeth. She didn't want to get herself riled up thinking about Lenae Randolph. "What do you think that's about?"

"Probably just territorial, right? She's writing about us and doesn't want any other reporters getting in on anything about our store. And she has the power to back people off, so she does."

Cindy thought about it. "That seems right." She really wasn't sure—her mind tended to stray toward the dark and dramatic. But maybe it was good that Jay was lighter, more optimistic. She needed someone to balance her out here.

"Wait," Jay said with a start. "Cindy. When Lenae called about the poisoned letter, she said she'd heard about it on the police scanner."

"Yeah," Cindy said. "So?"

"Well, the wine lady still doesn't know about the letter, and neither does the designer—because none of this has gotten any press attention at all. It's been days since Dylan was murdered."

"Right. Which wouldn't make sense if it were being discussed on the police radio. I've been thinking about this too. But it could just be Lenae getting territorial and calling in favors or dirt over other reporters." She shrugged, suddenly tired of it all. "Or maybe it was just a mistake."

"It couldn't be a mistake," Jay said. He took his phone out of his pocket and called Simon, putting it on speakerphone so Cindy could listen in.

"Detective Fletcher," he answered.

"You need to get caller ID," Jay said.

Simon laughed. "Jay," he said. "The police department desk phones are probably the same ones we had when *Columbo* was on the air. What's up?"

"I was checking to see whether you put the call about the poisoned letter on the police scanner."

Simon was silent for a moment. "No. I deliberately kept it off the scanner."

"Why?"

"Because Mary called me directly on my cell phone. And I was at the station, so I just grabbed the guys, and we headed over. I didn't want it on the scanner because that would make the situation public, and I wanted to protect you and your privacy and your business."

Cindy felt her heart warm. Maybe she was getting used to Simon, after all. Did this mean Simon liked Jay? Or was this whole speech just an effort to wear him down, Columbo style, while Simon focused his investigation on them?

"I appreciate that," Jay said. "Thank you. So there was absolutely no discussion of the poisoned letter on the police radio?"

"No," Simon said. "What's this all about?"

"Just checking," Jay said, and hung up. "Lenae definitely lied to us," he said to Cindy. "And I want to find out why."

It took Jay ten minutes to get to the small home where Lenae had lived for the past fifteen years, though finding it had been something of a challenge. Google and property records didn't turn up an address, which Cindy had once told him was common for older people who'd already put their homes in trusts for estate planning purposes. But he did find a photo of the home on a clickbait article about celebrities who lived in surprisingly modest homes. He'd then downloaded the photo from that slideshow and done a reverse image search to find it on a real estate site. And now, here he was, rather impressed with his sleuthing.

It was a mid-century ranch, but not a modernist one, in a development surrounded by similar homes—middle-class, style-free homes designed after World War II. Eight hundred and fifty square feet each, available in one of four styles from the company that had built the whole neighborhood.

With minimal coaxing at the door, he made it into Lenae's home. She had already changed into her pajamas but went to the kitchen to prepare him a cup of tea like a good host. While he waited for her, he looked around. The home was modest and cluttered with what used to be called "collectibles" but were now just called junk: Hummel figurines, limited edition Elvis Presley plates, that kind of thing. The key to collectibles, Jay had once been told by an antiques dealer, was that anything marketed as a collectible would never actually be valuable because everyone saved them and thus they never became rare.

Lenae returned to the living room with a steaming emoji-covered "I Love Hallmark Movies" mug for Jay and a small glass of milk for herself. He took the leather couch—the one recent piece of furniture—and she sat facing him in a plaid recliner. The table between them was covered with gossip magazines, sticky notes scattered through them. "My office," she told him.

When he asked her about the police scanner discrepancy, she shut him down immediately.

"I'm not going to discuss sources with you," Lenae said. "I won't discuss you being a source with anyone else, and vice versa."

"My life is being threatened," Jay said, "and so is Cindy's."

"And I'm a journalist," Lenae said. "Let me explain something to you. I might be an old woman, and the topics I cover might not be as important as Woodward and Bernstein's. But to me, they're important. And the standards of the fourth estate are important to me. That means I don't tell people how I find things out. Ever. Period. I'll go to jail for contempt of court before I reveal sources."

"Am I getting a morality lecture from a Twitter-famous tabloid writer?" Jay asked. He said it with a smile, so it was more disarming than it might have been if delivered by anyone else.

"Twitter-famous?" Lenae said. "What's that mean?"

"It means you became famous on Twitter. You're a social media celebrity."

Lenae waved a dismissive hand, her face wrinkling with distaste. "My great-grandson handles all that. He's twelve, and I pay him ten bucks an hour. I just do the writing and interviewing. Then I go on television and act like a cranky old woman who knows everyone's secrets."

"Isn't that what you are?"

She smiled. "Yep."

"My point is, I need to know how you knew about the letter, because it might be very important. It might literally be a matter of life and death." How funny—Jay never thought he'd have the occasion to say those words out loud before. He imagined most people didn't get the opportunity. It all felt surreal.

Lenae shrugged. "Can't help you there. Or, I should say, *won't* help you there." She sipped at her glass of milk, clearly for dramatic effect. "But maybe I can tell you something else that's interesting."

Jay didn't want to give up on the poisoned letter, but for now he'd take the bait. "Okay. What have you got?"

"Cypress was about to begin a big restructuring—a cost-cutting program, lots of jobs on the line. Maybe even including Dylan and Eydie's."

"Oh? How do you know that?"

"Hey," Lenae said, "I was just telling a nice young man that I'm a journalist and can't reveal my sources. Could you maybe ask him to explain it to you? Because I'm getting tired of repeating myself." She paused dramatically. "Oh, wait! You're the same young man I just told that to!"

Jay smiled. This was one tough lady. "Sorry," he said. "Would those two have known about it?"

Lenae nodded. "The rumors were circulating. And they were senior enough there that I can't imagine they wouldn't have heard."

"So they would've been desperate," Jay said. "Worried that if they didn't get the deal, they'd be on the chopping block. They also might have worried they were about to land a big consignment for Cypress and then get laid off before they could profit from it. If Dylan and Eydie had gotten the consignment from Yana, the company could've fired them, taken the stuff, and handed it to a bunch of junior people to handle, leaving them with nothing to show for their work."

"Which meant that stealing from Yana could've been a way to make sure they at least got something."

"Exactly."

"Very possible," Lenae said. She paused. "But what could all that have to do with Dylan's death? The company wouldn't bump him off, would they?"

"No, of course not." Jay didn't really want to sit around speculating with a tabloid reporter who'd lied to him, but that was how it worked. If he wanted her to pass information along, he'd have to humor her.

He continued: "Maybe Eydie and Dylan wanted to make an end run around Cypress and figure out some way to profit from the collection on their own. If that plan fell apart, Dylan might've threatened to tell Cypress, so Eydie killed him."

Lenae nodded. "Could be. Or maybe Eydie was worried there would be a layoff in her department. By killing the guy in charge of it, she could cut Cypress's payroll for them and make herself more attractive as an employee to retain. Especially if she then got to take credit for the Yana consignment."

"That would make sense too," Jay said. He decided to take a chance. "You know, Yana's son, Warren, knew Eydie's pet name. The one that people only called her when they were . . ." He blushed. "Well . . ." Lenae was a Hollywood tabloid reporter, but he still couldn't bring himself to say it, sitting on her couch, drinking her tea, and surrounded by all of her tchotchkes.

"*Now* we have a story," Lenae said. "Eydie's way out of Warren's league, of course. But maybe she was getting friendly with him to try to land the consignment."

"Any evidence of that?"

Lenae smiled. "It's all I can think of."

"And you think Eydie did that while also carrying on a relationship with Dylan?"

"What?" Lenae said. "Where did you hear that?"

"Oops."

"All right, buddy," she said. "Spill. One of my journalism rules is that sources who accidentally tell me part of something have to finish and tell me the rest, or the stuff they just told me before that I agreed to keep private won't be kept private."

"What?" Jay spluttered. "How is that a rule?"

She patted the coffee table, running her hand along a magazine with Teresa Giudice from *Real Housewives* on the cover. "House rules," she said. "We're sitting at my table."

Jay shook his head but agreed, and told her about the bar conversation with Eydie. It wouldn't hurt to get Lenae firmly on their side, and he wasn't going to do that by withholding information. Lenae nodded along the whole time.

"Well," she said, "nothing material exactly, other than that she's unbalanced."

"Or maybe she wants to *seem* unbalanced."

"Ah yes," Lenae said. "That is a thing. Pretend to be crazy so no one suspects they're capable of calculation, and then, *bam*"—she clapped her hands together—"they're more calculating than anyone, and nobody sees the evil coming."

Jay's phone rang. He saw that it was Cindy and excused himself.

"Where'd you go?" she asked.

That was the trouble with only having one car. And also taking it without asking. "I went to confront Lenae."

"You could've told me." Cindy didn't sound mad, just frustrated and tired.

"Sorry. I was mad at her. I'm here now."

"I need you to come back," Cindy said.

"Why? Is everything okay?"

"Yana called me. She wants to see us. Right now."

Jay walked further out onto the lawn to make sure he was out of Lenae's earshot. "What does she want?"

"To go over her finances. Well, she wants *me* to go over her finances with her, but she likes you and trusts you and wants you there. As do I."

"It's ten o'clock at night," Jay said, confused. "Can't this wait?"

"She wants to make sure her son won't know. I'm going to send an Uber for her so she can come to our house."

"Why don't we just go there?"

"No," Cindy said. "She's worried someone could be watching her."

Ordinarily, Jay would've thought that was overly paranoid, and perhaps a sign of a deteriorating mind. But given the circumstances, it made sense.

"How soon can you be here?" Cindy said.

"Give me half an hour. I don't want to run out on Lenae as if something important happened. She'll get curious."

Jay returned to Lenae, who seemed as distracted as he did. Which was just as well, but Jay wondered: Had she overheard the conversation? She was elderly and it seemed unlikely; but on the other hand, one didn't become a star gossip columnist without a talent for eavesdropping. Hell, maybe she had bugs planted around her own place. There were stranger things in the world. They said their goodbyes and he returned to the *Jurassic Park* SUV.

He put Barry Manilow on the radio, but he didn't sing along this time—he was too busy thinking. Lenae had met with Dylan Redman not long before everyone else did, which meant that she could have been the poisoner too. And maybe she'd decided to try to kill Jay because he'd been asking questions about the case. But in that case, why not Cindy too? Of course, Jay couldn't think of what Lenae's motive could be, but that didn't matter for now.

By the time he arrived home, he was no closer to answers, even if he had made it all the way through Barry's *Even Now* album for the second time that day. Maybe the meeting with Yana would help him and Cindy make sense of all these threads.

Or maybe not.

Jay walked into the kitchen to find Cindy drinking a mug of coffee. At near midnight, that wasn't a promising sign for how long they'd be up working with Yana.

"I can't believe it took her this long to finally let you look at her finances," Jay said.

"Money is the last taboo," Cindy said. "People post on social media about every disgusting thing they've ever done except their credit card debt. It's the only remaining bastion of shame in America."

To help set Yana at ease, Jay used the music streaming service to put on a Guy Lombardo album. It was a corny, Middle America big-band offering, but Yana had mentioned in one of their meetings that it was what she listened to when she wanted to relax.

Ten minutes later, Yana's Uber pulled up, and Cindy went out to the driveway to greet her.

Cindy led Yana straight to the living room, and Jay watched as the former actress gazed at the art Cindy and Esther had bought on their trips around the world.

She pointed to a sculpture of a tree with amethyst stones carved into leaves dangling from the branches. "I love that," she said. "Purple leaves, and yet it feels so real—evokes the magic of the forest."

"Esther bought that," Cindy said. "Amethyst is her birthstone." She squinched up her eyes a little, trying to keep from crying.

Yana put her hand on Cindy's elbow. "One of the hardest parts about loss is everything you've bought together reminds you of the person. Your home is filled with memories of the most important person you ever knew. So is mine. I know it hasn't been long for you, but you just have to trust me: over time, you'll cherish those daily reminders, and they won't make you sad anymore. It takes time, and it's a process. But eventually, they'll just remind you of the greatest love you could ever have and the blessing that it still is to have had that. At least, that's what it was for me."

Jay could see Cindy brighten. "Thank you," she said.

Yana winked. "And that," she said, "is all I'll say about it. I know it's difficult for you to talk about, and I don't want to impose."

"I appreciate that too."

Yana walked around the room for several minutes, looking at things, making comments, asking questions. After lingering to admire a series of Romero Britto Disney-themed paintings, she noted that the biggest regret of her career was never having had a chance to voice a Disney character.

"And not just because of Peggy Lee and all that money she made on *Lady and The Tramp*," Yana said, clearly stalling as the modernist digital clock in the living room changed colors and Friday became Saturday.

"And speaking of money," Cindy said, sipping coffee and stifling a yawn, "why don't we get started on those documents you brought?"

Yana reached into her Chanel purse, extracting a large manila envelope. Jay sat at the table a few feet away, scrolling through his cell phone, not wanting to seem too interested while Cindy looked at the documents.

"How often do you look at your statements?" Cindy asked.

"Oh, I never do," Yana said. "It's just so, so *boring*. I really just let Ben handle them. And now Ben is AWOL and my son is useless, and I just feel like a complete idiot. I'm from an era when men handled all these things. Which is a stupid idea, I know. And it's especially stupid because the women usually live longer." She was rambling a bit, clearly nervous. Jay had never seen Yana so on edge, her usual confidence rattled and shaken.

Jay watched as Cindy shuffled through the papers and explained what she was looking at: a few brokerage accounts for the assets she'd accumulated with her husband, one bank account where all the pensions and Social Security checks were deposited along with the transfers from the brokerage accounts that financed the expenses the Social Security and pensions didn't. Cindy leaned in over the papers, fully absorbed, while Yana drained a glass of orange juice Jay had brought her. Yana looked as bored as Jay felt when he was thinking about money.

But that's what Cindy was for. Jay knew how much Cindy loved studying financial statements. During their marriage, when they'd been confused and at times angry about how they felt and everything that was going on around them, Jay had retreated to their basement studio to record songs. Once, he'd gone upstairs to find her at the kitchen table, doing algebra problems for fun. Cindy had many talents, but sometimes Jay thought making sense of numbers was what she was put on earth to do.

After a few more minutes, Jay noticed Cindy's expression shift from tired to concerned. Her posture suddenly became more rigid and alert, as if she'd been shocked through with electricity.

"What is it?" Yana said, suddenly all attention. "Just tell me. I can take it. Tell me how everything looks. I know I don't have much cash left."

"Oh." Cindy looked relieved. "You knew that already?

"Well, I don't follow financial matters very closely, but I know enough to look at the numbers at the bottom of the statements."

Cindy nodded.

"It's okay, you know," Yana said. "I'm an arts person. People in the arts don't die rich." She laughed. "We're more cerebral than that. I'm more like Jay than I am like you, I bet. But I own the house and I own the costumes. What I want to know is, does anything in these statements look suspicious? Was Ben taking money from me?"

Cindy ignored the question. "Did you know you had a home equity loan?"

Yana looked confused. "Well, I mean, I—"

"You would have had to sign for it, Yana."

The actress shrugged. "If Ben or Warren told me to sign something to get money for expenses or the collection, I did it. I didn't necessarily pay much attention to what it was. What's money for, anyway?" She forced a smile.

"There are a lot of cash withdrawals from your checking account," Cindy said.

"Well, I wouldn't know anything about that either," she said. "I don't use cash."

"Are your son and Ben authorized to withdraw money from your checking account?"

Now, at last, Yana had started to break. She took a napkin out of the holder on the table and dabbed at her face. "I put them both on my accounts a couple years ago. I couldn't leave the house for a month after I broke a hip and had surgery, and it was just easier. Nothing bad happened, so I left them on in case something else like that came up in the future. I trust them." She paused. "*Trusted* them, I guess I should say now."

Cindy showed her the checking account. She pointed to a few lines—then read them aloud. The transactions had all been made in one day, three months ago:

Aces Food Mart—$1,000
Aces Food Mart—$1,000
Aces Food Mart—$1,000
Aces Food Mart—$1,000
Aces Food Mart—$1,000

"Do you know what Aces Food Mart is?" Cindy said.

Yana stared blankly. "No."

Jay had been searching the internet. "It's a convenience store in Las Vegas."

"Oh, Ben, what are you doing?" Yana muttered, her voice heavy. "That has to be Ben. I mean, it would make sense if it is, given his history."

"There's another thing I don't understand, Yana," Cindy said. "I'm looking at the brokerage statements, and the amounts are going down each month because of withdrawals . . . but all I see are the *total* withdrawals, not where they go. But the amount doesn't square up—you add all the deposits and subtract all the withdrawals, and it doesn't add up to the amount in the account. There are thousands of dollars each month being transferred out of that account, but that money isn't showing up in your bank account. Do you have another account?"

"I'm quite sure I don't," Yana said.

Jay looked at Yana, considering everything he was learning, and started to get nervous. Not for himself, but for her: Someone was taking advantage of a ninety-year-old actress, someone he was rapidly coming to consider a friend, and he didn't like it one bit.

Cindy hovered over the brokerage statement again. "This is even weirder. Are you investing more money into your brokerage account periodically?"

Yana looked frustrated. "No," she said. "Isn't that the point? I'm spending too much? Of course I'm not putting more money into my brokerage account. If I had money to put in my brokerage account, we wouldn't be talking about this."

"Well, *somebody* is putting money in your brokerage account." Cindy pointed to the page. "I did a few quick calculations in my head and—"

"You can do that?"

Cindy smiled. "I'm good at math. Anyway, the amount of money that's inexplicably missing from your account each month averages about ten thousand dollars. But there's also an unexplained transfer of about two thousand dollars into the account."

"So someone is stealing from me . . . and after they steal it, they give a little of it back?"

"It looks that way."

"Why would anyone do that?"

Jay spoke up. "Guilt."

Both women started at him. "What do you mean, 'guilt'?" Yana asked.

"If it's a gambling addict, maybe," Jay said. "I've had a lot of friends who were addicts over the years. Not gambling specifically, but other things. And addiction is usually about ambivalence—the person wants to stop but can't, and the will to quit comes and goes, and they feel genuinely terrible about the way they're treating people."

Yana nodded. "So he's stealing money from me, which he doesn't want to do but has to, and sometimes, when he's had a winning streak or something, he pays me back a little. But of course, it's Las Vegas, so it's never nearly enough to cover the losses."

Cindy nodded. "That makes sense." She leaned back in her chair and sighed heavily. "So, what should we do now?"

Yana looked terribly broken and sad. "I guess we need to sell the costumes more quickly than I realized."

Cindy nodded. "We're working on that, I promise. But the first thing you need to do is call your bank and broker and cut off everyone who has access on the accounts. In fact, we can call the emergency line and do that right now."

"Do I have to remove my son too?"

"I would," Cindy said. "You need to be on a tighter budget. You can give him what he needs in cash and checks."

With Cindy looking on, Yana called the twenty-four-hour numbers on the accounts, followed the prompts, and removed all authorized users other than the primary account holder.

Yana's overall effect was crestfallen—more upset than angry. The rage she'd so readily directed at Warren seemed absent in the case of a much larger betrayal by her longtime financial advisor. Jay wasn't sure what to make of that. Perhaps the devotion Ben had shown in other ways made him immune to Yana's rages in a way that a perpetually ungrateful son never could be.

"I can't believe this," Yana said for probably the fifth time.

"Is there anything I can do for you?" Cindy asked.

Yana thought about it. "Be my new financial advisor?"

Cindy smiled and put a hand on Yana's arm. "I'm retired from that—and it would be a conflict anyway. But I can certainly give you some names for other people who could help you—people I know and trust."

Yana nodded. "I can't think about any of that right now."

"You don't need to," Cindy said. "Would you like to spend the night?"

Yana shook her head, her swagger returning a little. "No," she said. "I would like to go home."

* * *

Jay held Yana's hand as he helped her into the *Jurassic Park* SUV. He started the engine. KWXY was playing softly. The singer was Julie London; the song was "Girl Talk"—the last of the great misogynistic hits of the 1960s. Jay winced at the sexist lyrics, a lament about women's interest in "inconsequential things that men don't really care to know," and turned it down. But Yana turned it back up.

Jay smiled. "I was worried it would offend you."

"Oh, I love that song. It was a different time. Plus, it's okay if a woman sings it. It's subversive—like she's mocking that image of women."

"Her husband wrote the song," Jay said.

Yana shrugged. "Maybe it's not subversive, then. I still like it." She paused. "Maybe I like it because I feel like I deserve it. I've been such a moron with my money—I really do feel like a cliché of a '50s woman who trusted her husband with everything and then got burned."

"He was very good with money," Jay said.

"He was. And I suppose I was like a child. He liked me that way. *I* liked me that way: talented and beautiful. And he managed our lives, so all I had to do was be talented and beautiful."

"And a heck of an investor," Jay said. "You put together a pretty amazing collection."

Yana smiled at that, regaining a bit of her luster. "I suppose that's true."

"It'll be okay," Jay said, just to say something. He didn't like silence, and it felt particularly uncomfortable with a semi-distraught Yana sitting next to him in the car.

"Will it?"

Jay nodded. The song changed to Vic Damone, singing Antonio Carlos Jobim's "Meditation." "Yes," he said. "We'll sell your costumes, and that'll solve everything. The collection is worth a fortune."

Yana put her arm around his shoulder. It felt bony but also surprisingly firm and warm, full of life. "I trust you, Jay," she said. "I want to give you the whole collection to sell for me. You and Cindy are the first people I've trusted in a long, long time. You know, Jay, I think I love you."

Jay giggled nervously.

"I don't meant it like that," she said. "I know you're gayer than Vincent Minnelli. I just mean . . ." She thought about it for a moment before saying finally, "You delight me. You make me smile. You're talented. I feel like you don't have an agenda. You're a *good* person—the first one I've had in my life since Fred died."

"I try to treat everybody well," Jay said, pulling into the driveway at Yana's house. "And Cindy and I have nothing but your best interests at heart. We can talk about the collection soon. We don't need to hurry. Just try to rest and relax. And don't worry about anything."

* * *

When Jay got home, Cindy was not, as he expected, asleep. In fact, she was buzzing around the house, still full of energy.

"Poor Yana," she said.

"What a mess," Jay moaned.

"The only thing I don't understand is what, if anything, all of this has to do with Dylan's murder."

"Well," Jay said, "if Dylan had figured out that Ben was stealing from Yana, Ben would have had every reason to kill him."

"But why would Eydie lie about a conversation she heard us having with Dylan?"

"To try to divert attention from herself? And get us arrested so we wouldn't be competition for the consignment."

Cindy nodded. "Or at least to make sure word of that conversation got back to Yana, so we wouldn't be competition for the consignment. She figured if Yana thought we were bad people, she wouldn't give us the deal."

"And Warren being tight enough with Eydie to call her by her little pet name?"

Cindy smiled. "Just a little more client development—all about building relationships and getting deals done. Eydie wants that consignment, and she's probably especially desperate to impress her bosses now that there's a restructuring going on."

"You're right." Jay pulled out his phone and started to dial.

"Who are you calling?" Cindy said.

"Simon."

"It's three in the morning."

"It's important."

"He'll think it's a booty call."

Jay smiled. "Okay, maybe it's not as important as that would be—but it is information that could help find Dylan's killer, clear us, and save—"

He was interrupted when Simon picked up on the fifth ring.

"Jay," he said. Sleep blurred his tone, making it soft and confused. "What time is it?"

"Late," Jay said. "Or early, depending on your perspective. I'm with Cindy. We have information about the case."

Jay handed the phone to Cindy and listened in as she explained what they'd found going over Yana's financials.

"Interesting," Simon said finally, after grunting along to her retelling of the night's events.

"That's all you got?" Cindy said. "Can't you—I don't know . . . *do* something? Is that enough to get a warrant for Ben Sinclair?"

"Not without a complaint from Yana."

"Man, Simon," Cindy said, "you're just killing us. You need to hurry up with the case. We're dying here." She hung up before Simon could respond.

"That went well," Jay said.

Cindy smiled. "Get some rest. We're gonna need to be even more charming with Yana tomorrow."

"I think you need to hire a lawyer," Mary said, "and stop talking to the police."

Jay was sitting in the living room with Cindy and Mary, and he'd never felt more tension between them.

"We can't do that," Cindy said, her teeth gritted. "We hire a lawyer, and you know that'll get leaked to the papers—and we'll be back in the headlines, and the public will be even more sure we're the killers. It'll be the end of our business. We have to keep talking to Simon, and we have to try to figure out who killed Dylan, because we can move a lot faster than the police can."

Mary shook her head. "Maybe your freedom is more important than your business."

"We're *innocent*!" Jay said, trying not to yell. "Hiring a lawyer will tank the business and drain our bank accounts, and it'll just mean that clearing us takes even longer. We need to help Simon."

Mary threw her hands up in the air. She was getting heated herself—something Jay wasn't used to. "And look at where all the help you're giving him has gotten you so far!"

"You know what, Mary?" Cindy said. "We don't have time for second-guessing right now. We have to go meet with Yana to shoot the videos that, if we can somehow get out of this mess with Simon over Dylan Redman, will save our skins."

Without another word, Cindy stormed out to the car, leaving Jay alone with Mary, who looked as if she wanted to cry.

"I'm sorry," Jay said. "It's just . . . tensions are a little high right now. With . . . everything."

Mary was quiet for a moment. "It's not your fault," she said. "It's nobody's fault. Tell Cindy to break a leg with the video shoot—which I know you're going to. We're gonna get through this. Together. The three of us. Like we always have." She sighed, giving him a warm and teary smile. "We love each other too much not to."

Jay gave her a hug and joined Cindy in the car. A few minutes later, they were speeding toward Yana's house, the SUV's trunk filled with the camera equipment Cindy had let Jay buy, draining most of their last remaining funds. But they'd decided it was worth it. Nailing the videos presented their best shot at selling the pieces Yana had consigned to them—bringing in some desperately needed revenue and a shot at the rest of the collection. Of course, that was before Yana had told Jay the night before that she wanted to give the entire collection to them anyway. Oh, well—they'd saved the receipts, just in case.

As they drove, he despaired over how little progress had been made on the case. Ben was still proving elusive, and it didn't sound like the information about Yana's financials would be enough to get Simon working harder to find him. For all the talk about the surveillance state, Jay thought, it was surprisingly easy to disappear if you really wanted to. Meanwhile, Simon had told them, the forensics on the poison were also proving to be a dead end. The police had been in touch with local pharmacies and chemical companies, and none could report any unusual purchases of sodium fluoride recently—not that that meant anything. It was a compound that could last forever, which meant the poisoner could've procured it long ago—or bought it or even stolen it from someone else who'd had it in a closet for decades. Nothing Simon said put Jay at ease as to whether he and Cindy were suspects either. He'd been hoping Simon would tell him to relax, that they had nothing to worry about—but for whatever reason, Simon wasn't eager to take that bit of tension out of his life.

They arrived at Yana's house and carried the camera equipment into the living room that Jay had spent the last two days transforming into a TV studio. Her black leather sofa had been moved in front of a picture window with sparkling views of palm trees, and large white sheets of paper had been placed on stands behind the camera Cindy would be using to film.

Yana was always glamorous, but today she was resplendent. She'd been to the nail salon, and her white hair had more volume than ever, like she'd brought out a special wig for the occasion. While Jay set up the cameras, Cindy did her makeup, draining decades from her face.

"My God!" Yana examined herself with the mirror Cindy had handed her. "What is your secret?"

"A lady friend of mine named Elizabeth Arden."

Yana winked at her. She was fully *on*, ready for the camera.

"You ready, Yana?" Jay said.

"Ready when you are, CB," Yana replied.

"What?" Jay said.

"CB was Cecil B. DeMille, the movie director. He was shooting a half-million-dollar scene with tons of pyrotechnics, so they could only shoot it once. The explosion went off, and everything went great. He called out to the camera guy to see how the shot looked and the camera guy hadn't been paying attention. He yelled back, 'Ready when you are, CB!' He'd missed the entire scene. From then on, 'Ready when you are, CB' was a movie industry term used to describe general incompetence."

Jay laughed like it was the best joke he'd ever heard. It kind of was. "You ready to tell more funny stories on camera?"

Yana gave him a thumbs-up, and Cindy started filming.

A few minutes in, Jay darted behind the tripod to check out some of the test shots she'd taken. "Do I look okay?" he asked Cindy.

"Dapper as ever."

"Thanks," he said. If there was one word he went for when he got dressed every morning, it was *dapper*. Today he was wearing one of the pinstriped suits he'd worn while wowing audiences in Las Vegas, along with a bow tie he'd gotten when the Liberace Museum closed.

He stepped back in front of the camera, and Cindy started rolling as Jay recited the script he'd memorized—just the introduction. The rest of the interview would be a free-flowing conversation, and he'd edit it down to just the best parts.

"Hi, I'm Jay Allan with Hooray for Hollywood Movie Memorabilia in Palm Springs, and it is *such* a pleasure to welcome you into the home of the legendary Yana Tosh, one of the great vixens of mid-century classic films like *The Hollow Wall*, *The Bishop's Move*, and of course *The Red Lady*. What you probably *didn't* know is that after Yana was done stacking up all those awards and rave reviews, she started a different collection: the greatest collection of movie costumes in the world. And today, we're here to give you a chance to bring a little part of it into your home. Yana, thanks so much for joining me. Why don't you start by telling us a little about why you felt assembling this fantastic collection was so important?"

Yana smiled and put her hand on Jay's knee, looking at him steadily while she talked. Jay loved the shot. Rather than talking into a camera, she was showering her energy on Jay, and the viewers would be able to see her true charisma. That, Jay had promised Cindy, was sure to drive viewers to make big offers for the pieces they were selling.

"Jay," Yana said, "these films meant so much to me. I was always conscious of the fact that we were creating—inventing, really—an art form, maybe the only art form that was original to America. I've been gratified to see that view catching on lately. I mean, you see what's on TV and in the art house theaters now. Classic movies are bigger than ever. And the costumes, for me, were a way to preserve and showcase the craftsmanship that went into building that."

Jay nodded. "I'm a big film buff myself, Yana—as you know from working with me to put together this sale of your collection. And I've always wondered about the relationship actors have with costumes. I mean, as an actress, how involved were you in the actual costume design? Or did you just show up on the set and put the outfits on and then take them off and forget about them?"

"A lot of actors think of costumes that way, but for me, it was never like that. You know, you learn a lot about who someone is from the way they dress. That's why I'm always yelling at my son to dress up more for job interviews—or I did, back when he bothered with job interviews."

Cindy cackled behind the camera, and Jay immediately yelled, "Cut!" He tried to be annoyed with Yana for disrupting the shoot, but then leaned toward her, laughing. Yana, however, hadn't laughed at all. She asked Cindy if she was ready to resume shooting.

"Yeah, in five, four—" Cindy began, but Jay was still smirking.

"Let's give my cohost a moment to compose himself," Yana said. "I could use a drink anyway."

She got up, shooed off help, and went into the kitchen. Cindy and Jay heard chopping sounds, and Yana emerged a few minutes later with two vodka sodas, each with a lemon twist.

"Drinking on the job?" Jay said.

"It's just soda," Yana said. "No vodka. But don't you think it'll be a good visual? The ninety-year-old movie star sipping a drink and talking about her collection?"

Cindy nodded. "Yeah, that's good."

"I don't know," Jay said.

"Hey," Yana said, affecting an old Brooklyn accent, "it's my collection. The drinks stay in the picture."

She handed one to Jay and sipped hers primly, then reclined on the couch, the picture of relaxation. A cool lady of a certain age, Jay thought, was the ticket to riches. Angela Lansbury. Betty White. And now, he hoped, Yana Tosh.

"God," Yana said, staring at Jay, voice acerbic, "you remind me of Warren. I guess that's why I couldn't help but start talking about him."

Jay was taken aback. "I thought you hated Warren!"

Yana looked out the window, her voice pained and full of regret. "He was such a nice little boy—so funny and compassionate. That's why you reminded me of him. Then . . . well, something happened. And now he's nothing like you."

They sat in silence for a time. "I'm sorry," Jay said.

Yana snapped out her mood—as if she'd willed herself to put everything aside to be camera-ready, just like the pro she was. All of the personal drama stayed backstage and off camera. "What can you do?" she said. "Let's get back to work."

"Okay," Jay said. "We'll pick up with the question about your relationship with costumes. Loved the first part of the answer, but maybe let's leave out the Warren part."

Cindy started the camera rolling again, counted down, and yelled, "Action!"

"I think a lot of actors do just look at costumes as something to change into before they go on the set," Yana said. "Maybe that's the problem with acting today—everyone sees it as just a job. For me, it was never like that. You can tell so much about a person by how they dress. The costumes were everything to me. I would make sure they were sent to me months in advance, and I'd wear them around the house."

"You wore your costumes around your house?" Jay said, eyebrows raised.

"Oh, sure. And to restaurants and bars. I once wore a nun's habit to a Yankees game—we had box seats, of course."

"Now, Yana," Jay said. "I don't mean to sound rude, but why would you wear a nun's habit to a ball game?"

"I wanted to inhabit the character," she said. "It's called method acting, Jay. It's the way I learned to act, and it's the only way I know to do it. I don't want to just *play* a character, I want to *become* a character—for weeks before we start shooting. Feel what it was like to be that person, see the responses she drew. *That's* what acting is: becoming another person. And that's how I started the costume collection. I'd grow so attached to the character that I'd want to keep a little piece of her. And not just the costumes. I'd save other stuff—a stationery set that was in the character's home, the hair product we used, whatever. Little things I obtained to make me feel more like the person I was playing. Even stuff that didn't get used in the movie."

"And the studio people were okay with you taking things?"

Yana waved. "You have to understand, nobody thought the items were special back then. They were all custom-made for me, never to be used again."

"And now they're all worth a lot of money."

"Yes," Yana said. "It's wonderful, isn't it?

From there, they discussed a few of the pieces Hooray for Hollywood was selling, starting with a robe worn by Sydney Greenstreet in *Casablanca*. The robe was enormous—sized as extra-extra-large, and Yana joked that he was the only star whose name didn't need to be written on the labels. The robe was distinctively elegant, with a golden-brown sash and green tassels.

"Now, I should note," Yana said, "that this robe didn't actually appear in the movie. It's from a scene that was cut."

Jay was impressed. He'd been through the provenance in her filing cabinet that corroborated that information, and it would, of course, lower the value substantially compared to a piece that had made the final cut. But it was a stand-up move for Yana to point it out herself in a promotional video.

"What I like about that," Yana said, "is that you can make up what he said while he was wearing it—and no one will ever be able to prove you wrong. Sometimes I'll put it on and do that myself, alone in my walk-in closet, in front of the mirror."

Jay sized up her petite physique, then looked back at the enormous robe she was holding on her lap. "You," he said, "wear *that*?"

She smiled. "Well, on me it's more like a blanket. But it's a lot of fun. Sydney played Signor Ferrari in that film, a mob boss. You can make the most wicked threats in it!" She patted Jay's shoulder playfully.

A few hours later, they had everything they needed, and Jay couldn't have been happier—partly because he knew, from the luminous look on Cindy's face, that he'd delivered everything he'd promised. Yana Tosh, film star–turned-collector, drinking a vodka soda, reminiscing about her life, making jokes, touching the objects she loved. Jay had never seen anyone so happy. The weight of everything that was going on around her seemed lifted by her love of films and the treasures she had. There was also, he could sense, genuine pleasure at how much joy her pieces would bring to their new owners.

As they were leaving, Yana was still on a high, energized by the camera and the stories. "Boy," she said. "That was fun. I should give you the whole collection to handle. I'm getting tired of that Eydie Jackson woman calling me."

"Eydie?" Jay asked, shocked. "Have you been speaking with her lately?"

"Yes," Yana said.

"Well," Cindy said, "if you want to tell her you've decided to go in a different direction, she'll probably stop calling. If you're firm about it."

Yana smiled. "Oh, I don't know about that. I'm terrified to tell her anything negative. What with the murder investigation and all."

Cindy shrugged. "She'll get over it."

Jay looked at Yana nervously and caught a similar expression on Cindy's face. He wasn't sure what to make of it: Was Yana really afraid of Eydie? Or was it possible that she was still toying with them over the consignment?

Cindy sat at the dining room table with Jay and Mary, with printouts of the store's financials between them in one stack, and copies of their original business plan scattered all over the table. Bob Hope was in the kitchen, having his dinner, while Mae West napped by the window.

"This meeting of the executive board of overseers of Hooray for Hollywood is now in session!" Jay said.

Mary laughed. "The executive board of overseers consists of everyone involved in the business?"

Jay nodded. "All hands on deck in a time of crisis! We must consult the business plan!"

Mary said, "Was there a page in that business plan presentation for all of our possible customers thinking we're cold-blooded killers?"

"No," Cindy said. "But you sure can see the impact in the difference between the sales projections and the sales results." She sighed. "I just feel awful. People are afraid to do business with us."

"All of this money stuff is overwhelming," Jay said. "I don't know an EBITDA from a profit margin!"

Mary touched his hand. "I'm beginning to wish I didn't either."

"All right," Cindy said. "Enough of the mutual misery society. We're going to make this work. I was going through the financials. I can afford to float the business another fifty thousand dollars."

Jay shook his head. "Cindy, we agreed—"

"I know," Cindy said. "I know what I said in the beginning—but that was before I knew how important this business would be to us."

"And how good you two are at it," Mary added.

Jay pointed to the stack of financial statements. "How can you possibly look at those financial statements and think we're good at this, Mary? Are you going senile, my love?"

Cindy smiled and grabbed the papers and pounded them on the table. "You know what I see when I look at these? I see potential. I see the three hardest-working people I've ever met, busting their tails because they believe in something—and they got handed some bad luck to start, sure, but they're not the type of people who give up, because they believe in themselves. We're not giving up. We're . . . we're just *not*. I can afford to put in a little more. Final answer. Boom. Done! We are not giving up on Esther's dream. The name for the store was Esther's idea, you know."

"You never told me that," Jay said.

"I didn't want to lay on a guilt trip," she said. "But now I see you dejected, so I'm laying on the guilt trip. This is for Esther. If you can't fight for our dream, fight for hers. We're going to win. I just know it. Esther will not let us fail."

Jay hugged her. "I love you so much. And you know—"

Cindy pulled away. "This was not an invitation to talk about Esther."

Jay nodded. "Understood."

Cindy took a sip of the iced tea Jay had brewed in advance of their meeting. Like everything Jay made, it was delicious. "What is this tea?" she asked. "How many calories are in it?"

"It's Dragonwell Sweet Tea, from a recipe in the back of a Laura Childs Teashop Mystery."

"And the calories?" Cindy pressed.

Jay made a lip-zipping motion with his fingers. "Part of the recipe is you can never know how many calories are in it."

Bob Hope had finished his snack, and Mae West had left her hammock in the living room to join the activity, now napping beside him on his doggie bed in the corner. Everyone said cats and dogs didn't get along, but Cindy thought Bob Hope and Mae West must have been friends in past lives. She made a note to google that. A photo of them together, if one existed—of the actors, not the pets—would be a fun decoration for her office. Mae West's back was pressed tightly against Bob Hope's stomach, where she was curled up with her paws in front of her eyes.

"So we've solved the business part of the problem," Mary said. "For now, at least."

Cindy smiled. "Only because I have a childlike faith in our abilities in the absence of all evidence. And we had some backup money. I got lucky on the GameStop trade."

"GameStop trade?" Jay shouted. "Isn't that exactly the kind of thing you, the financial expert, are always telling me not to do?"

"Well, yes," Cindy said. "But the shoemaker's sons go barefoot—and I needed a little mindless excitement to distract from all the very mindful excitement in our lives. So I put five grand in. Now it's fifty grand, and we're back in business."

Jay nodded. "So that whole speech was really just nonsense, and you're actually just tossing in your gambling winnings?"

Cindy shrugged. "Nah. I probably would've dipped into savings anyway. It's what Esther would have wanted."

Jay's gaze softened. "Either way," he said, "I love you for it."

"And I love you," Cindy said. She grew serious. "And now that we're putting even more money on the line, we need to solve this murder more than ever—because there is *no way* the business survives if we just sit around and wait for the cops. At this point, frankly, I don't even have faith that they're going to figure this thing out. It feels like every lead lately has come from our own gumshoe work."

"But isn't it dangerous?" Mary said.

"Manifestly, yes," Cindy said. "But anyone have a better idea?"

Mary spoke, softly at first, before gaining confidence. "Someone tried to poison Jay. Probably Ben Sinclair, because he's missing. He's been gone a couple of weeks now, though, and no one has been able to get a trail on him. If he's not the killer, maybe he's actually another victim."

"You think somebody *killed* him?" Jay asked.

"Could be," Mary said. "He was a smart guy, a numbers guy. He might've figured out who killed Dylan."

"So he's either dead or he fled," Jay said. "If he's not dead, and he's not the killer, why did he skip town?"

Mary said, "Because he knew what he knew and was afraid someone would kill him next."

"But why would he leave with a bunch of costumes and a painting?" Cindy asked.

"For money? Just in case?"

"Could be," Jay said. "But maybe there's an innocent explanation."

"Sure," Cindy said. "The costumes could've been from his own collection. And we have no idea what that painting was. It could've been the Virgin and Child—or not. Simon asked Yana about it, and she didn't think anything else was missing. If you were going to leave town in a hurry, the first thing you'd grab would be something valuable, monetary or otherwise. And there's another thing that's bothering me."

"What's that?" Mary asked.

"The financial irregularities aren't enough to explain it," Cindy said. "If Ben needed money, he would've stolen costumes, pure and simple. Not a five-thousand-dollar painting."

The land line rang. "I'll get it," Cindy said, jumping up.

It was Detective Fletcher. "Simon," she said, "we're just in the middle of lunch. Can I call you back?"

"No," he said. "I'm afraid it can't wait. I need you to come to the station."

"Just me? Or Jay too?"

"Who's at the house with you?'

She told him, then waited a few seconds. She heard someone shout in the background. It sounded like a woman's voice.

"Let me just put you on hold for a second," Simon said.

Hold music started—soft piano, wildly at odds with the typical work police departments did. They should've gone with Tom Waits, Cindy thought. Or maybe "Bad Boys," the theme song from *COPS*.

"Okay, bring Jay down to the station too," Simon said when he returned.

Somehow, Cindy had never been to a police station. She didn't scare easily, but she couldn't help but feel intimidated by the imposing structure and brutalist concrete, totally out of step with everything else in Palm Springs. She noticed that every time she drove by, its very architecture seemed to announce that it was the end of the Palm Springs vacation dream. Maybe, she supposed, that was the point.

"You ever been in a police station, Jay?" she said, just to fill the air on the drive over.

Jay grinned. "Twice."

"You?" she said. "Why?" She parked, and they got out of the car.

"In my early days of being out," he said, "I fell for the wrong guy. I bailed him out a couple times, and then he bailed on me."

"Ah," Cindy said. "But *you* were never in trouble."

"Nah," Jay said. "I just attract trouble—or am attracted to it, I suppose."

The mood changed as they entered the police station. The palm trees out front seemed out of place, but they were short—as if they hadn't been there long and were part of some recent effort to put a friendlier face on policing. The American flag towered over them, motionless in the hot, dry sun.

As soon as they arrived, a young, no-nonsense cop sent them into separate interview rooms.

Simon went into Cindy's room first. He was out of uniform, wearing a polo with the Palm Springs Police Department insignia on the chest, and she saw even more clearly what Jay liked about him. His arms rippled with power, and he had achieved that combination of leanness and musculature that you rarely saw on straight guys, who couldn't lay off the carbs with quite that much discipline. That was her experience anyway. Then again, The Rock did pretty well for himself.

"Ms. Cooper," Simon said, sitting in the chair across from her. The table that separated them was blue Formica, but it was more chipped than blue. The harsh fluorescent lighting made Cindy want to say whatever it took to get the interview to end.

"Cindy," she said. "Just call me Cindy, Simon. Whatever happens in this interview isn't going to change my relationship with you or your relationship with Jay, because none of us did anything wrong."

"Why don't you tell me exactly what Mary told you about the letter she got," he said, ignoring her. "The one that was addressed to Jay."

"She already told you about it."

"And now I'm asking *you*."

Cindy sighed. He wasn't making this easy. She heard a commotion outside and looked toward the window. The shades were drawn but broken, so you could still see through them. A drunk college kid was being hauled, with the help of three cops, through the station. Cindy noticed the Burberry pattern on the kid's collar. A trust fund baby, she thought. Someone who would never face any real consequence from whatever he'd done to land him here. For him, it was just an awkward night that would make a good story for his friends.

"Can I get you a drink?" Simon said.

"No, I'm fine. Sorry. Just distracted." She told him everything she could remember that Mary had told her about the letter.

He took notes the whole time and didn't look up when she was finished.

"So what is this about?" she asked.

"We heard back from the feds," he said.

"The feds?"

"Sorry, the postal inspectors," he said. There was something funny about referring to post office workers as "the feds," although postal personnel were federal employees, Cindy knew, as legitimate as any others. "We sent the poisoned letter to them so their lab could evaluate it in ways that ours can't. We obviously looked for fingerprints and that kind of thing, but we hoped they could trace it to a particular post office, maybe find a machine it ran through, security footage of someone dropping it in a box—that kind of thing."

"What'd they find?"

"Well, that's the problem."

Fletcher picked up his pad and shuffled through it until a single piece of copy paper fell out. He handed it across the table to her. It was a high-resolution photocopy of the envelope addressed to Jay. "The postmark," he said.

She looked down at a Las Vegas zip code, along with the date. It was a stamp, not a high-tech printer, so it was smudged a little. Possibly, it had gotten wet somewhere between Vegas and their mailbox.

"I don't see anything odd about it," Cindy said, "but I'm no philatelist."

His eyebrows went up.

"Stamp collector," she said. "Someone who cares about postmarks and things like that. I'm not one of them."

"And yet you know what the word means?"

"Some people just know a lot of words, Simon."

He grinned, but awkwardly, clearly trying to cut the tension. "Just making conversation."

"Don't. Tell me what the postmark tells you."

"It hasn't been used in Las Vegas in ten years," he said. "They changed it—some sort of national security thing or, more likely, just a more fraud-proof postmark. They want to make it harder for people to slip things into the mail and get them delivered for free."

"That's an actual problem?"

"People will do anything for money. If you're running some direct mail scam, dumping lots of mail with fake postmarks into boxes is a good way to cut expenses and raise your profit margins. The point is, that letter wasn't mailed from Las Vegas. It wasn't mailed at all. Someone just dropped it in your mailbox. Do you have any sort of security camera that would've spotted it?"

Cindy felt a pang of disappointment—the end of any easy solution to the puzzle that was consuming her life. This news made everything more complicated. It didn't exactly rule out Ben Sinclair as a suspect—his disappearance still made him a likely culprit—but it did nix the Las Vegas gambling connection. Unless, Cindy thought, it was a double fake: Ben Sinclair pretending to frame himself to make it look like someone else was guilty. It was dizzying to think about, reminding Cindy of the complicated scams she'd had to unravel to get new clients out of bad investments.

"No security camera," Cindy said.

Simon shook his head, dejected. A smart guy, Cindy thought, but he was looking for an easy answer, and he didn't seem to be getting one.

"So where does this leave our investigation?" Cindy asked.

"*My* investigation," Simon corrected. He was quiet a moment, staring at the wall behind her. "On the one hand, it's nice because it takes the feds completely out of it. You know how in movies there's always tension between the local police, whom the feds think are dumber than a second coat of paint, and the feds, who all went to Ivy League schools but have no common sense? Well, in the real world it's exactly like that. But since the letter was delivered locally, with no connection to the mail system, the Postal Inspector's Office is washing its hands of the whole thing."

Cindy tried to smile. "Well, that's good for you."

"Is it? No one to get in my way, but also no one to blame if the investigation goes south."

"You can solve it," Cindy said. She wasn't really in the mood to give a pep talk right now, but she would if that was their fastest way out of this mess.

Simon stood up and walked toward the door, opening it for her. She headed toward it.

"I had another detective interview Jay while I talked to you."

"Oh," Cindy said. "Did you feel that your personal connection made it inappropriate for you to question him?"

Simon closed the door in a hurry, leaving them both standing in the interview room. A group of cops walked by, one of them glancing through the window to see what had happened that the door had closed so suddenly.

"And what, exactly, is that supposed to mean?" Simon asked.

"Just making a little joke."

"Don't," he snapped. "I'm a detective, first and foremost, and nothing will ever come before that."

Cindy smiled at him. "I think you like Jay. At least a little bit." Simon didn't say anything, so Cindy kept talking. "I understand the case creates lot of conflicts."

"I don't—"

She slapped at his hand, teasing him. "Don't say anything. I just want you to know that Jay is special. He's the most special person I've ever met. I'm a full-on lesbian, a Kinsey six, but if ever there was a guy who would win me over, it was Jay. Heck, he's so freakin' perfect, I married him, anyway."

Simon sighed. "Your point?"

"My point is you should go for it—while you can. Believe me, life doesn't wait. But you should also be very certain that you never do anything to hurt him or even make him a little bit sad. Because if you do, I have his back. And neither of us killed Dylan Redman, no matter what you might think. The only person I'd ever kill for is Jay. So be nice to him. He's worth it."

She winked at him, opened the door, and hurried down to the lobby, where Jay was waiting.

"Well," he said, as they left the station, "that was interesting. Are we allowed to talk about it?"

"I don't see why not," Cindy said.

To clear their minds, she suggested a long Palm Springs drive. It had been one of her favorite things to do when she'd first moved here, but Jay had been so busy since he'd arrived that he'd had little time to see his new town. They drove along the freeway, taking in the majestic views: mountains and, in the foreground, windmills. They were tall and white, and if you rolled down the windows, you could hear a faint hum.

"I love the windmills," Jay said.

"They're important for the planet," Cindy said. "But ugly."

Jay shook his head. "To me, anything that's making it so all of this can last longer is beautiful. You think about it that way, and you can appreciate the geometry of the wind turbines, you know?"

"You are so open-minded," Cindy said. "I worry your brain is going to fall right out of your head one of these days."

They turned off I-10 and onto Highway 62, and there was no other change from interstate to highway that led to such a dramatic difference in the view out the window. The mountains and turbines gave way to a desert oasis: enormous prehistoric rocks, dunes, and cacti. Then she noticed Jay was looking at his phone.

"Oh, crap," he said.

Cindy's foot slammed down on the pedal, a nervous reaction, and the car accelerated. "What is it?"

"Lenae is out with a story on the letter," he said.

"What?" Cindy yelled. She pulled the SUV over into the breakdown lane and took her own phone out. With the car stopped, the hum of the turbines was more noticeable, as was the sound of the cars speeding by.

It was just a short item:

DECEPTION AND INTRIGUE SURROUND AUCTION HONCHO'S MURDER

In the continuing saga of the murder of Dylan Redman, Cypress Auctions' memorabilia vice president, a poison-laced letter mailed to a person of interest in the murder was found to have not been mailed at all, sources say. The postmark on the letter was fake, and sources say it was dropped in the mailbox. An official spokesman for the Palm Springs Police Department declined to comment.

"Oh," Jay said. "Well, that's actually rather innocuous, thank God. Doesn't even mention us. I still don't know where she's getting her information, though. When did that come out?"

Cindy looked at the time stamp. "Eight hours ago."

"I wonder who the source was."

"The police," Cindy said, pulling back out onto the road.

"But it says the police declined to comment."

"No," Cindy said, reaching for her phone again while she drove. "It doesn't say that."

"Focus on the road," Jay said.

"Hey, king of the shotgun seat," Cindy said, "settle down. I got this."

Jay took the phone out of her hand and read it again, this time aloud. "Ah," he said. "I see. It says an official spokesman declined to comment—which would suggest that perhaps an *unofficial* spokesman was more forthcoming."

They went to lunch to distract themselves, and then went bowling at Palm Springs Lanes, a fun-looking place, but one that catered to a group of senior citizens who went bowling to win, not to have fun. They followed that with dinner at The Pink Cabana and afterward stopped at Hooray for Hollywood, just to check on things and to grab a few posters Jay wanted to hang in the in-law suite he was making into a true home.

When they got to the shop, the voicemail button on the office phone was blinking. Cindy ran over and listened, hung up, and called out to Jay twice, to divert his attention from the posters he was flipping through. He stared back at her.

"That was Yana," Cindy said. "Ben Sinclair is back in town."

"He's *back*?"

"They got together for lunch, apparently. She says he claims he was just stressed out from everything, embarrassed over how sloppy he'd been with things, and needed to get away. He thought about staying away—that was why he packed so much stuff—but he decided to come back."

"Did he tell her where he was?"

"Didn't sound like it."

"Well," Jay said, "let's find out."

Bright and early, Cindy called Simon to tell him Ben Sinclair was back in town.

"I am aware of this," he said.

"Oh?"

"Give me a little credit, Cindy," he said. "I'm a detective, not a moron. I had a unit watching his apartment, and they called me as soon as he pulled in."

"Did you talk to him?"

"Yes."

"Did you find out where he went and why?"

"No."

"No?"

"He wouldn't tell me."

"You mean you didn't make him tell you."

Simon laughed. "I know you think you know more about policing than I do, but—"

"That's not what I was saying."

"Of course it was. But my point is, I went and talked to Ben Sinclair. He didn't want to talk to me. I asked him a few questions, and he was vague and didn't say much. And that's all I can do for now. He hasn't been charged with a crime, and we don't have any evidence he committed one. Skipping town is weird, but it's not illegal. I can't make him answer questions."

"*You* can't make him answer questions," Cindy said.

"I don't like where you're going with this."

"I'll just go to talk to him," Cindy said. "Make sure he's okay, you know?"

Before Fletcher could tell her not to, Cindy hung up and got in the car, leaving Jay and Mary to tend to Hooray for Hollywood.

* * *

The drive was, as usual, filled with traffic, giving Cindy plenty of time to worry. She had always been a numbers person, and the nice thing about math was that there *was*, always, an answer. If you wanted to calculate your losses on an investment, you could do that. You might hate looking at the number that resulted, but at least you could see the number. And there was, for Cindy's brain, comfort in that. She thought of her favorite Agatha Christie quote: *"The truth, however ugly in itself, is always curious and beautiful to seekers after it."* That was in the book of quotes Esther had made for her. She thought of Esther's beautiful handwriting and the little love notes she'd always left in the lunches she packed for Cindy. Her meticulous penmanship always made it seem like everything would be okay—like the universe would always provide her with the order she so craved. Things would make sense because they needed to. But of course Cindy knew, especially now, that wasn't how it worked.

When it came to people, and especially emotions and relationships, things didn't have to make any sense at all. In fact, the rule there seemed to be that things *wouldn't* add up. So: Ben Sinclair was back in town. Okay, but why? And why had he left?

She knocked on Ben's door, and he opened it quickly, then started to close it. Cindy caught just enough of a glimpse to see that Sinclair's time, wherever he'd been, hadn't been good for him. He was unshaven and looked exhausted, like he'd consumed his missing days with panic and anxiety. He was wearing a light blue T-shirt, khaki shorts, and flip-flops.

"I just want to talk," she said. "I'm trying to help. I'm not looking to get you in trouble."

"What good does it do me to talk to you?" he said.

"How is the approach you've been taking working out for you?"

He didn't say anything.

"I'm not the police. I'm just a nice person who cares about Yana and wants to get to the bottom of what's happening. I'm not looking to hurt you or anyone else."

The door opened, slowly, into a living room, and to the right was a staircase that looked like it led up to two bedrooms. It was sparsely furnished but clean, and the first thing Cindy noticed was the art—large, Chinese scroll paintings lined the back wall of the living room. Ten scrolls in all, each depicting a different fish. There were goldfish, koi, and a beautiful oscar—a black and orange fish that looked like a Halloween decoration.

"Beautiful paintings," was the first thing she said to Ben once she got inside. Might as well try to defuse the tension.

"Thank you," he said, still on edge.

"Are they antiques?"

"No," he said. "I bought them from a street artist on a trip to China with Yana a few years ago. Stuff like this is so cheap there. Look just like they're antique, don't they?"

Cindy nodded. "I don't suppose you want to tell me where you've been? People have been looking for you—worried about you."

His face was expressionless. "No."

Cindy nodded. "I want you to know that I don't think you had anything to do with what happened to Dylan Redman," she fibbed.

"I appreciate that."

"But I do want to ask you about Yana's finances."

Ben smirked. "On the advice of my past attorneys, I'm not going to talk about that at all with anyone. Including you. It's not personal."

"Look, I used to be a financial advisor. I know how things can get messy and complicated, and how innocent record keeping can become a full-blown—"

Ben cut her off and started to walk her back toward the door. "I'm fine talking with you, Cindy, but I'm just not going to get into that kind of discussion. Not now and not ever. Yana's financial dealings are private. You're a financial advisor—you know that. If you want to talk about Yana's collection, of course, I'm happy to—"

"I went over her books with her," Cindy said. "At her request. There was money being transferred out of the bank account and into a brokerage account, and I can't figure out what the brokerage account is."

He looked annoyed. Good. Maybe that would inspire him to tell her what he knew. "Yana is just confused. She has another account she uses for some expenses. She probably just forgot about it or couldn't find the paperwork. She is ninety years old, after all."

"God, I wish people would stop throwing her age around as if that makes her a senile old bat. Do *you* have the paperwork, then, Ben?"

He was silent for a moment. "I'll ask Yana the next time I see her."

Cindy laughed, harsh and disbelieving. "You've got to be kidding me. You're still involved with her affairs? After you left without telling anyone?"

"As far as I know," he said. "I went and talked with her. She didn't say that I was, but she also didn't say that I wasn't. I think she was just happy I was okay."

"You're unbelievable. Did you explain why you skipped town?"

"Well, I'm back now, aren't I? What does it matter? I don't owe anyone an explanation. What was that commercial for that airline? *'You are now free to move about the country?'* That's me. It's just no one's business."

"There's a murder investigation happening, Ben. And a second attempted murder—the poisoned letter."

"I guess you just don't get it, do you?" he said. "I fled because as soon as Yana told me you'd asked about my financial history, I knew you or Jay would tell that detective. I didn't do anything wrong, and I don't want to get in a jam over a mistake from more than a decade ago."

"Ben—"

He cut her off. "And I knew they would start digging into me, and I just couldn't stand that. I still have some pride, hard as that might be to imagine. I was also, frankly, worried my presence would make Yana's life a living hell—that the investigation would center on me, and you're proving me right. So I figured I would just leave—let her go on with her life, let everyone think I did it. I'd move somewhere, start over. I don't have anything left, you know. It's all gone."

"The gambling addiction?"

He didn't say anything.

"I'm not here to judge. I've done dumber and worse." One of the things Cindy had learned from working with clients on their financial affairs was that telling people you'd done dumb things with money, too, was the best rapport builder there was. In Cindy's case, it wasn't true—she'd always been good with money, unless you counted her new business. But it was a harmless lie. "When you left town, where'd you go?"

"For the fortieth time, I don't need to tell you that."

She nodded. "Fair enough. Why'd you come back, then?"

"When I saw the story that the letter wasn't really from Las Vegas, I knew that would take the attention off me. I figured I might as well come back and do what I could to help Yana."

"From what I heard, it sounded like you left with some costumes," Cindy said. "Were they Yana's?"

He shrugged. "Yana gave me costumes sometimes. It was a way to give me an occasional bonus—things I really liked. And like I said, I thought I was leaving for good. Why wouldn't I take them with me?"

"You still have them?"

He shook his head. "Pawned them as soon as I got out of town."

"You took a painting too."

"Lots of people have paintings. And now I think it's time for you to go."

She wished she'd brought Jay. She'd been too abrasive with Ben, too quick to try to get answers, and now he was shutting down. Plus, he was angry. Cindy was alone, and Ben wasn't exactly physically imposing, but . . . who knew what he was capable of?

She followed his suggestion and went back to her car.

* * *

The phone rang twice while Jay was in the store, but he was too absorbed in editing the Yana Tosh videos to answer it. Mary had left for lunch. The door opened, and Judy Garland belted out "That's entertainment!"—a bit of gadgetry he'd rigged up earlier in the morning. Maybe it was a bit much. He'd leave it to Cindy to decide.

"I'm here to help you," Simon announced.

Him again.

"I don't think I can take any more of your *help*, Detective," Jay said, emphasizing the word like it was a curse. "Any good friend would advise me to hire a lawyer, even if all I do is pay him five hundred dollars an hour to tell me to stop getting *help* from you."

"If you don't want to hear what I have to tell you, I'll leave now." Simon stared at Jay, maintaining direct eye contact. Jay wasn't sure what that conveyed. Suspicion? A predatory desire to manipulate him, like Mae West toying with a mouse before clawing it? If this was Simon's way of flirting, Jay thought optimistically, Detective Beefcake would still be single by the time he and Cindy got out of prison for a murder they didn't commit.

Still, that unbroken eye contact sent a shiver down his spine. "Okay," he said. "What do you have . . . *Detective*?"

"First of all," Simon said, a small grin twitching at his lips, "I thought we agreed you would call me Simon."

"Then please tell me, *Simon*, what trap you're trying to lay for me."

Simon shook his head. "No trap. Just something I've picked up that I want to share with you." He paused. "I really shouldn't."

"What?" Jay asked. "You want me to beg for it now?"

Simon shook his head, a confused look on his face, as if wondering how the conversation had taken such a quick turn. "Tomorrow at two o'clock, Eydie Jackson is going to meet with Yana Tosh at her home."

Jay's chest pounded. The two priorities in his life right now were making sure he didn't get charged with murder and getting the Yana Tosh consignment. Now the guy who probably wanted to charge him with murder was here to tell him he and Cindy might be losing the consignment.

"How do you know that?" Jay said.

Simon smiled. "I'm a trained professional, Jay—went to school for it and everything. I find stuff out. It's what I do."

Jay started to reply, then stopped himself. He wasn't sure what to do with this little tip. Plus, he didn't want to say something dumb that would make Simon think he was a loser. It was funny how that never changed. When he liked a guy, he was always terrified that every word he said would make the guy think he wasn't cool. It'd been true when Jay was twelve, pining for straight boys, and it was true in his forties. Except . . . when had his push-and-pull with Simon turned into probably—no, definitely—liking him?

"Look," Simon said, "it's probably better if neither of us says anything more about it. I just thought you should know."

He turned and headed toward the door, but Jay followed him. "Simon, wait. Why *are* you telling me this?"

Simon shrugged. "Maybe I'm rooting for you guys to get the sale."

"I'm all ears, Mary," Jay said, smiling. "What's on your mind?"

He was sitting at the counter, flipping through an auction catalog, and Mary had just popped out of the backroom to tell him she had something to say. "I heard that little exchange back there," Mary said, "and I think that you should just ask Simon out."

Jay looked at Mary, admiring the warmth in her face. It was the face of a woman who'd devoted the nine decades of her life to serving others, not to her own vanity. To him, she was more beautiful than anyone who spent her time at spas or salons.

"I'm playing hard to get," Jay said, laughing. "Or at least, it'll look that way. Probably not very smart to make a move until he's completely cleared me of, you know . . . murder."

They'd just closed the store for the day, and were having dinner—steak-and-cheese subs Jay had gotten from the Subway next door. The horror movie table was finally gone, delivered to its new owner, so they stood eating on paper towels spread out on the counter.

"I was sad when things ended with your last . . ." Mary trailed off.

"Boyfriend," Jay finished. "That's all it was. And it shouldn't have even been that."

"All I want is for you to be happy, not lonely," Mary said. She had been widowed thirty years ago, her husband lost to cancer.

"I *am* happy," Jay said. "I have everything I need: you, Cindy, and Mae West—though I must confess, I'm also becoming fond of Bob Hope."

Mae West was with them in the store that day, climbing on everything, but such a meticulous self-groomer and careful walker that there was no concern about her damaging any of their wares. It had taken some coaxing, but Jay had finally gotten Cindy to concede that Mae could be a valuable addition to the store's branding. The valuable breakables were in a display case. Bob Hope, on the other hand, couldn't be trusted at Hooray for Hollywood. If he ever became a mascot for the store, he'd need to be represented by a portrait.

"You say that," Mary said. "And I'm sure it's true. But it's good to have love in your life too, Jay. You're too young to give up on that. I think I also gave up too young. I couldn't imagine being with anyone else, even though I knew he would have wanted that for me."

"How do you think Cindy is doing with her loss?" Jay said.

Mary thought about it. "Honestly, she won't talk to me about it. She's doing the whole high-functioning-Cindy thing, like she always does. But you know she's hurting."

"Is there anything I can do to help?"

"You are," Mary said. "You're doing a lot to help. Just your presence and love and support. That's what she needs. You're a talker—if it were you, you'd want to talk about it. But that's not her. And it probably isn't going to be. And that's okay. You just keep on loving her, and she'll be okay. I just know it."

Cindy walked in, dressed in gym clothes, and Mary quickly filled her in on what they'd been discussing—minus the part about her grieving process, of course.

Cindy nodded. "Do you know how lucky the two of us have been to have you in our life all those years ago—and to have you back now? You're like the best guardian angel ever."

"I just want you to be as happy as you make me," Mary said.

Jay put his sandwich down on the paper towel and hugged Mary. "We love you so much, we want you all to ourselves. But don't worry about me, please. I promise, I'm not giving up. I'm trying to get to a place where I don't need someone else to be happy. A romantic companion could be a nice add to my life, but not a necessity."

"Do you feel like you're in that place?" Cindy said.

Jay nodded. "It's not that I don't miss being with someone. But you and Mary are the best friends I'll ever have. I could meet and fall in love with the greatest man ever, and I hope to do that someday, but the relationships I have right now will always be the most important things in my life."

Mae West came over and pawed at Jay's leg. Her claws sunk in just enough that it hurt—as though she were protesting his claim that his current relationships were all sunshine and lollipops. He pulled his leg away and tried his best not to look at her. It wasn't that Mae West wanted to hurt him, Jay knew. She was just playful, and it seemed as if any time he talked about her and how wonderful she was, she felt a need to assert her menacing side. As her namesake had put it, *"I used to be Snow White . . . but I drifted."* Jay took a piece of the steak from his sandwich and tossed it to her. She scurried away with it.

"Let's put on a movie," Cindy said.

"Oh!" Jay exclaimed. "I love that idea."

When they'd first opened the store, Jay had bought a projector that could show movies on a screen, which had itself been used in a few episodes of *NYPD Blue*. He'd purchased it from a prop house that had gone out of business, but the piece wasn't worth much. Few people used projector screens anymore, and *NYPD Blue*, sadly, was not a particularly coveted brand.

"What should we watch?" Cindy said.

It was Mary who answered, which was unusual for her. She'd been watching movies with Jay and Cindy since they'd toured together, and she'd always deferred to their choices. "*The Mirror Crack'd,*" she said.

"Ah," Jay said. "Because of the missing painting."

"You never know," Mary said. "Sometimes things jog your mind in the strangest way. I'll be reading a Joel Osteen book at night, something about the importance of forgiveness, and then—bam! I'll know exactly what to do next on the quilt I'm working on. The human mind is mysterious. Maybe the movie will crack the case." She grinned. "Besides, I just want to see it."

Jay went over to the popcorn machine they'd gotten at a flea market a few weekends ago. It had been used in one of the Jerry Lewis Cinema theaters built in the '70s, and featured retro colors and styling, along with the comedian's face on it. The popcorn machine was a rare cross-collectible: it appealed to movie buffs, Jerry Lewis fans, and Wall Street types who liked to accumulate mementos of high-profile corporate failures. That was one way to make something valuable, Jay had learned. Get two distinct groups of collectors desperate to own it for completely different reasons. Double the demand without increasing the supply.

Bonus: It was a good popcorn machine. Jay made two bags, dumped them into the vintage red, white, and blue popcorn bowls Mary had bought at a thrift shop, and turned off the lights.

Settled into the chairs that once surrounded the horror movie table, they watched as the film opened with Angela Lansbury as Miss Marple. A stellar performance, Jay thought, and the only time she played that role, though it was just a precursor to the mega-stardom she found a few years later with *Murder, She Wrote.*

Half an hour in, they all spotted the painting Jay and Cindy had seen, ever so briefly, in Yana Tosh's home.

"I don't understand it," Cindy said. "Where did that painting go?"

Jay started to speak, and Mary paused the movie. "Maybe it's more valuable than we thought," he said. "It's from a movie with a lot of big stars, and it's a rare prop that plays a pivotal role in the plot. It's not like a dress that someone just happens to wear in a movie. That painting is the reason—"

"Come on, Jay," Mary said, "don't give away the whole plot."

Jay laughed. "Sorry, Mary. We're trying to solve a murder here."

Mary shook her head. "And I'm just trying to solve the murder in the movie." She reached across to Jay's bowl and took a few pieces of popcorn. "I'll be right back," she said. "Just have to wash my hands."

When she returned, she reached into her tote bag for a scarf she was knitting inspired by one she'd seen in *Mary Poppins.* Disney movie-themed scarves had been big sellers for her. "Okay," she said. "Now, where were we?"

Cindy looked at Jay. "I think you might be right, Jay. Plus, we're in the middle of a major Agatha Christie renaissance. Two new big-budget movies, a bunch of high-end streaming shows. There's even an Agatha Christie card game now. I'd figured that painting was probably only worth a few thousand dollars, but now I'm not so sure."

Jay pulled out his phone and searched for experts in rare Agatha Christie memorabilia. The first couple of pages were full of London-based experts, and the time zone difference meant he wouldn't be able to reach them right away. He could always email them later, and probably would, but he preferred someone located in the United States. He didn't want to wait; there was no time to spare. He clicked onto the third page of results and gasped.

"What?" Cindy said.

Mary leaned over to see, and they both crowded over Jay's shoulder, squinting for a better view, their faces illuminated by the light the phone gave off in the dark store. Jay finally shooed them away and read aloud. It was a short profile of Dylan Redman from Boston University's student newspaper, dated twelve years earlier, when Redman had been a senior English major. It described the thesis he'd written and his career plans. The writing had, Jay thought, the laboriousness typical of a college newspaper:

Redman, an English major, plans on a career in the world of art and antiques, where he thinks his view of prewar pop culture as a major aesthetic milestone in American life can have an impact. "I'd like to have people see how important these things are and recognize that there's an opportunity to build a collection for very little money. At least right now."

He likes the opportunity of a lucrative career that memorabilia provides, but literature will always be his first love—even if his tastes are at odds with those of his professors. Asked where he sees himself in ten years, Redman laughs. "I'd like to one day be the top Agatha Christie memorabilia expert in the world."

Jay continued his web search, but couldn't find any more mentions of Dylan Redman in relation to Agatha Christie. Cypress had sold a few first-edition Agatha Christie books over the years, but nothing that would have involved Dylan. The movie memorabilia department hadn't sold anything from films based on Christie's works, and a magazine piece on Redman's personal collection contained no mention of her.

"Seems like just a weird coincidence," Cindy said. "A throwaway line."

"You think so?" Jay wasn't sure.

She nodded. "Dylan was talking about the importance of recognizing early-twentieth-century pop culture figures as historically significant. He tossed out Agatha Christie as an example. That's all."

"Come on, Cindy," Mary said, looking up from her knitting. "You're no fun. And besides, it doesn't do us any good to assume it's a coincidence."

"But I think it *is* a coincidence."

Mary sighed. "So what are we going to talk about, then? How do we advance our investigation right now if we assume that?"

"*Our* investigation?" Cindy said. Jay smiled.

"Well, yes," Mary said. "You two are smarter than Simon, that's clear. You're his best hope at solving this. Plus, you have me to help." She winked and took another piece of popcorn, carefully using a tissue to grab it so her hands wouldn't get buttery.

"Okay," Jay said. "So let's assume the painting is connected to our investigation somehow. But what would be the connection between Dylan's knowledge of Agatha Christie, a missing painting from a movie based on Agatha Christie, and Dylan's murder?"

They sat in silence for a time before Cindy spoke. "Maybe he tried to steal the painting—or knew something about it, or"—she snapped her fingers—"maybe Dylan told them the painting wasn't worth anything and tried to buy it from them cheap. But they saw through it and got mad. Or maybe he tried to make a deal for it and cut Eydie out of the transaction. So she lost it and killed him."

Mary nodded. "I like the way you think."

"Thanks," Cindy said. "I'm just spitballing here."

"Well, it's better than nothing," Jay said.

He put the movie back on, hoping that distracting themselves with the rest of the film might, as Mary suggested, kick-start their brains to come up with some more useful ideas. They watched through to the end, Mary grumbling periodically about how Jay and Cindy had ruined it by giving her a clue about the painting.

"The thing about Christie," Cindy said, "is that you don't read or watch the movies just to find out who did it. She's still one of the most famous mystery writers in the world, because so few ever came close to having her psychological insight."

"That was some dark stuff we just watched," Jay said. "You know, I never really thought of Miss Marple like that. She always seemed rather twee to me—all those doilies and stuff."

Cindy winked. "That's what people always think when they haven't read Christie. But her works are full of bite and cynicism—a dark portrayal of humanity, set in the genteel English countryside. It was Miss Marple who said, after all, *'The worst is so often true.'*"

* * *

When he and Cindy got home, Jay retreated to his suite and scooped Mae West onto his lap. She purred and he tucked her favorite blanket around her—a bright blue afghan that had belonged to his grandmother. Immediately she began kneading it, purring at an increasing volume as she massaged it with her paws. It was an activity of pure contentment, and one that had concerned Jay when he'd noticed she was still doing it as an adult cat. But a vet explained that, while it was rare, some cats did like to "knead" blankets well into adulthood. It was generally a harmless relaxation method. Jay smiled whenever he watched her at it. Funny, he thought, that cats came with their own instinctive method of meditation. If only humans were programmed like that, so much suffering could be avoided.

Mae West's heartbeat and the white noise of her purring helped Jay focus on the death of Dylan Redman. All he and Cindy had right now, he realized, was a group of weird, sketchy people and events. No possible explanation for what had happened.

Mae West jumped off Jay's lap and ran over to the window. She stared into the night, and Jay was paranoid enough to run over and look too.

It was just a bird. He walked back to bed, and Mae West remained by the window, staring. After a few minutes, Jay pulled out his Kindle and started reading *And Then There Were*

None. He'd planned to be asleep by eleven, but reading the first page of an Agatha Christie at night meant a guaranteed book hangover—every bit as regrettable the next morning as a regular hangover, but more worth it.

He texted Cindy well after midnight: "Want to crash Eydie's meeting with Yana? Just say we were stopping by to look at stuff?"

He saw the icon indicating when Cindy was typing. It stopped, then started again. A few minutes later, he finally got the return text from her: "That's what I would do, but it's very much not what you would do."

Jay smiled and typed out a reply: "I'm an aggressive businessman now."

Cindy texted back a thumbs-up. "Let's do it."

The next day, Cindy carefully maneuvered the SUV into Yana Tosh's driveway at the exact time Simon had told Jay that Eydie would be there. She and Jay were uninvited, of course, but showing up punctually at least wouldn't make them look desperate—or worse, rude—to Yana. At least, that's what she hoped.

Eydie Jackson was in the driveway, just stepping out of an Infiniti, rental car agency stickers in the window, prompting a smirk from Cindy. There was nothing lamer, in her opinion, than renting a luxury car to impress a potential client. The other guest was more interesting: Lenae Randolph, emerging from a competing Mercedes SUV. Something about that stuck out to Cindy, and then she realized what it was: Lenae's transportation was a big upgrade from the 1990s Wagoneer she'd shown up in for her first meeting at Hooray for Hollywood. On its own, a new car wasn't suspicious—but the abrupt jump in price was. Maybe it was just a rental, she thought. Maybe Eydie had insisted on Lenae driving a nicer car if they were meeting with Yana together. Cindy didn't have time to keep thinking about car values, though. Lenae and Eydie had greeted each other and were walking now toward Yana's front door, side by side.

"What's *she* doing here?" Jay hissed, motioning for Cindy to leave the car running. "Let's take a minute to make a plan."

Cindy shrugged. "How can we make a plan? We had one, but now that plan is toast because we have absolutely no idea what Eydie and Lenae walking in together means."

"Well, we know one thing they have in common," Jay said. The car was still on, and the stereo kept playing Barry Manilow's "Copacabana." Cindy was too anxious about the meeting to bother protesting the music.

"Yes," she said. "Either they both lied *to* us or *about* us. Lenae told us she found out about the letter attempting to poison you from the police scanner—which we know wasn't true. And Eydie lied to the police about the conversation she heard us having with Dylan Redman."

"There's a lot of that going around," Jay said. "Everyone involved in this situation has lied relentlessly."

"And now these two are showing up together," Cindy said. "Probably to lie some more."

Cindy turned off the engine, and she and Jay headed toward the front door. Eydie and Lenae noticed them walking behind, and both women turned, but neither said anything. Cindy smiled at that. They probably assumed Yana had also asked Cindy and Jay to come, and while they surely weren't happy about it, it was too late to do anything about it now. Though Lenae was a feisty one, Eydie was savvy enough to know that confronting them would just make her look bad in front of Yana.

Wordlessly, and with smiles faker than an annuity salesman's, the four of them arrived at the door together. Before anyone had a chance to ring the bell, they were greeted by Yana herself. Behind her was Warren, and, somewhat surprisingly,

Ben. Whatever he'd told her about his disappearance and reappearance had apparently been enough to allow him to remain as at least a friend, if not a trusted advisor. Cindy shuddered at that.

"Eydie!" Yana crowed, her voice more cheerful this time. "Lenae! Thanks for coming out to talk."

"Thanks for having us," Eydie said.

Yana stood back. "Well, you said you had a proposal for my collection—and I can't just ignore that, can I? Come on in, and let Ben know what you'd like to drink."

"Hell is empty," Cindy whispered to Jay. "And all the devils are here."

"Don't go all Shakespeare on me," he whispered back. "I was thinking more *Mean Girls*: *'She doesn't even go here.'*" He nodded toward Eydie.

Cindy and Jay trailed in behind Eydie and Lenae, and Cindy prepared to deliver the little speech she'd planned for Yana. The one about wanting to stop by to see more of the collection and take some B-roll for the video Jay was working on. And good golly gosh, what a complete coincidence that they'd pulled into the driveway at the *exact same time* as Eydie and Lenae!

Cindy took Yana aside, but the former starlet spoke before Cindy could steer the direction of the conversation. "I'm so glad you two are here," she said, rolling with the surprise. Given the way everyone in her inner circle seemed to be double-crossing one another lately, she didn't even seem to question Cindy and Jay showing up. "You know, you're still the best people I've met in this godforsaken memorabilia trade," Yana whispered. "But Eydie said she had a new plan she wanted to unveil to me, a way she could sell my pieces for more money than anyone else. I just have to listen to that, don't I?"

"Of course you do," Cindy said. "You'll want privacy for that, I'm assuming—we can go in the other room. Or come back later?" She felt like she had to at least suggest it.

A mischievous grin took over Yana's face. "No," she said, "I don't think I do want to give them privacy. Let's have you and Jay there for it—an old-fashioned bake-off! Like a casting call. God, it takes me back—all the awkwardness and tension of people vying for the part."

Cindy and Jay followed Yana into the living room, where Eydie and Lenae were already seated, sipping iced teas that Ben had prepared. There seemed to be a tacit agreement among all involved not to comment on Jay and Cindy's presence. Eydie had apparently concluded that she could only make herself look bad by being openly sharp-elbowed. And Lenae—well, who knew what her angle was? The situation was almost surreally awkward, Cindy thought, but it worked in Yana's favor. Both of her suitors would have to play off against each other, and everyone had to be on their best behavior.

Yana started to tell Jay and Cindy about a movie she'd made with Humphrey Bogart, but their conversation was interrupted by Eydie, who came and stood in front of Yana with a small bag in her hand. Eydie was dressed as provocatively as ever, like she'd forgotten she was selling a vixen's collection, not auditioning to play one in a movie. Cindy chastised herself for being catty, but still. Eydie was dressed like a harlot: deep red, Betty Boop lipstick and a plaid miniskirt. The white blouse went well with her deep tan, which Cindy recognized as a spray job rather than the product of the sun.

"Yana!" Eydie crowed, throwing her arms around the actress. Cindy saw that Yana was taken aback by the display of affection, but she recovered quickly. "Before I forget," Eydie added, "I wanted to give you a little treat Lenae and I picked up for you."

She handed over the small gift bag—pink and white, with a palm tree coming out of a cupcake for a logo: Palm Springs Cupcake Factory. "Factory" was a bit of self-deprecation, Cindy knew, as the bakery was famous for its large, meticulously handcrafted pieces that cost up to twenty dollars each.

The cupcake they presented was roughly four times the size of the ones Cindy remembered from birthday parties when she was a kid. A bright, juicy orange slice peeked out from the top, as if reaching to emerge from the puffy dollop of frosting that coated it.

"It's an orange creamsicle cupcake," Lenae said finally after an awkward silence. "They're my favorite."

"Very thoughtful of you, my dear." Yana gave a Pan Am smile, then picked up the bag and put it in the kitchen. When the former starlet returned to the living room, Cindy allowed herself a smug smile of her own, knowing that giving Yana Tosh a dessert, of all things, betrayed just how little they knew her at all.

Warren turned to Eydie. "It's nice of you to bring my mother a cupcake," he said. "We do appreciate your generosity. And I'm sure it's not at all an effort to try to charm your way into a consignment that she's made fairly clear she isn't inclined to give you."

What was with the tone change? Cindy thought. Had Warren and Eydie had a falling out? Had he caught on to "Eedles's" financially motivated flirtations?

She smiled, not taking the bait. Cindy knew how aggressive the young woman could be, but Eydie wasn't going to show it here. She was too smart, or at least cunning, for that. "I've come up with a new sales plan that I think will dwarf anything a local, small business start-up can do."

Cindy opened her mouth, but Jay gave her a warning look. They could offer their rebuttal later, but there was no advantage to coming off as threatened or defensive.

Yana nodded at Eydie noncommittally. "Okay," she said. "I'm all ears."

Eydie reached into her Chanel bag and pulled out a small iPad, motioning toward the couch. Lenae joined her, and Yana sat in the middle, with the rest of the group sitting in chairs across from them. It felt like a reality TV set, Cindy thought—everyone gathered together for maximum tension and drama. Conversations that should've been private made public just for effect.

"Our plan," said Eydie, "is to combine the traditional, time-tested resources of Cypress with the media skills and online following of Lenae Randolph, to give you the best of all worlds: the credibility that can only come from Cypress, and the exposure that can only come from the top celebrity writer in the world."

Yana smiled, and Cindy wished that the woman was a worse actress so she'd have a clue whether it was real or faked. "I'm intrigued."

"Mom," Warren said, "this is stupid. You have the most valuable Hollywood stuff in the world. No matter how you sell it, Lenae is going to have to write about it. I'm not saying Cypress is bad, and you know I don't think we need to be selling right now anyway, but—"

"There is no *we* here, Warren," Yana snapped.

Warren looked annoyed but regained his focus quickly. He probably had a lot of practice bouncing back from Yana's put-downs. "I'm just saying, you don't need to sign with Cypress to get Lenae."

Yana looked at Lenae, who suddenly looked uncomfortable, which was not her usual state. Eydie reached across and touched her shoulder. "Talk a bit about what you're envisioning," she said.

Lenae cleared her throat. "I've decided that, you know, after a long time of really trying to be an outsider who thinks she's above the hubbub of commerce and marketing, that it makes sense at this point to take the Lenae Randolph brand in the direction of a more immersive, partnership-based media world. And Cypress, with its sterling reputation and enormous reach, is a perfect fit for my first deal. I'm looking forward to bringing my readers a big, exclusive series of stories as part of a new brand partnership—a way to generate a new revenue stream, something to keep the money coming in if my online ad revenue slows."

It was a carefully rehearsed pitch, meant for maximum manipulative effect. Cindy carefully dialed back the simmering rage brought by every word. When she spoke, her words came out calmly. "So what you're saying is, you won't cover Yana's collection if it's sold through Hooray for Hollywood, because Eydie has offered you a kickback."

"Come off your high horse," Eydie said. "It's called sponsored content. There's nothing wrong with that. It's the way all media works now, and it's a chance for Lenae to get her retirement fund together. Not immoral in the least."

"We don't need lectures about morality from a lying drunk like you," Jay said. Cindy winced. Jay prided himself on his composure and never liked to say nasty things—but Eydie and her smug, dishonest self-dealing had finally broken him.

"Good lord." Yana stood up, shaking with some combination of rage and anxiety. "All of you, shut up. This isn't about any of you, and it's not even about me. It's about my *collection*, and its ties to cultural *history*, and you are all acting like entitled brats—children, really. And I already have one of those. My God, selling this collection off and giving the pieces new homes was supposed to be a fun last hoorah for me—a way to show the world what I've built and what it means to me. What it *should* mean to *them*."

Cindy looked at Jay, who stared at his feet like a chastised child. She felt bad too—like they were all making Yana's life very difficult.

Yana continued, "And you come in here with your schemes and your greed and your agendas. I'm tempted to send you all home and keep the whole thing to myself. Maybe you can try again after I'm dead, and you'll only have my thankless son to annoy. You disrespect me, and you disrespect my collection."

"Mother, you're upset," Warren said, walking over to hold her hand, with the first real show of compassion Cindy had ever seen from him. "Let's go get you a drink."

Ben followed, and the three of them disappeared into the kitchen, Yana muttering under her breath. The woman was angry in a way that Cindy hadn't experienced before. Yes, Yana had been offended when she'd confronted her with information about her financial advisor. She'd felt patronized, as if her independence, judgment, and personal life were all being questioned. But now she just seemed truly, purely livid.

Cindy excused herself to run to the bathroom, and then walked by the kitchen as slowly as possible so she could hear a bit of the conversation. If she was already in the doghouse, a little eavesdropping couldn't hurt *too* much.

Cindy heard Ben whispering to Yana. "The Cypress offer is quite compelling," he said. "They have the reach to find the buyers. I think you really need to consider it."

"I don't even want to hear it," Yana said. "Leave me alone. I am going to have a snack, and I will deal with this later."

"What do you want, Mom?" Warren said.

"For you to leave me alone." Her tone was icy. It was shocking for Cindy to hear a woman of her age still capable of instilling fear, but there it was: Yana Tosh's power remained undiminished.

Ben and Warren rejoined the rest in the living room while Yana foraged for food. Cindy returned to the living room, deciding it was best not to push things with the woman right now, or even offer sympathy.

"I think," Jay said, "that it would be best if we don't speak of the costumes right now."

There was nodded agreement, and awkward small talk filled the room for the next few minutes. Warren yammered on about the Los Angeles Dodgers, and Jay joined in. Jay was a renaissance man, Cindy thought: a gay entertainer and movie buff, but he knew the name of every player on every Major League Baseball roster going back thirty years.

"I hadn't expected you to be such a baseball fan," Warren said.

"I'm a fan of beauty," Jay said. "A beautiful song, a beautiful painting, a beautiful play. A beautiful man in a baseball uniform. If I can see beauty in something, it's special to me."

Warren went into the kitchen to check on his mother, and the next thing everyone heard was a primal scream.

Warren's.

"Mom! Oh my God!" More yelling, crying. Everyone ran into the kitchen. Through the crowd, Cindy could see enough to be scared: The elderly woman lay prostrate on the floor, a half-drunk glass of water on the counter and, next to her, the quarter-eaten cupcake. Cindy and Jay moved in and lifted Yana off the floor, bringing her to the couch in the living room, while Ben Sinclair dialed 911.

"Is she responsive?" Warren said. "Does she have a pulse?"

"I'm not sure," Jay said. "The paramedics should be here in a few minutes."

"Please just stay with her," Warren said. "I'm freaking out. I can't watch."

He walked back into the kitchen, staring out the window down the driveway. Eydie and Lenae stood in the living room, looking more inconvenienced about the consignment than upset. Cindy sat on the couch next to Yana, stroking her hair and whispering kind words. There wasn't much movement from the starlet, who lay flat on her back, but Cindy felt her chest, and sensed a hint of light breathing. She knew she hadn't felt the same rapport with Yana that Jay had—though few people connected with anyone the way Jay always seemed to—but it was still painful. Yana was so full of energy and life, never more so than at her most intractable and imperious. Seeing her in a state of utter vulnerability was jarring and painful.

Cindy looked up from Yana, one hand still on the woman's shoulder, and had a good enough view to see Jay walk toward the kitchen. Warren was in there on his hands and knees, picking up the pieces of cupcake with his right hand and placing them in his left.

"Just leave it, Warren," Jay said. "We can deal with it later."

Warren looked up at him, startled by his presence. "My mother just hates messes. I don't want her to come to and see this—she'll be mad at herself and at me."

"I really think you should leave everything as-is for the police." Jay gently took the bits of cupcake from Warren's hand and placed them back on the floor.

"Oh," Warren said, understanding now. "You think that—"

"I don't think anything other than that we should leave things as they are," Jay said. He guided Yana's son by the shoulder back into the living room. Warren's eyes kept darting back toward the kitchen, and Cindy watched as Jay practically dragged him back to the couch and his mother. Cindy squeezed over to let Warren sit next to her and then resumed stroking Yana's hair, singing gently to her in that voice that, she remembered fondly, had once brought comfort to so many: *"I come to the garden alone, while the dew is still on the roses. And the voice I hear, falling on my ear . . ."*

The last time she'd sung this song, it had been to Esther, right at the end. For the first time, she let herself think about that—let the memory rush over her body as she sang, imbibing her voice with emotion. She held it together, though, because she had to. She knew Yana needed her to. The room went silent, and Cindy sensed why: Everyone was listening to her. She loved that. Missed it, even.

A few verses in, the door opened, and four paramedics joined them with a stretcher. One checked Yana's vitals, while the other asked Warren about what had happened and Yana's general health. Cindy was surprised by how up to date Warren was. Whatever issues he had, he obviously cared about his mother and paid careful attention to her medical history.

"Did she have any allergies?" one of the men asked Warren.

Warren thought about it. "I think mild lactose intolerance, but nothing that would explain . . . *this*."

The paramedics placed the legendary Yana Tosh on the stretcher and started to wheel her out. Before they reached the door, Simon Fletcher joined them, along with a few other uniforms. With a quick nod to him, they left with Yana, leaving Simon with the group.

And that was when it hit Cindy: they were all in the middle of yet another attempted murder.

In a way, Cindy wished she'd joined Yana in the ambulance. She knew it wasn't her place—that Yana was in good hands with the paramedics and, hopefully, with her son—but she was sad she couldn't keep singing to her. *Maybe I'm crazy,* Cindy thought, *but I really did think my singing was helping her.* Instead, she sat with Jay and Ben, along with Lenae and Eydie, in the now silent living room. Simon paced between them.

It was Ben Sinclair who spoke first. "Do you think she'll be okay?" He looked shaken and broken.

"I don't know," Simon said. "She's ninety years old and unresponsive. For now, at least. The good news is, the paramedics of Palm Springs are the best in the business."

"Do you think someone poisoned her?" Ben said.

"I'm an investigator." Simon flipped through his notebook, scribbling with the Bic pen he'd pulled out of his pocket. "I go where the facts lead me."

"But you must be suspicious," Ben said. "There's been a lot of weirdness going on here—Dylan dying of poison, then the poisoned letter that was sent to Jay, the same poison both times. And now this. Test her and find out if she ingested the same poison."

Simon just looked at him, his expression as unreadable as ever.

"If Yana has sodium fluoride in her system," Cindy supplied, "you need to find out."

"Somehow," Simon said, "I already thought of that."

"Sorry," Cindy said. "I don't mean to tell you how to do your job."

"You sure do it a lot for something you don't mean to do."

"I'm just desperate," Cindy said.

Simon softened. "I know."

She leaned over to catch a glimpse through the kitchen doorway of the other cops who'd arrived. They were examining things, placing the bits of orange creamsicle cupcake in a series of evidence bags, along with the bag the cupcake came in.

"Is what happened to Yana consistent with sodium fluoride poisoning?" Jay asked.

Simon ignored the question. "Why don't you tell me what happened?" he said. "Why you're all here, how Yana was, what happened before she passed out, how you found her. That kind of thing."

For the next few minutes, everyone put aside their differences to explain the situation to Simon. Cindy was astonished by how open Eydie and Lenae were about the pitch they'd put together to corner Yana into giving them the consignment. In a way, Cindy thought, the nakedness was almost admirable: no pretense of morality, no impulse to make excuses. After some preliminary discussion, Simon took them out to the porch one by one for separate interviews. Then they gathered again in the living room.

"As you can see, Detective," Eydie said, "the people who would have been most incentivized to kill Yana Tosh were Jay and Cindy, because they had just found out they were going to lose a consignment."

"Yana hadn't made any decision," Cindy said, remaining calm. "And it was *your* cupcake."

"Which you probably poisoned to try to pin it on us," Lenae supplied.

"How would we have poisoned it?" Cindy said.

"It was in the kitchen alone, and everyone was going in and out," Lenae said. "Anyone could have." She paused, then continued. "Someone poisoned that cupcake, and the goal was to kill Yana Tosh."

"We didn't even know Eydie was going to bring a cupcake with her," Cindy pointed out. "How could we have poisoned it?"

Lenae ignored the question. "And Warren liked you guys, because it would've taken you forever to sell the stuff. You were his kind of dealers—slow and incompetent."

"Incompetent?" Jay said.

Eydie laughed. "Yes, incompetent. A pair of rookies. Yana consigns the whole collection to you, and there'll be plenty of costumes left for him to inherit for his stupid little museum. Because you're amateurs who won't be able to find buyers as quickly as Cypress can."

Lenae grabbed her phone out of her purse. "I have quite a scoop on this little story," she said, furiously pecking away with her fingers. She looked at Jay and Cindy, who sat next to each other at the coffee table. "I don't think this is going to be the kind of press you two were looking for when you came to me begging for a story."

"Whatever, Lenae," Jay said. "Are you really so desperate for attention that you'd sell out your journalistic integrity like this? Obviously I was wrong about you."

"What's that supposed to mean?" Lenae asked harshly. But she did put down her phone.

Suddenly, Cindy remembered Jay's description of his visit to Lenae's home. He was never one to mock people's lifestyles, Cindy knew, but even he had been struck by her rundown residence. There was nothing wrong with choosing to have a modest home filled with trinkets, but was Lenae in severe financial straits? What else could explain her conduct here?

Cindy stared at Lenae. "You live so modestly," she said, "and yet this little partnership with Eydie you've put together suggests Hetty Green–level avarice."

"Who in the world is Hetty Green?" Lenae snapped.

Cindy smiled, remembering the biography Jay had given her a few months ago. "The Witch of Wall Street. She was a famously good stock trader in the early 1900s, the first famous woman in New York City finance. But she was famously stingy, mean, and greedy."

Lenae didn't say anything. Ben Sinclair also remained deathly silent, and Simon cleared his throat.

"We'll know more soon—once we get a report from the hospital on how Yana is doing and what caused her medical emergency. In the meantime, I'd appreciate it if all of you would keep your phones on so you can be available if I need anything more from you."

With that, he stood up and left, and the deputies followed behind him. Cindy and Jay seized the opportunity to make their exit, avoiding any further conflict with Lenae and Eydie.

When they got out to the car, it was Cindy who spoke first. "Yana was eating the cupcake," she said. "That was the last thing she was doing."

"And Eydie and Lenae are the ones who brought it," Jay said. "Did we find out which of them bought it?"

Cindy shook her head.

"Even if one of them bought it, the other could have poisoned it," Jay said.

Cindy shook her head. "They arrived in separate cars, so that seems unlikely."

Jay turned down the radio. "Unless the one who brought the cupcake told the other one of her plan to bring the cupcake—in which case the other person could've grabbed it for a second on the way in and poisoned it. If you were looking to frame someone, poisoning a cupcake they brought as a gift and had in their possession almost the whole time isn't a bad bet."

"Or anyone else at the house could've gone into the kitchen and poisoned it."

Cindy stayed focused on the road. A coyote darted across, and she slammed on her brakes. Jay was thrown forward a bit but recovered quickly.

"Sorry," Cindy said. "Didn't have time to warn you."

"It's okay," Jay said. "Glad you saw him in time."

Part of living in Palm Springs was living with wildlife. It was one of Cindy's favorite things about having relocated here full time. Palm Springs had a few wildlife preserves, and the climate and large expanses of undeveloped land led to impressive biodiversity. The combination of nature with the glitz of a mid-century Hollywood retreat offered the best of all things: both nature and nurture.

When they got back to the store, the lot was empty except for Mary's car. They walked in to find their friend at the desk, thumbing through a vintage magazine. Cindy decided to hold off on telling Mary what had just happened. No need to upset her too.

"What have you got there?" Cindy asked.

"Well, I didn't know what to do," Mary said, anxiety in her voice. "A nice older woman came in with a big box of old celebrity magazines. She wanted two dollars each for them. I told her you weren't in, and asked if you could call back, but she was insistent. I know we always need new inventory, so I bought them with some of the cash in the register. And I don't know enough—"

Cindy went behind the counter and put her arms around Mary. "You paid two dollars each for those?"

Mary nodded. "I hope it's okay. I'm just not an expert on these things."

"Did she leave a name and number?"

"Yes, but she wanted to make a deal now. I counted them up and gave her a hundred-and-fifty dollars, because there were seventy-four magazines. I rounded it up, just to—"

"Mary, relax," Jay said. "You did perfectly. You're a valued member of our team, and we trust your discretion. You needed to make a decision, and you made a decision."

"Was it an okay price?"

Cindy winked at Jay, and thumbed through the magazines. Excellent condition, with some of the biggest stars of the 1950s on the covers: Rock Hudson, Doris Day, Frank Sinatra, Deborah Kerr, Perry Como. "More than okay. I would have offered her five dollars each. That's why I asked if you had the woman's name and number. I want to call her and send a check for the difference. We're not looking to make windfall profits or take advantage of people. We want to pay fair prices for things and earn a fair profit."

Jay laughed. "Excuse me, ma'am, where is Cindy Cooper, cutthroat financial wizard?"

"I want us to make a lot of money, but we're not going to do it by underpaying for vintage movie magazines." Cindy grinned mischievously. Partly, she really did want to be a good neighbor who gave people a fair price. But she had another motive too: "Not to mention, she'll tell everyone about Hooray for Hollywood, the most ethical memorabilia dealers in the world. Maybe she'll even post about it on Facebook."

"I don't know about Facebook," Mary said. "She had to have been in her eighties."

"No one under eighty is on Facebook anymore," Cindy said. "My point is, it'll be good business to surprise her with a bonus check. And if she has more movie stuff, she'll know who to call."

Cindy went into the office with the woman's phone number and emerged a few minutes later with an envelope and a check. She placed the check in the envelope and left it on the desk with the rest of the outgoing mail for the day. Done.

The store phone rang. Jay was closest, so he picked it up. It was Simon Fletcher. Cindy leaned in to listen.

"Simon," Jay said, "any word on Yana?"

"She's in serious condition," Simon said. "Heavily sedated, so we'll know more once they dial down the drug dosing. She may pull through, but she may not. It's hard to say. At her age, any number of things could go wrong. We'll know more soon."

"Any word on what caused it?"

Silence on the other end of the phone.

"Hey, you called us," Jay said.

"You were at the party," Simon said. "What more can I tell you?"

Jay's face reddened, and his voice rose. "Look, if you're still treating us as suspects, you're a lot stupider than I thought, Simon Fletcher. And if Cindy or I was the one who poisoned her—"

"How do you know for sure it was poison?" Simon suddenly sounded tense.

"If it was a completely innocent incident, you probably wouldn't be calling me and hesitating on whether to give me any details."

The detective laughed. "Look at you," he said, "using that deductive reasoning."

"Condescend to me a little more, Simon," Jay said. Cindy felt herself wince. "Which is a little rich, when you think about it, because you're obviously flailing on this case. You're making zero progress, and things keep getting worse. But who knows? Maybe Cindy and I can bail you out."

Simon cleared his throat. "There was sodium fluoride in the cupcake," he admitted. "But it wasn't baked in. Someone laced it by sprinkling it on top. Now, do you have any idea why Eydie or Lenae would've done that?"

"So it was the same poison all three times," Jay said.

Simon ignored him. "Answer my question."

"Maybe they'd worked out a deal with Warren that he would give them the consignment if Yana died. But that doesn't fit with the way Warren was acting. Unless he was intentionally hostile to them, to throw us off the scent."

Cindy took the phone from Jay. "Hi, Simon. It's Cindy."

"I didn't realize you were there."

"I listen in on all your conversations. Perhaps whoever poisoned the cupcake thought that Warren would eat it, given that he seems to have more of a sweet tooth than his mother. And then the goal would be to kill Warren because he was the one interfering with the decision to sell. But it would look like the cupcake was *supposed* to kill Yana. That would be some sixteen-dimensional chess."

"Whoever we're dealing with is big on misdirection," Simon said. "I wouldn't rule anyone or anything out because it's too complicated." He paused, and when he spoke again, his voice had a note of chagrin to it. "If you think of anything else, let me know."

"Of course. 'Bye, Simon."

"Oh, and one more thing."

"Yes?"

"Tell Jay not to be so sensitive."

The next morning, Cindy took Jay and Mary out for breakfast at the diner next door to Hooray for Hollywood. The diner's decor was a perfect fit for their store—a true 1960s theme, with a jukebox and signed photos of oldies stars like Rick Nelson and Lou Christie. Plus plaid tablecloths and waitresses who called everyone "honey." They were seated at a booth by the window, where they could watch the steady flow of traffic going in and out of the dollar store. *People like new and cheap these days,* Cindy thought. *Old and expensive is a tough niche.*

"I still think all of this comes back to Ben Sinclair," Cindy said, "even if he's not the actual murderer. We know he's a crook and a gambler, and he disappeared for a while for no apparent reason. We don't know where he went or what he did while he was away. Not to mention, he had a lot of costumes with him when he left. No one has acted more suspiciously than he did."

"Eydie lied about us to the cops," Jay supplied.

"That could be explained by her desire to destroy our business and get the Yana Tosh collection herself. I'm not ruling her out, but I think Ben Sinclair is the one to dig into. And that's what I'm going to do."

When they got back to the store, Cindy disappeared into the office and started searching for "Ben Sinclair financial advisor." In the golden-age private eye novels she devoured, investigative techniques tended to involve a lot of following people around, hanging out in bars, and travel. All of that was great, and sometimes still needed, but the true crime books she'd read lately showed how much things had changed. Detectives—private or otherwise—started their investigative work on the internet, with the same search engines middle school students used for essays on rabbits and the *Titanic*. The best resources in the world were now available to everyone.

She scrolled through the results. One was from five years ago, an obituary for Theresa Sinclair, age seventy-nine, who had died in South Florida. At the bottom of the listing on the website for a funeral home, it read, "She is survived by her son, Ben Sinclair, a Palm Springs financial advisor, and her daughter, Delilah McGovern, an arts reporter at *The Boston Globe*."

Cindy's cursor hovered over the name. After a few more clicks, she found the sister's listing on the newspaper's website, accompanied by an email address, but no phone number. She thought about dialing the main switchboard and asking to be transferred, but decided it wasn't worth it—if Delilah wasn't at her desk, Cindy would have to leave a voicemail. And nobody checked voicemail anymore. She started typing an email:

Hi Delilah,

I hope you are well. My name is Cindy Cooper, and I'm the co-owner of Hooray for Hollywood Movie Memorabilia, a vintage memorabilia store in Palm Springs. I know this is a strange email, but I'm kind of at a loss for what to do next. Some strange things have been happening with your brother Ben's employer, Yana Tosh, and I'm concerned that he will be blamed for them because of his past behavior. I know he's had his struggles, but I also know how much he cares about Yana. If you could give me a call, perhaps you can help me to help him. I can say more by phone.

She closed with her name and cell phone number, then hit "Send." Next she went back to the search results and found nothing else of interest about Ben Sinclair.

She got up and walked into Jay's backroom, where he was watching footage from his interview with Yana.

"If she doesn't make it," Jay said, sounding sad, "this will be the last-ever footage of her."

Cindy headed over to the record player and shuffled through the albums Jay had in the bookcase next to it. She stopped when she found one she hadn't listened to before: Lawrence Welk's *Songs of Faith*. A strange choice for Jay. She took it out of the cover and placed it on the turntable, adjusting the needle and turning the volume up as a series of crackles filled the room. She loved vinyl records—swore by them. The opening bars of "Ave Maria" played, a full chorus accompanied by too many strings—as though the song were being strip-mined for kitsch and sentimentality. It wasn't good, in her opinion, but it was oddly affecting. So maybe that did make it good.

"Why are you playing that?" Jay asked.

"Just curious," Cindy said. "I was surprised that you had this. It doesn't really seem like you."

"I never listen to it." He shrugged and at last looked up from the computer, pressing "Pause" on the video. The computer lingered on a frame of Yana Tosh, leaning in for a playful peck at Jay's cheek.

"That's a great shot," Cindy said.

"Yes," Jay said, his voice touchingly emotional. "She's going to pull through, and we're going to do the sale, and Simon is going to find out who killed Dylan and tried to kill me and Yana. Soon this day will all just be a weird memory."

"Where'd you get that Lawrence Welk album?" Cindy said.

"It was my parents' favorite," he said. Cindy could see that he was tearing up now. Jay's parents had died in a car accident when he was in junior high school, and he almost never talked about them.

"Oh, Jay, I'm so sorry." She walked toward the phonograph and lifted the plastic covering, but Jay's voice stopped her.

"Leave it," he said. "It's okay. I should let myself think about them more."

"They would be so proud of you," Cindy said. "Proud of the music we made, and the music you made on your own after I went into finance, and proud of the business we're building. Mostly, they'd be proud of what a wonderful, compassionate, moral man you are."

"They might not be so cool with the gay thing," Jay said.

"It was a different time. People were raised the way they were raised, and their beliefs reflected their time and culture. You can't judge their 1980s beliefs against our 2020s standards. Your parents would've been the first people to evolve on those issues. I just know it."

"You really think so?"

Cindy joined Jay by the computer and hugged him. "I'm absolutely positive."

They sung along with the last few bars of "Ave Maria" and kept going with the rest of the album: "The Lord Will Understand," "Somebody Bigger Than You and I," and "Give Us This Day." Without any need for discussion, Cindy flipped the album over after that song. Out in the main office, the phone rang, but Mary answered it. They moved on to "He," a song Jay and Cindy had performed dozens of times all over America. It was the first time Cindy had listened to it, much less sung it, since their divorce.

They were interrupted by a knock on the door. Jay silenced the record player while Cindy called for Mary to come in.

"It's Warren Limon," she said, handing Cindy the phone. "He said it was urgent."

Cindy nodded her thanks and took the phone. She'd barely gotten a chance to offer a greeting before Warren machine-gunned her with what sounded like a planned speech. It took her a few seconds to emerge from the time warp she and Jay had been in so she could follow what he was saying.

"With my mother being incapacitated, I'm sure you understand. I want you to halt all progress on listing the pieces she gave you and return them to me. I can be there to pick them up in a few minutes, if you're around."

"I understand your position, Warren," Cindy said carefully. Warren was distraught, and she couldn't let her own frustration or emotion come through. If there was ever a time to be calm, professional, and businesslike, this was it. "And I am so sorry for what you're going through with your mother. But you must understand our obligations. Yana is our client, and unless she's been declared medically incapacitated and you've been legally authorized to take charge of her affairs, I'm afraid I can't return anything."

"My mother is very sick!" Warren shouted. "Probably dying." He let loose a string of obscenities, and Cindy interrupted him—unnerved by his temper but wanting to assume the best of him.

"I understand you're upset, Mr. Limon, and please know that your mother is in our thoughts. In the meantime, her items are safely stored here. We won't be listing them for sale immediately, so there's no urgency to get anything back to you or to her. When the time comes, whatever the outcome, we will work things out. Please know that your family is in my thoughts."

He was still screaming when Cindy hung up.

"That sounded pleasant," Jay said.

Cindy frowned. "I feel terrible for him. He's going through a lot, whatever kind of person he is."

"His mother's death would put a stop to her plans to sell the costume collection," Jay said. "Just before she was about to sign with us—or, perish the thought, Eydie and Lenae."

"Oh, I know," Cindy said. "And he was in the kitchen with her and the cupcake too. He could have poisoned it. Not as easily as whoever bought the cupcake, but—"

"Ben Sinclair was in there too."

Cindy nodded. "This is like one of those awful logic puzzles where one of the big clues, it turns out, doesn't actually tell you anything. The poisoned cupcake doesn't narrow our pool of suspects at all. Not even a little bit. It could have been any of them. It would've been easier for Eydie or Lenae to have done it. But that also makes it more likely someone else would've used that method to frame them. What better way to get away with murder than to poison a gift given to your victim by someone who's also a suspect?"

Her cell phone rang.

"Is my brother in trouble?" the woman said after the briefest of greetings. It was Delilah McGovern, Ben's sister.

Cindy paused, unsure how to respond. "I don't know."

A sigh. "If you see him, please tell him I'm on my way. We'll sort this out."

"Delilah—"

But the call had ended.

* * *

After closing time, Cindy decided she wanted to do a little more research on Lenae Randolph. She'd been through pages of internet results, but she knew there was so much missing. Those big newspapers Lenae had written for over the years had been through so many restructurings and bankruptcies that the archives were rarely available online.

She needed to know more about the gossip maven and what drove her. The key piece that didn't make sense was that Lenae lived and dressed simply despite having a big media profile—presumably with the revenue that would come with that. She'd displayed no signs of greed as far as Cindy could tell—until she'd abruptly abandoned all journalistic integrity to throw her marketing muscle behind Eydie in exchange for a cut of the proceeds. Cindy couldn't get her head around the idea that someone who didn't appear materialistic was now acting out of pure greed to help a repulsive creature like Eydie. What could Eydie possibly give Lenae beyond money? Charm and friendship were not among her offerings.

It was time, Cindy decided, to go to the best place in the world for finding information: a local public library. A ten-minute drive later, the Palm Springs reference librarian led Cindy past the large plant installation in the middle of the reading room, past rows of seniors reading newspapers and kids doing homework, over to one of the two microfilm reading machines that were still there.

"Thanks so much for showing me how all this works," Cindy said.

The librarian, a handsome man in his twenties with a name tag identifying him as Daryl, smiled. "Oh, it's a pleasure. We don't get many requests for the microfilm anymore."

"They still teach it in librarian college?" Cindy asked.

He smiled. "For now."

It took her several minutes to browse through the indices of a few defunct Palm Springs magazines and newspapers, looking for issues with feature articles about Lenae's life and career. That, Cindy decided, was the best approach. If the answer to her questions about Lenae's motive was contained in one of the thousands of columns she'd written, Cindy didn't have time to find it today.

She skimmed articles for an hour, calling Daryl back to retrieve new rolls of microfilm when she needed a different article. Sitting in a library and reading articles on microfiche was meditative, she decided—the tactile nature of the research made the thrill of discovery sharper. It wasn't as convenient as the internet, but maybe that made things more fun.

By the time Cindy packed up, she hadn't found much. Lenae had never married, which was unusual for someone of her age, but she did have a daughter and a grandson. She had lived in Palm Springs, as far as Cindy could tell, since at least the 1950s, and studied journalism at UCLA back when the field made little room for women.

One thing was interesting, though: a photo spread from the early 1980s showing her in a full-length fur coat in front of a Mercedes, her hand so loaded with bling that it looked like a jewelry commercial. Lenae had told Cindy she didn't value material things, and based on the way she lived now, that seemed to be the case.

But it hadn't always been. Back when she'd been a much smaller celebrity, she'd clearly lived a lot higher. It didn't make sense, but Cindy couldn't come up with any real information beyond that. Like so many things in the world of Yana Tosh, there were lots of problems, but the solutions were evasive. Something had changed in Lenae's past, and now the change had reversed. The once-materialistic showboat had suddenly become a frugal proponent of simple living. And now she was trying to swing a big deal for a cut of Yana's collection, and she was driving a flashy new car before the deal was even signed.

What had changed in her life—and then changed again?

It was nearly eight o'clock, and Jay and Cindy were in the living room, watching *Murder, She Wrote* on the Hallmark Movies & Mysteries channel. It was an early episode: A millionaire entrepreneur had supposedly been murdered on his yacht by one of his daughters, but Jessica Fletcher, of course, discovered that he hadn't been murdered after all.

"This was such a great show," Jay said as the second commercial break began.

Cindy nodded. "Unexpectedly socially progressive too. In the best possible way. A show starring a mature woman who lives alone and is perfectly content and happy and productive. She creates her art and solves crimes. There's never any hint of her needing a man to complete her."

"I never thought of it that way," Jay said.

"That's what's so great about it," Cindy said. "Especially the light touch. Much more impactful that way."

Jay could smell that dinner was ready, and he went into the kitchen to plate it. He opened one of the cupboards and found a set of plates he hadn't seen before—Royal Doulton, he noticed, after a quick, discreet look at the base of a serving bowl.

Bone china with a leaf-themed gold border. Cindy caught Jay looking, and he quickly placed it back, mildly embarrassed.

"How many sets of fine china do you have?" Jay said.

"Twenty," Cindy said, as though it were the most natural thing. "I keep bringing old ones out of storage. They remind me of Esther—I can remember how excited she was when she found them. Whenever she went to an estate sale, she looked for another set. She couldn't stop buying them. She grew up with nothing, so I guess fine china made her feel fancy—you know, Old World class, back when people cared about stuff like that."

"I didn't realize Esther grew up poor," Jay said. "And then she went to Harvard Law School and became a powerhouse lawyer?"

"And the first openly gay partner at her firm," Cindy said. "She was a remarkable person."

"How often do you miss her?" Jay said.

"Every second." Cindy paused. "Okay, if I'm really lucky, I can go five seconds without missing her, but only if I'm distracted by something really important."

"Do you think it'll always be like that?"

Cindy walked over to the counter and pulled the book of inspirational quotes that Esther had made for her near the end. Jay had accidentally looked at it when he saw it on the table once, not realizing what it was, but this was the first time Cindy had ever shown it to him. He counted that as progress. She flipped a few pages until she found what she was looking for.

"Here," she said, pointing to Esther's calligraphic script. "*'No one ever told me that grief felt so like fear.'* C. S. Lewis. One of my favorite writers."

Jay thought about that. "Is that what it's like? You're afraid?"

"Of course," she said. "Esther was my soul. Still is. Hooray for Hollywood was her dream. It's why I stopped waiting for the perfect timing and just opened the darn store. I had to. For her memory. It was a way to feel like I was with her, building this business with her. But at the same time, the idea of trying to do anything difficult without her to lean on—I mean, that's scary."

Jay was silent, rubbing her back.

"Does that make any sense?" Cindy said.

"Of course it does."

"So I'm not crazy?"

"No, you're not crazy—you're grieving. And I love you more than you can imagine, and I'm so honored that you're sharing a little of what you're going through with me." He was silent for a bit. "Do you feel like, maybe, you're feeling a little bit better?"

Cindy nodded. "When I'm down, it's as bad as it was the moment I found out. But it's not every minute of every day now. I'm always thinking of her, but it isn't always painful. Sometimes it's actually nice memories. I'm getting these little peaceful intervals now—and I just cherish them, and I know Esther wants me to have them."

"I can't tell you how glad I am to hear that. And I'm always here anytime you want to share more."

Cindy smiled a little at that. "And I think I'm done sharing for now. This is about as much opening up as I can take—"

"It's a lot for you."

"Yes, it is," she said. "And it made me hungry. So let's eat."

The meal was a sausage and broccoli rabe pasta from a Wolfgang Puck cookbook. He'd made the pasta himself—the first time he'd tried his new pasta maker—and Cindy admired how fresh it tasted, with none of the excessive firmness of the store-bought stuff. They ate and half-watched *Murder, She Wrote*, which was almost worse than not watching it. The well-plotted mysteries were most satisfying when you watched carefully, and they didn't lend themselves to multitasking. Maybe, Jay thought, that's why well-plotted mystery shows weren't so popular anymore. They weren't good for catching while you scrolled Instagram.

They were just settling in for tea and dessert—more of the Agatha Christie *Murder on the Orient Express* tea from Harney and Sons, along with a key lime pie Jay had picked up on the way home—when the doorbell rang.

"Are you expecting anyone?" Cindy said.

When Jay said no, she got up and walked toward the door. Jay followed her. "Look through the peephole before you open it," he warned. He hated how on edge he was all the time, and he couldn't wait for the Dylan Redman matter to be resolved, no matter the outcome.

Cindy smiled. "You're not exactly a chapter in *Profiles in Courage*."

"Just being careful."

She nodded and checked through the peephole.

"It's a woman," she said. "Not someone I recognize."

Jay stepped forward for a peek. Their visitor was short and thin. Long black hair with wisps of white.

"Ask who it is," he whispered.

"Who is this?" Cindy's voice was polite, but she made no move to open the door.

"It's Delilah McGovern," the woman said. "You called about my brother."

"How'd you find my house?"

"I'm a reporter," Ben's sister said. "I can find people. That's my job. I'm sorry if it's weird I showed up in person, but I'm harmless, I assure you."

Cindy didn't respond, and Delilah kept talking. "Look, I'm sorry. I can see now how just showing up would be unsettling and rude. But your email unnerved me, and I want to know what's going on."

Cindy hesitated.

"Please," Delilah said. "Just let me in. Do I seem threatening?"

Well, that was something that somebody who *was* threatening might say too. But there were two of them and one of her, and Cindy had sent a vague and alarming email.

"Just let her in," Jay whispered.

Cindy opened the door, and Delilah McGovern walked in. She carried a large tote bag with a Boston Red Sox logo. It held notebooks, magazines, and a few pieces of clothing.

"Did you come right from the airport?" Jay asked after introductions were made.

Delilah nodded. "I took a taxi right to your house. I wanted to come to the store first because it would be less weird, but I checked the hours and saw that I would be too late. I also thought about going to a hotel and coming to see you in the morning, but I couldn't wait that long. I hope you understand."

"Well," said Cindy delicately, "I'm glad you're here."

Delilah sighed. "I'm clearly not in the best frame of mind right now. He's my brother, and I love him. I just . . . I need to know what mess he's gotten himself into now. I found out about Dylan Redman's murder. I know Ben works for Yana Tosh, but he isn't mixed up in a murder somehow, is he?"

Cindy looked at Jay. He turned off the television and went into the kitchen, emerging with a glass of sweet tea for each of them.

Delilah downed her drink in a single gulp and put it down on the coffee table. Jay retreated to the kitchen to refill it, then rejoined them.

No one had answered Delilah's question. "How close are you to your brother?" Jay asked, as carefully as possible. Man, he hated this.

Delilah frowned. "Not close at all. We haven't spoken in years. He's cut me out of his life—I send him Christmas cards and don't hear back. I can't seem to make any progress with him. It's like he doesn't want anything to do with his own sister. That's why I came to you rather than him."

Jay studied the woman. Her features were drawn, and her posture said "dejected"—as if she'd given up. Jay hoped that wasn't the case. "Do you have any idea why that would be?"

Delilah took a sip of the sweet tea, as though it contained the courage she needed to explain her situation. "I—I really don't know."

"Delilah," Cindy said gently, "we can't help you unless you tell us something."

"I was hoping *you* would tell *me* something. I'm a reporter, after all. I'm used to asking the questions, not answering them."

"If Ben is in trouble, you probably know more than we do about why," Jay said. "You haven't used your reporter skills to try to find out? Done a little sleuthing?"

Delilah shook her head. "I'm an arts reporter," she said. "I cover galleries and museum openings. I got here quickly because I happened to be in San Francisco for a story. A controversy over whether Disney belongs in a fine arts museum—that's the kind of thing I cover."

"*Of course* Disney belongs in a museum," Jay said passionately. "What's the question?"

"Focus, Jay," Cindy said.

Delilah smiled weakly. "I think my reporting instincts abandon me when it comes to my own brother."

They were all silent for a few moments. "If you had to guess at the reason Ben is upset with you, what would it be?" Jay asked. "What was the last big argument you had with him?"

He watched as Delilah thought about it. The woman's eyes misted slightly, and she touched them with her index finger, first one and then the other. Cindy passed her a box of tissues. "I've always been more practical than Ben. I started local, knowing I wanted to work for a big paper eventually. I moved up the ranks and got my big break as a metro reporter at *The Boston Globe*. That was twenty years ago, and I've been there ever since, maxing out my 401(k) each month, buying a home with twenty percent down, cutting coupons. Slow and steady, getting promotions every ten years. Ben's more of a free spirit."

"He was a financial advisor, though," Cindy said. "It doesn't get much more buttoned-down and practical than that."

"Well, that was, now that you mention it, what our fight was about, actually."

"What was the nature of the disagreement?"

"He decided to give up his practice, which was thriving," Delilah said. "He shut it down to just be a full-time—" She paused, searching for a word. "A full-time personal assistant-slash-consigliere for some B-list actress from the 1950s."

Jay looked at Cindy, unsure what to say, but the situation was clear to him: Ben was avoiding his sister because he hadn't come clean with her. Ben Sinclair had lost his career to a gambling addiction, and Yana was the safety net he'd landed in. It wouldn't be an easy thing to tell Delilah, and it wasn't the kind of information the woman should learn from strangers. But there was a murder investigation they needed her help with. Their lives and new business depended on it, to say nothing of justice and all that high-minded stuff.

"Delilah," Jay said slowly, "from what you're telling us, I don't think Ben was completely honest with you about what happened with his financial advisory career."

"What?"

"He didn't mention anything about a regulatory investigation . . . or that he'd surrendered his license to avoid having it stripped by a disciplinary panel?"

Delilah stared at him, her cheeks flushed and her eyes furious. "I can't imagine that's true. Who told you that?"

Cindy excused herself to run into the home office and print out the FINRA filing.

"We'll have the document for you in a second," Jay said, "Just try to keep an open mind as you read it, and we can try to figure out what it all means. I'm sorry we're the ones to tell you this, but please know that we want to help."

Delilah sat there, clearly agitated and sipping her tea. *How could she possibly still be thirsty after the multiple glasses she'd already gone through since her arrival?* Jay wondered. Mae West walked over to Delilah and nuzzled against her leg, then jumped up and perched on the chair's armrest.

"If she's in your way, I can put her in the bedroom," Jay offered.

Delilah allowed a small smile. "It's fine. I like cats. And yours is beautiful. She seems to notice when people need comfort."

"Yes," he said. "That's Mae West for you: a dazzling combination of selfishness and empathy."

Walking over, he scooped the cat up and placed her on Delilah's lap. The purring ensued a few seconds later, and Delilah stroked Mae West softly, her eyes filled with sadness now. A few moments later, Cindy came in and handed a printout of the FINRA report on Ben Sinclair to his sister.

Delilah read through it and looked up, eyes rimmed with tears. "Why wouldn't he have told me?"

"He was probably ashamed," Cindy said. "A lot of people, when they've had a crisis, retreat from the people they love because they don't want to lie to them. But they can't bear to tell them the truth either. So they just . . . disappear."

Delilah shuffled the papers. "Benjamin cared about his clients. *A lot.* They were his life. Why would he steal money from them?"

Cindy stood up and sat on the floor next to Delilah's chair. "Did Ben ever tell you about his gambling problem?"

"Gambling?" Delilah said. "Definitely not."

"He told us that gambling is what got him into trouble. He needed money, and he ran out of other sources, so he resorted to . . . this." Cindy nodded toward the papers.

"Why wouldn't he have just come to me for money, then?" Delilah said.

"Did you have money?"

"I mean, not a lot—but if he'd been desperate enough to rip off clients, I would think he would have called his sister for help first. Are you sure it was gambling?"

"Yes," Cindy said. "When I came across this information, I confronted him about it because I wanted to know whether he was someone we could trust. And frankly, Jay and I were looking for suspects in Dylan Redman's murder."

"So you thought you'd dredge up dirt on my brother and try to redirect suspicion toward him?"

"It wasn't like that."

Delilah didn't answer.

Jay could see that Ben's sister felt betrayed. Her response to adverse information was denial. He could only hope that the poor woman would progress through the stages of grief until she came, ultimately, to acceptance. And she really needed to double-time it through those stages, because there was a murderer on the loose, and she might be able to help him and Cindy figure out what was happening.

Delilah suddenly put down the papers and sat up straighter. "Well, there's one thing I can tell you. I know this for sure, with every ounce of my being: my brother was not a gambler."

Before Jay or Cindy could muster a response to Delilah's statement, the doorbell rang.

The visitor was—of course—Simon Fletcher.

Cindy contemplated asking Delilah for privacy, but decided against it. Ben's sister seemed sincere and badly shaken by what was happening in her brother's life, but she also seemed smart, resourceful, and accomplished. She deserved to know about the case.

After a brief visit to sniff at Simon, Mae West returned to Delilah's lap, purring and kneading the blanket Jay had given her. Simon looked at Delilah, then back at Cindy. He seemed at a loss for words.

"It's fine, Simon," Cindy said. "Anything you want to tell us, you might as well say in front of Delilah. We have nothing to hide."

In truth, Cindy's motive was twofold. Mostly, she didn't mind having Delilah hear whatever information Simon had for them, but she also thought demonstrating openness might inspire Delilah to be more forthcoming about her brother's past. Or what she knew of it, anyway.

"So there's good news," Simon began. "Yana Tosh is alive. She's not in great shape just yet, but her doctor says she's pulled through. They'll keep her at the hospital for a few days, to monitor her, but she'll be home soon with what appears will be no lasting damage."

"Thank God," Cindy and Jay said in unison.

The detective raised an eyebrow. "I suppose this is a special sort of relief to you?"

Jay rolled his eyes. "Stop it. Your implications are offensive and, more importantly, dumber than a late-stage Adam Sandler movie. We care about Yana. She's a friend now. That's all this is about."

Simon stared at Jay, ignoring his angry tone. Cindy admired that about the detective. He was a man who focused on substance and wasn't easily emotionally rattled. Sparring with him was like playing tennis with a backboard.

"So none of your relief is because Warren Limon wasn't going to sell the collection if he inherited it?" Simon asked eventually.

"Come on," Jay snapped. "With that logic, why would we have poisoned Yana? If you think we're glad she's alive because it's good for our business, you should eliminate us as suspects."

"From what Eydie and Lenae told me about their last meeting, Yana was quite intrigued by the pitch they made."

"Actually," Cindy interrupted, "I don't think Yana was buying what they were selling. Ben and Warren might've been, though—which would mean a dead or incapacitated Yana Tosh would've been in Eydie and Lenae's best interests."

"My brother never would have thought that way," Delilah snapped.

"I didn't mean it like that," Cindy said.

Delilah shook her head. "Then what did you mean?"

Simon jumped in. "I'm sorry, ma'am. We're just speaking hypothetically."

Delilah, surprisingly, softened. “I understand. I know you have a job to do.”

“You should be looking at Eydie and Lenae,” Jay insisted again. “*They’re* the ones acting super weird.”

Simon didn’t say anything.

“Yeah,” Cindy agreed. “Why don’t you go harass them?”

“I already tried,” Simon admitted.

Jay cackled, more harshly than he might have intended, Cindy thought. “Oh? And they threw your annoying butt out, the way we should have just now?” he said.

“No,” Cindy said. “They didn’t throw him out. They told him that he needed to direct their inquiries to their attorneys—as any sane person in such a situation would.”

Simon gave a hint of a smile. “As a matter of fact, yes. They did.”

“Well, there you go,” Cindy said. “They won’t talk because they’re involved in something sleazy. *They’re* your criminals.”

“Or maybe they’re just smart,” Jay quipped as he walked back into the room, carrying a large tray of brownies, after a quick trip to the kitchen. He offered them to Simon first, explaining that the cupcakes were from a Giada De Laurentiis recipe.

Simon took one off the tray, and Jay handed him a napkin. He bit into it and moaned with pleasure, bits of gooey warmth dripping from his lip. “Now this,” he said, licking his fingers in between bites, “is *quite* the bribe.”

“If we wanted to bribe you, we’d offer you a date with Jay, not a brownie,” Cindy said.

Simon laughed uncomfortably and took another bite of the brownie, likely so he wouldn’t have to answer.

“Don’t be awkward, Cindy,” Jay said. “And, honestly, I’m not so sure I’d want to go out with Detective Fletcher anymore. He’s being boorish.”

"So, now you've just admitted that you *did* want to go out with Simon," Cindy crowed.

Jay blushed, and Simon studied his brownie intently, as if it, too, might be a suspect in the murder. Delilah was the only one who didn't seem affected by the moment, glancing between the three of them as if she were caught in the middle of the world's stupidest soap opera. "Hello? We were talking about my brother?"

"Right," Jay said, all too pleased to switch topics of conversation. "You were saying that he wasn't a gambler after all. But how can you know that for sure?"

Delilah shuffled in her chair, causing Mae West to hop off her lap, disturbed, to go look out the window. A car with a loud muffler drove by, prompting her to run from one end of the long, room-length window to the other in hot pursuit.

"I don't know how to say this nicely," Delilah said, looking at Cindy and Jay, "but I think you're out of your minds to be talking to a detective. It's none of my business what you get up to, but I'm not discussing the subject further until Detective Fletcher has left for the night."

Simon nodded. "I understand."

"See how lucky you are to have stupid suspects like us, Simon?" Jay said. "We just prattle on with you right here."

"Touché." Simon smiled and got up to leave. Jay walked him to the door—an interesting move, given the awkwardness a few minutes ago, Cindy thought. She heard them talking in hushed voices, and then Jay returned.

"What was that about?" Cindy asked.

"Simon's mad at us," he said. "He's not happy we sought out Delilah—thinks we're interfering in his case and putting ourselves at risk playing Miss Marple."

Delilah shook her head. "It was my choice to come here."

"Yes," Cindy said. She looked at Jay. "Which do you think Simon is more upset about—us interfering in his case or maybe our putting ourselves at risk?"

Jay thought about that. "I hope mostly the latter."

"I think so too," Cindy said. "It explains why he stopped by to tell us about Yana—he cares about us."

"We'll probably never really know what his motives are."

Cindy smiled. "You are the most optimistic guy in the world except when it comes to whether a guy might actually like you."

Jay shook his head, worried they were being rude to their guest. But one look at Delilah showed she was grateful for the distraction. "My luck with guys would suggest my pessimism about them is mostly justified."

It took a few minutes, and another round of Jay's sweet tea, for everyone to settle back in before they could get back on the topic of Ben. With Mae West perched on the armrest, Delilah finally added to her story.

"I remember, years ago, I invited Ben to join my husband and me on a trip to Las Vegas. We were going for a quick, end-of-year weekend getaway, and I thought, you know, my brother liked Céline Dion, and maybe he would join us and we could try to reconnect. I sent him an email and didn't hear back, which was normal for him. So then I called him. He must not have recognized the number because I called him from my office line—so he picked up. I told him about the trip plan, and he got all sad and said he didn't want to go to Las Vegas."

"Did he say why?" Jay said.

"As a matter of fact, he did," Delilah said. She dabbed at her eyes with the napkin Jay had offered her with the brownie.

Cindy retrieved a box of tissues from the cabinet in the bathroom and handed them over.

Ben's sister blew her nose and continued. "He said that casinos made him sad. He had a friend who, years ago, got into a lot of trouble with gambling. Seeing people gamble just reminded him of that. He said he understood that a lot of people enjoyed it and that it could be harmless fun, but it wasn't for him. So that's why what you're telling me doesn't make any sense."

"Delilah," Cindy said slowly, "do you think it's possible that the friend your brother was telling you about was himself?"

She laughed—a sad, hollow thing. "I don't think my brother is deep enough to speak in that kind of metaphor."

It soon became clear to Cindy that they had exhausted their ability to help Delilah—and that she was too estranged from her brother to provide much more insight. Twenty minutes later, after Jay had called around and made her a reservation at The Parker, Delilah left.

"Did you pay for her hotel on your card?" Cindy asked.

Jay nodded. "She was too distracted and upset to even notice. She'll figure it out when she gets to the hotel. I want her to stay in a nice place and get some rest. Poor thing."

The two of them remained in the living room, shuffling through their joint movie collection. Cindy owned hundreds of films, but Jay's move-in had added at least another thousand easily—including a couple hundred VHS tapes for films that had never been digitized. Luckily, he'd also brought a vintage VCR for those. They'd briefly kept their collections separate—his in his part of the house, hers in the living room—but the collections had merged slowly until they'd finally decided to put them all together, once and for all. To Cindy, it seemed heavy with symbolism. They'd split their possessions in half twenty years ago, but the thing that first brought them together, their love of art, had morphed into a different kind of shared life with just as much meaning.

They flipped through DVDs for about twenty minutes, discussing the pros and cons of each film. For them, debating which movie to watch had always been as much a part of the experience as watching whatever it was they chose. In the end, they settled on *Heavenly Creatures*, the 1994 Kate Winslet movie based on the 1954 tabloid sensation murder in New Zealand, when two fifteen-year-old best friends had teamed up to murder one of their mothers, to avoid being separated. In a twist too odd for fiction, one of the girls had served five years in prison and emerged with a changed name to become Anne Perry, the wildly successful historical mystery writer.

"Quite a second act," Jay said when the credits rolled. "To go from that beginning to bestselling novelist."

Cindy grinned. "That transformation has nothing on what we're going to turn Hooray for Hollywood into. I can just see the headline: '*WASHED-UP SOAP OPERA HACKS TAKE STAR TURN AS WORLD'S LEADING MEMORABILIA DEALERS.*'"

"You forgot the part about us being washed-up stars from *decades* ago."

"They can say whatever they want as long as they spell our names right and drive traffic to our store."

Jay leaned over to give her a hug. "If that happens, everything I've ever accomplished in my life will have been because I had you as a partner."

"But first," Cindy said, "we need to wrap up this murder investigation—and land the Yana Tosh consignment."

"And how do you propose we do that?"

Cindy was silent for a time. The truth was, for the first time since this all began, she was out of ideas. Ben's sister had been less helpful than she'd expected, and it felt like they were really at a dead end. "We'll think of something," she said finally. "It's what we always do."

She wished she had as much self-confidence as she was trying to project.

Bleary-eyed from a long night of movies, Jay accomplished little in his first few hours at the store the next day. He edited some of his Yana Tosh videos, but he was rapidly reaching the point of diminishing returns. He'd watched them so many times that he couldn't see them with fresh eyes, and his changes were as likely to make things worse as they were to make them better. Still, Jay was a perfectionist—he couldn't help himself.

Judging from the silence in the store, both he and Cindy were working their way through different ideas, each stuck in their own bubble. They were both, he thought, nearing the end of their ability to manage it all. If things didn't get back to normal, and soon, he didn't know what they'd do. Forget the store—it was starting to wear on both of their already tenuous grips on sanity.

"It would be good to go see Yana," he said finally.

"Yes," Cindy agreed. "I'd been thinking that."

Jay picked up the phone and dialed the hospital, asking for her room. The operator patched him through, but it was Warren who answered. Warren's reception was cool—not rude exactly, but also certainly not appreciative of the call. Which was unsurprising given the conversation he'd had with Cindy earlier.

"How is your mother?" Jay said.

"She's in stable condition," Warren said stiffly. "In theory, she'll make it. But at her age, a lot can go wrong, so it's very scary."

"I'm sorry you're going through this," Jay said.

"Thank you," Warren said. "And I have to let you know that in the meantime, I'm suspending all activity related to the sale of the initial pieces she gave you. I hope you and your partner won't try to fight me on this."

"Warren, as Cindy told you, we have a contract with Yana, not you. Unless we have a legal order not to, we are going to carry out the sale as she instructed."

"She is not in a state to make decisions right now, and I'm ordering you to desist from the sale," Warren said. "If you need a letter from a lawyer, that can be arranged, but I'll expect to be compensated for the expense."

Jay turned on his calming voice, the one he'd used in Las Vegas to try to ease drunk, boisterous showgoers into leaving, or at least keeping their voices down. "This decision was made *before* her current state, Warren. You know that. I'm not looking to fight with you, but I hope you can understand that we have contractual obligations to honor here. You're threatening us with legal action, but your mother could sue us just as easily if we decided to break our agreement with her."

Warren didn't say anything.

"Look, if Cindy and I—or even just one of us—could meet with her briefly, maybe we could work this out. If she's at all lucid, then maybe—"

"Let me see how she's doing later and get back to you," Warren interrupted. "Might be a couple of hours."

Jay hung up and returned to puttering around the store. He was mostly finished with the first round of videos; all that was left to do was to upload them to the internet and send them, along with the press release he and Cindy had written, to the media outlets on their list.

It was a problem that Lenae Randolph was no longer on that list. Jay tried to put all thoughts of the sale out of his mind, using a tactic he'd learned in therapy almost two decades ago, when he was still recovering from the end of his career and marriage. Whenever he found himself caught in a thought loop on a problem that couldn't be dealt with immediately, he forced himself to visualize a police officer ordering him to stop. Often that worked, though this time the police officer visual was distracting because he pictured Simon, and all the confusion and ambiguity that came with their cat-and-mouse game. He tried to give himself something else to think about. This time, he replaced Simon and Yana with *Star Trek*.

Jay picked up a small jewelry box that contained a piece of Vulcan jewelry used in an episode of *Star Trek: Enterprise. Star Trek* was always a hot collectible category, but the later pieces were less valuable. By the 2000s, when this prop had appeared, everyone involved in the shows was aware of the lucrative Trekkie prop market. That meant everything now was saved, and in some cases duplicates made, so that members of the crew could get a quick payday. The result was a flooded market, with the worth of Vulcan jewelry in the hundreds rather than the thousands of dollars. That wasn't great for business, but Jay preferred it that way. It meant more people could have access to pieces that meant something to them, and serious collectors could still chase the earlier pieces.

He had just set the piece of Vulcan jewelry back in the display case when the door opened. As if summoned, Simon Fletcher strode into the room. He took off his hat as he entered, revealing that shiny head. Cindy said a quick hello and retreated tactfully to the office, leaving Simon alone with Jay.

"Simon," Jay said.

"Jay," Simon said.

They looked past each other uneasily, the tension of the last couple of weeks bubbling into the silence.

"I wanted to ask you," Simon said, "about—"

Jay cut him off. "Look, Simon, we've told you everything we know about Yana and her collection. At some point, it becomes annoying and, quite frankly, insulting."

Simon smiled at him.

"You're smiling," Jay said. "I don't find this entertaining."

"I wasn't going to ask you about the case."

"What were you going to ask me about, then?"

Jay was still standing behind the jewelry case, and Simon had been slowly making his way across the store. As he stepped up to the counter, he made eye contact with Jay for the first time since he'd arrived. It felt electrifying, like Jay had just accidentally brushed up against a live wire.

"I wanted to ask whether you might want to get dinner," he said. "With me, next Friday. There's a show I think you'll like."

"What show?"

Simon paused, as if trying to summon confidence. "A Judy Garland impersonator. But he's supposed to be good—a Palm Springs legend of sorts. It's at The Purple Room, where the Rat Pack used to play."

"I've never been."

"It's Palm Springs history. You'll love it."

Jay hesitated. "Isn't this a conflict?" he said. "If Cindy and I are still, you know, suspects?"

"I don't think either of you was involved. And if I did, I wouldn't tell you—and might even take you to a show to put you at ease while I grilled you to incriminate yourself."

"So I can't assume I'm in the clear?"

Simon winked at him. "I suppose not."

"You really are so romantic."

"Just tell me if you want to go. Two Fridays from now, at eight o'clock. Show's at nine, but we should get there early."

Jay smiled. He was dying to say yes but still nervous about the case—and, well, he figured it couldn't hurt to play a little hard to get. Besides, he'd noticed that Simon wasn't asking him out *this* week, perhaps giving him enough time to allow the case to die down and clear Jay for real. "I'll think about it, Detective. I promise."

"It's *Simon*, Jay." But then, after a brief and awkward silence, Simon nodded, put his hat back on, and left the store.

After he'd left, Cindy came out of the office.

"While you were talking to The Rock over there," she said, "Warren called back. He says his mother isn't up to having visitors, and reiterated that we need to halt the sale. He read me a few lines from a letter his attorney drafted to us. It'll be delivered by courier today. He really is thick."

"Do you believe him?" Jay said. "Do you really think she's not up to seeing visitors?"

Cindy thought about it. "I'm not sure."

"Warren is making this impossible," Jay said. "We have an obligation to our client, but now her son, who never wanted to sell the collection anyway, is using his mother's illness, which could have been caused by him, to try to halt the sale. I'm worried about Yana. And I don't trust Warren." The thought bubbled up to his lips before he had a chance to stop it. "Do you think that she could be in danger? Being left alone with Warren like that?"

"I'm sure Simon wouldn't allow that to happen if he thought Warren was the primary suspect." Cindy sounded calm, but when Jay glanced up at her, he noticed a mischievous look in her eyes. "But I think we should talk to Yana anyway."

"And how do you propose we do that?"

Cindy had a little twinkle in her eye. "I have an idea."

* * *

They drove by Warren's house on the way to the hospital, just to see if he was there. That would make things easier—providing certainty that they wouldn't have to deal with him when they arrived to see Yana. But Warren wasn't home, so they continued on to the hospital anyway. It was an older, brutalist-style building, with low roofs and plenty of parking.

The receptionist at the front desk, a middle-aged woman with fluffy black hair, frowned when they said they were there to see Yana Tosh. A worn plastic tag attached to her chest identified her as a volunteer named Vivienne. "Is she expecting you?"

Jay looked at Cindy.

"No, but we're friends of hers." Cindy pointed to the keyboard Jay was carrying. "We wanted to play some music for her, cheer her up a bit. It can get a little mundane being cooped up in a hospital bed."

The receptionist took the IDs they'd presented and typed away a bit on her computer. "You're not on her list of approved visitors," she said.

Cindy nodded. “We just want to surprise her. You're welcome to come sit in with us, Vivienne. You'll enjoy the music too, I promise.”

Vivienne nodded, a small smile cracking through. “I have a break coming up,” she said, nodding down the hall at another volunteer who was walking toward her. “But you have to promise you won't do anything that will create a problem. I could be terminated, and volunteering here is my life.”

“I get that,” Cindy said. “Bringing comfort to people who are sick is a sacred thing. That's why we're here too.”

Jay knew that was true. The music thing wasn't just a pretense to see Yana and make sure she was okay—though it was also that. After the poisoned cupcake incident, Cindy had told him that she really believed singing to Yana had helped her healing.

Vivienne led them down the hallway toward Yana Tosh's room.

When Cindy and Jay followed Vivienne into the small but private hospital room, Yana was sitting bolt upright in bed, reading a Miranda James mystery novel. The former starlet was hooked up to all kinds of monitors and tubes, but her eyes sparked with recognition.

Luckily, Warren was nowhere in sight.

"Jay! Cindy! What a lovely surprise." She sounded drained and tired, closer to a hundred than ninety, where on prior occasions she'd seemed more like seventy. Maybe she was recovering from the poisoning and would soon be back to her usual self, but Cindy feared the Yana they'd known and come to admire and care for was gone, never to return.

"Yana," Cindy said, "how are you?"

"A bit out of sorts," Yana said, "but my son has been here, taking care of me. You see who comes and who doesn't when you're sick. And so far, it's been you and Warren and Ben."

"Have Eydie and Lenae been to see you?" Cindy asked, ignoring Jay's wince.

"Crickets on that front, I'm afraid," Yana croaked.

Cindy thought about pressing that point but decided it was better to get straight to the official reason for their visit, especially with Vivienne looking on. Jay had already set up the keyboard in the corner of the room, unfolded the little stool it came with, and plugged the cord into a wall outlet, and now he was adjusting the volume knobs.

"You brought an instrument," Yana said, sounding pleased. "And here I was thinking you were here to talk business."

"We don't need to worry about business right now," Cindy said. "We just wanted to play music for you—it's been proven to help people with healing."

Yana nodded. "As for business, by the way, I want you to continue on with the pieces as directed. And I'm still leaning toward giving you the rest of them too."

Vivienne was seated in a chair by the window now, and Cindy was glad the hospital volunteer was there. If it came to it, and she hoped it didn't, they would have a neutral observer who could testify that Yana was of sound mind and had, without any prompting, asked them to continue with their selling efforts.

Jay started to play a few chords on the keyboard, as if hoping to dissuade her from saying anything more about the consignment. Cindy loved him for that. They had come to play for Yana, after all, and that was what she wanted to do too.

"I appreciate that, Yana," Cindy said, taking Jay's hint. "But you know, since you've never heard us play—"

"Not true!" Jay said. "She heard me in Las Vegas."

Yana leaned back in bed, looking more relaxed now. Clearly the prospect of music was already improving her spirits in the way they'd hoped.

"We mostly do the Great American Songbook," Cindy said, nervous. "You know, the stuff Sinatra sang." Jay liked improvising and going with it, but Cindy liked control. For her, art was about trying to replicate the same thing perfectly every time.

Yana waved. “I love Sinatra, but Sinatra isn’t for me right now. I need something peppier. Do you have anything by Elvis?”

Jay nodded and began to play—a complicated piano run to open, the kind of show-off thing that Cindy knew his Vegas audiences loved, and jazz clubs rolled their eyes at. He started to sing “Can’t Help Falling in Love.”

Cindy had never sung it, but she joined in after a few bars, improvising a harmony. When a song was that familiar, it wasn’t hard to riff. Once they finished, Yana leaned forward, clapping, and Vivienne joined in. Cindy loved it. It had been decades since anyone had clapped for her, and even if it was just two people performing in a cramped hospital room, it was a thrill. Someone once said applause was the food for an artist’s soul, and Cindy hadn’t realized how much she’d been starving for it.

“Like Elvis reincarnated!” Yana said. “Bravo!” She had perked up immediately, showing more energy during their three-minute performance than she had since before her poisoning. Maybe it was working.

Jay smiled from behind the keyboard, and Cindy bowed.

Yana looked at Vivienne. “Vivienne, dear, I don’t want to bother the nurse with this, but is there any chance you could get me a cup of tea? I haven’t had caffeine in almost a day, which is the longest I’ve gone without it since I was fifteen and doing my first screen test for MGM.”

“Of course.” Vivienne left in search of tea.

Jay played another florid run on the keyboard. “From the movie *Loving You*,” he announced. “As sung by Elvis Presley, here’s”—he rolled his voice—“‘Let Me Be Your . . . Teddy Bear’!”

He pounded away at the keyboard, giving that swaggering Elvis styling to the little country-pop number that he explained had been a number-one hit for Elvis in 1957—"back when he could've made a number-one hit out of a Lord Byron poem if he'd wanted to," as Jay put it, prompting a laugh from Yana. Cindy wondered how many times he'd used that joke in Vegas. Probably thousands.

"I had no idea," Cindy said when Jay was done, "that you could do Elvis like that."

Jay shrugged. "You play cocktail lounges in Las Vegas, you learn a lot of Elvis." He grinned. "Especially if they let you put a tip jar on the piano. Did I play an Elvis song that time you saw me, Yana?"

Yana stared off into space, trying to remember. "You know, I remember that you were great, but I'm afraid I don't recall what you sang. I'm sure you did Elvis songs at least one of the times I saw you."

Vivienne returned with a Styrofoam cup of tea and handed it to Yana, who sipped it and immediately made a face. "Lipton?"

Vivienne nodded.

Yana rolled her eyes. "The great Yana Tosh cannot be seen drinking Lipton tea. Wait until the tabloids get hold of this! The decline and fall of a once-proud woman."

"Oh, I'm sorry, Yana," Vivienne said. "I'm afraid that's all we have here at the hospital. Would you like something else? I could run next door and—"

Yana waved. "I know the options are limited. If bland food and cold, weak tea could kill . . . well, hospital death rates would be much higher—I'll put it that way."

"How many times did you see me in Las Vegas, Yana?" Jay broke in. "I'm just wondering."

Yana looked at him, obviously surprised by the question. Cindy was surprised too. Jay didn't often let his ego show.

"You said you were sure I'd played Elvis at least one of the times you saw me. How often did you go to Vegas?"

Now Cindy cringed. Whatever point he was diving toward, she hoped he got there soon. Or didn't.

"What is this, an interrogation?" Yana said, suddenly tense. "I told you, I was a fan of yours. I loved your Vegas show, but I didn't buy any of your albums because I'm so old I don't even listen to CDs—just records." She took a sip of the tea and reached to put it down on the nightstand. Cindy hurried over to take it from her.

"I think maybe our patient has had enough visiting time now," Vivienne said, rushing from her chair. "She needs her rest."

"I'm fine," Yana said sharply. "Vivienne. Darling. Could you please get another cup of tea and leave the bag in? I can forgive the Lipton if you steep it longer."

Vivienne nodded and left the room. Cindy wasn't sure if it was an honest request or if Yana was trying to get rid of the volunteer, for some reason. She seemed much edgier now, alert and with a calculating gleam behind her eyes. Or maybe Cindy was just imagining it, since Jay was also being more alert and calculating than she'd seen him in . . . well, ever.

Yana turned back to Jay. "You were saying?"

"How much time have you spent in Vegas?"

"I really don't know," she said. "I don't have a personal assistant to keep my appointment book anymore. It's a short flight from Palm Springs, and there are a lot of great shows. And Hollywood memorabilia conventions, of course. I got some nice stuff in Vegas."

Jay's mood seemed dramatically changed from when he'd been doing his Elvis routine. Cindy knew that creativity always fueled his thinking. Some people thought best by studying. She thought best when she was running. For Jay, the best ideas came to him when he was creating art, musical or visual. And she could see that something was falling into place in her best friend's mind.

"Yana, we met with Ben's sister," he said.

"Oh? Why?"

Cindy took a seat in the chair that Vivienne had vacated. It was an old armchair—comfortable in a frumpy sort of way, big armrests and a bird-themed print on the fabric. Ethan Allen, 1980s, she thought. A nice bit of coziness in an otherwise sterile hospital room.

Vivienne came in and handed Yana a fresh mug of tea, this time with the bag in it.

"A real live mug," Yana said. "Ceramic and everything."

Vivienne smiled. "They have them in the staff room. I figured you'd like it more than the foam cup. Sadly, though, I should go back to the desk. You're okay here with your visitors? I was going to bring you a piece of cake, but I know you don't eat that kind of thing."

Yana nodded, and the volunteer left.

Cindy perked up. "That's right—you were emphatic about that when I met you at the gym. You told me you hadn't eaten desserts since you'd been on the MGM lot."

Before Yana could respond, there was a voice at the door.

"What are you doing here?" Warren Limon entered the room and closed the door behind him.

And suddenly, Cindy thought, the room felt very small.

Cindy could see immediately that Warren was furious to find her and Jay in his mother's hospital room. It was a response she could have anticipated based on his phone calls—but anticipation was one thing. Actually seeing someone red-faced and panting in fury, with the full weight of that fury directed at you . . . that was harder to prepare for.

"We came here to play for Yana," Jay said, pointing to the keyboard.

"I didn't hear any music when I was walking down the hall."

"We took a break," Cindy said icily. She tried to keep the tone of her voice even; this would all go more easily if everyone kept their cool. But after days of being bullied and harassed by Warren, having things all out in the open now—and being able to vent her frustration for the first time—felt like a dream come true.

Now Cindy saw Warren as he had the potential to be: scary. He wasn't physically imposing, of course. But there was a rage there, the simmering fury of someone whose life hadn't worked out as he'd hoped, who'd been reduced to living off his mother, manipulating her and undercutting her wishes for her legacy.

"Well, break's over," Warren said. "And I think it's time for you two to leave. My mother and I have a lot to discuss." His voice shook like a rattling doorknob in a room engulfed in flames, the door about to fly off the hinges.

"Oh, for goodness sake, Warren," Yana said, "Cindy and Jay are just visiting. They played some Elvis songs for me, which was fun, and now we're reminiscing about Las Vegas."

"They're not trying to get you to agree to give them the rest of the collection?"

"No," Yana snapped. "They're not vulgar and opportunistic like you. Besides, we all know that they don't need to *try* to do anything. I know perfectly well what I want, and I've been clear about it from the beginning." She said it all without a smile, barely able to look at her son anymore.

Warren visibly softened. The fear-driven, fight-or-flight menace in his eyes receded. "Okay, Mother," he said. "That's fine."

"What brings you here?" Yana said.

Warren smiled. "I left a note at the desk that if you had any visitors, I was to be notified. I got a call, maybe ten minutes ago, and hurried over."

Jay looked at Yana. "You were saying, Yana? About the Hollywood memorabilia conventions in Las Vegas?"

"Oh, yes," she said airily. "A lot of fun. Beautiful stuff."

"Did you ever sell anything there?" Jay asked. "Any pieces from your collection you didn't want anymore?"

Yana's head jerked forward, her posture suddenly military-grade upright. "Why do you ask?"

"Just a harmless question." He held up his hands. "I didn't mean anything by it."

She relaxed—a little. "Well, of course I did, now and then. You know, selling one thing to buy another. Or maybe trading.

Like when my son needed money for poker." Just like that, back to tension-filled venom.

Warren smiled. "Just a little harmless fun."

"You know what I hated about your poker playing, Warren?" she said. "It showed me how delusional you were. You couldn't just play the slot machines, a losing game with no illusion of skill, and be addicted to that. No, you had to play *poker*"—she spat the word—"a game where you could trick yourself into thinking you were smart. Which, of course, you never have been. You managed to get your father's looks and my math skills. What an absolute waste."

Warren was about to respond, but Cindy broke in before he had a chance. "If you sold something at a convention," she said, "I bet you must have really missed it afterward. I mean, I know how much you care about all of the pieces in your collection."

"Well, sure. That's the nature of a collection, isn't it? You buy something because you love it, and parting with it is always bittersweet. But you try to find joy in how much pleasure that object will bring its new owner, and you keep a little piece of it in your heart."

Cindy went over to examine the blanket Yana had covering her. Mary had crocheted it for her, based on a blanket seen on an episode of *Little House on the Prairie*. She and Jay had brought it to Yana on one of their earlier visits, to sweeten the pot and give their enterprise a bit of a thoughtful, homey touch. Apparently it had done the trick if it meant enough to Yana to have somebody bring it to her in the hospital.

"It's beautiful," Cindy said.

"Yes, it is," Yana agreed. "And it's keeping me warm here—I do get chilly sometimes. Like all old ladies, I suppose. God, I hate being old."

"Mary's so talented. It looks almost identical to the one in the episode." Jay laughed. "We could honestly sell it as the real thing—if we had documents tying it to the episode and a conscience-free brain."

Yana smiled. "Luckily, you have neither of those."

"You seem tired, Mother," Warren said, his voice suddenly angry again.

"Shut up, Warren," Yana said.

Cindy now knew exactly what had happened. Things had begun to fall into place while she was watching Jay play the piano, and then crystalized when she looked over at Yana swaddled in her *Little House on the Prairie* blanket.

It was funny how watching Jay's mind work at the piano helped Cindy think. She knew how brilliant and creative he was in that artistic role, and it reminded her of how she felt in the office, going over a new client's financial statements, piecing together the problems created by a prior advisor.

The biggest, most satisfying epiphanies came when she found signs of deception.

The combination of their strengths put it together. The realization that Yana didn't normally eat sweets, Warren's protectiveness, Yana's frequent trips to Vegas, the dated postal mark that meant the poisoned letter wasn't actually mailed, the reproduction Chinese scroll paintings Cindy had seen in Ben's condo. Then there was the missing painting and Dylan's interest in Agatha Christie memorabilia. None of those meant much on their own. But all put together . . .

Cindy stared at Yana, arriving at what was now, after all this time, striking her as the only possible explanation for what had happened. Her heart raced with excitement—it really was like building a financial model in a spreadsheet. You had all these disparate ideas and pieces and thoughts and emotions, and you juggled them in your mind, mostly—maybe a little bit on paper—and finally you put them all together. And when you did it right, the pieces came together in a way that achieved everything you'd hoped for. No other arrangement made sense. The only difference was, putting together a great financial plan brought with it a true sense of peace—you had at last arrived at the solution that would give the client their best life. And while this solution certainly brought satisfaction—and relief—it also carried with it rage and a sense of betrayal.

Yana slowly shrugged the blanket off and slid her legs out from under the covers. Cindy watched as Jay rushed over and offered her an arm as she made her way to the bathroom. Then he ran toward the bed, discreetly checked her purse, and was back where he'd been standing by the door by the time Yana returned.

What was that all about? Cindy wondered. Warren seemed deep in his own thoughts, too focused on the earlier conversation to notice.

"Did you ever have copies made of those pieces you had?" Jay asked, glancing over to Cindy with a meaningful glint to his eyes. "Like the replicas Mary makes? Sometimes I've considered asking her to make one for us after we sell a piece, because I miss having the real thing around so much. With the sentimental value you attach to your own collection, I imagine you must have had the same temptation, at least once."

Yana shrugged. "Maybe. Never had it done, but I really couldn't say whether I've *thought* about it. There are ninety years' worth of thoughts in this brain, you know." She sounded bored now—or perhaps like she was trying to sound bored. It was hard to tell with a talented actress.

Cindy ignored her denial. "Did you ever, by any chance, tell people those pieces were real—and hide the fact that you'd actually sold the originals?"

"What are you talking about?" Warren moved quickly to position himself between Cindy and his mother.

"She was asking your mother," Jay said calmly. "Not you."

Warren stared at Yana, eyebrows furrowed, blinking in an almost cartoonish portrayal of confusion. Yana still didn't say anything, pursing her lips together.

"What is all of this about?" Warren said. "I don't get it."

"That's no surprise," Yana snapped. Of course, she couldn't resist the chance to get in another dig at her son.

Cindy rolled her eyes. "When we first met, Yana, you told me you didn't gamble."

"I did?"

"Yes." Cindy started to pace. "We were pitching you on why you should use Hooray for Hollywood. That we were the upstarts rather than the pedigreed certainty that Cypress represented. And you said, 'I don't gamble. I *never* gamble.'"

"It's a figure of speech, Cindy," she said. "I was speaking metaphorically. Do they not teach that in English class anymore? I wasn't being literal."

"Maybe not," Cindy said. "But it's funny how gambling has been a little motif of this big mess you're in."

"*I'm* in?" Yana said, a hand fluttering to her heart. It was almost like she was hamming it up.

"Yes," Cindy said. "All of us are in it, sure. But you especially."

Warren started to speak, but Cindy interrupted him. "When I was in therapy, after the divorce and all of the tabloid stuff, my therapist and I talked about how the language we use reflects our unconscious thoughts. It's true that saying 'I never gamble' could be merely a figure of speech. But just now I started to think about it. You told me that Ben Sinclair was a gambling addict. Heck, Ben didn't even dispute it. But his sister claimed he wasn't."

"Ben hasn't spoken to his sister in years," Yana said. "How on earth would she know?"

Cindy stared at Yana. "In my experience, someone with the gambling addiction you claimed Ben had would have resorted to hitting his sister up for money. The addiction would have overcome his pride. That's how addiction works. But he never did. The whole time, Ben Sinclair never asked his sister for money. Don't you think that's odd?"

Yana didn't say anything. Warren opened his mouth, but again, Cindy steamrolled him. "In fact," she said, "the reason Ben told his sister he didn't gamble was that a close friend of his had a gambling problem. Now, who could that close friend have been?"

"I'm sure he was just deflecting," Yana muttered.

"*You're* a close friend of his, Yana," Jay supplied, giving Cindy a much-needed break. "And you're a close friend of his who spent a lot of time in Las Vegas—enough to have seen my show multiple times. And while I like to think my show was good, it was hardly Sin City's star attraction. If you saw it a few times, you had to be in Vegas *a lot.*"

Yana stared blankly ahead, her face empty of emotion. "Okay," she said, "I'm not conceding any of these points. But let's say I do enjoy a little gambling on occasion. What does that have to do with anything?"

Before Cindy could speak, Jay jumped in, his mind clearly working overtime, filling in some pieces she had been missing. It reminded her of how they'd worked together on stage back in the day, the way they could play off each other's ideas, silently communicating. There was even a slight flush to his cheeks. "I think you had a serious gambling problem, Yana. And to offset your losses, you've been selling costumes and replacing them with counterfeits you ordered from China. I think that's why you went on trips there with Ben—and that's where he got those beautiful scroll paintings he showed me. I thought they were antiques, but they're not. In fact, he told me how easy it is to get reproductions there."

Yana rolled her eyes. "Jay, this is a lot of nonsense. You've been single too long. You need a boyfriend."

"No, you need a—"

Cindy broke in. "Focus, Jay. Yana, I think the unexplained transfers out of your bank account on the docs you showed me were from you to your counterfeiter, and the transfers back in were rebates or discounts the counterfeiter gave you. Ben Sinclair was a mega-fan of yours. Heck, that's how you met him: He was the last president of your fan club. But he was also more than a fan. He cared about you so much, he looted other clients' accounts to give you money so that you wouldn't have to sell your costumes. He betrayed his clients and destroyed his career for you. But you ended up having to sell the costumes anyway."

"Here we go 'round the mulberry bush," Yana muttered. "I'm waiting for you to tie this back to Dylan Redman's murder."

"Mother," Warren said, "don't say anything more. These people are crazy. They'll be out of here soon, and they sure aren't getting your collection now."

Cindy kept talking. "Dylan was interested in collecting Agatha Christie—Jay and I know that from a little interview we found online. And he was a dealer who might've known what was out there on the market, even if he wasn't a participant.

I think you sold that *Mirror Crack'd* painting Elizabeth Taylor gave you years ago, and had a forgery made for your collection. It was a minor painting, not something you thought you'd have to worry about. But unfortunately for you—although mostly unfortunately for Dylan—he recognized it as a piece that had already been sold. Maybe he even knew the new owner. And he told you that and threatened to out your secret. Maybe he even told you that he'd expose you if you didn't give him the whole consignment, and on generous terms. And you couldn't have that uppity little millennial dictating the conditions of your sale, could you? So you poisoned his coffee and killed him."

Warren stood in the corner, staring at his mother, tears in his eyes—as if in a trance. Yana sat in bed, unmoving. There was a look of icy calm on her face, like she wasn't reacting at all, just watching herself playing a role she'd played too many times to be shocked by it anymore.

"Jay," Cindy said, "go get security, please. And call Simon."

Jay left the room, leaving Cindy alone with Warren and Yana. For a brief moment she was terrified, but then . . . nothing happened. Yana continued to sit there with the same frozen expression, and Warren stayed in the corner, his head buried in his hands. Silent tears rolled down his face, as if he hadn't even noticed Jay leave. Jay returned a few moments later with hospital security. And it wasn't long after that before Simon was on the scene. He must have been somewhere nearby.

"So it was Yana Tosh," Simon said, as though his suspect wasn't even there, breaking the awkward silence that had reigned in the room ever since they'd called him in.

"Yes," Cindy and Jay said in unison. Jay continued, voice clipped and emotionless: "That's who it has to have been. It's the only scenario that makes any sense. I'd been thinking about how weird it was that she ate that cupcake—she doesn't eat desserts. The only idea that made sense was that she wanted to make it *look* like someone poisoned her. So I ran with that theory. And then I saw Mary's replica blanket, and . . . it all just clicked over Elvis."

"Mary's involved in this?" Simon said. "I knew she seemed shady!"

"No," Jay said, rolling his eyes. "Not at all. Her craftwork just showed Cindy and me what was possible."

Cindy nodded. "And as Sherlock Holmes said, *'Once you eliminate the impossible, whatever remains, no matter how improbable, must be the truth.'* It was Mary's blanket that made us realize the pieces could be copies."

Yana lay in her bed without expression, seemingly exhausted from the day's events. Warren hovered over her, stroking her head—the first genuine display of tenderness between them Cindy had seen so far. Maybe he was doing that to distract her from what was happening; maybe he was doing it to distract himself. Yana briefly roused herself enough to reach into her purse on the nightstand for a tissue. She blew her nose, then reached again into her purse, bringing out a pillbox, and popped an ibuprofen.

"We still need motive," Simon said. "Why would she do all of this?"

"Yana Tosh had a gambling addiction," Cindy explained. "We have some pretty strong evidence that she's been selling off her collection piecemeal, probably over many years, to finance it. Dylan Redman realized the *Mirror Crack'd* painting was a forgery because he was an Agatha Christie aficionado. He knew the real one had been sold. He told Yana that—probably threatened to tell other collectors, too, if he didn't get the consignment. But she didn't want to be told what to do, diva that she is. So she poisoned his coffee and hid or destroyed the painting in case Dylan had a chance to tell anyone about it before he died."

"Whoa, there," Simon said. "Why would a ninety-year-old lady with no record have a stash of sodium fluoride on hand?"

Now Cindy was enjoying this. She liked Simon and wanted him and Jay to get together, but she was taking great joy in explaining his own case to him. It wouldn't do to have Jay's new boyfriend be smarter than her, after all. "Oh, but that's the genius of it," she said. "She was an actress. And she collected mementoes from her roles—the costumes, yes, but also anything that would help her get into the mind of the person she was going to inhabit."

Jay smiled grimly. "She had the poisons because that was how she prepared for films, what made her great. Like her story about wearing a nun's habit to a baseball game to get in character. And she played a lot of scheming, evil women—some of whom were poisoners. She probably studied sodium fluoride for a role she played—knew exactly how much would kill Dylan Redman and how little to use to put herself in the hospital without any serious risk of death. I'm sure it gave her some feeling of power, knowing that she had all that lethal poison just sitting back at her house. I have no doubt she used that for her roles. And it also allowed her to walk around a chauvinistic film industry with her head held high, knowing that she could sprinkle a dash of sodium fluoride in a sexist director's drink and be done with him if things ever went too far."

Simon nodded. "And sodium fluoride is a poison that would last forever."

"Yes," Cindy said. "Plus, don't forget that old postal mark. Remember how Yana played a mail carrier in a Hallmark movie in 2005? That's when she got it. How many people would have access to the equipment to do that? Probably no one involved in this case—other than a very method actress who once played a mail carrier."

Simon nodded, allowing both of them a look of admiration. “I definitely didn’t dive into her filmography all that deeply. I guess it’s a good thing I had two film buffs meddling in my case, after all.”

Jay turned back toward Yana, his gaze blazing with venom and fury. Cindy had never seen him like this before. It was traumatizing, honestly, and she knew she would remember this version of her best friend and former husband for the rest of her life.

“You never could bring yourself to get rid of those trinkets you bought for your method acting, could you, Yana? Your collection . . . well, you could sell that, because it was just transactional, wasn’t it? But your own props from your own roles? Those were personal. And I bet you liked having that poison sitting around, didn’t you? Did it make you feel powerful?”

Simon slid in front of Jay, blocking him from Yana’s gaze—or perhaps her from his—and deflecting the tension back onto him. “You’re saying she was planning to sell fake costumes,” Simon said. “Well, I don’t know much about costumes, but I know in art, people are always on the lookout for fakes. Sure, you might get away with it a couple of times, but—”

“Maybe,” Cindy said. “But the problem is, she has the provenance. If you have all of the original documentation to accompany well-done fakes, people will fall for it. Jay and I certainly did. When a seller has all those letters and invoices and costume department files, it doesn’t occur to buyers that they could be looking at fake pieces.”

She paused for breath. “Heck, Yana even had a letter from Elizabeth Taylor, gifting her the Agatha Christie painting. She sold the originals first because that was easy and risk-free. She probably sold them to dealers and pawn shops—took a discounted price because she was holding on to all the records pertaining to the provenance. That's why she sold the real ones but kept the original documents. If someone didn't believe her, she could just walk away, and she hadn't done anything illegal because *those* pieces were real. And the way pieces moved from studio backlots to collectors over many decades is so disorganized that pieces are sold all the time without provenance—as long as they appear real, which hers certainly did because they were. Then she planned to sell the fake ones later, which was easy to do because she had such meticulous documentation for the provenance. The perfect crime, really."

Simon looked over his shoulder at Yana, who slowly and silently sipped her tea. "That explains everything else too," he said. "Her son didn't want her to sell the collection because he knew—or suspected—that it contained fakes."

Cindy turned to Warren. He was expressionless, like his mother.

Simon continued: "He cared about her, and he didn't want her to get caught. So, he figured he'd deal with the mess after she died, and he'd have plausible deniability if he got caught, because they were his mother's forgeries. Ben Sinclair leaves when Dylan gets killed—and makes sure he's seen carrying costumes, probably ones Yana had given him as gifts—so that people will suspect him, but not be able to find him. But when the heat never turns up on him, there's no warrant for his arrest, and the investigation proceeds in another direction, he returns. Once Ben realized his absence couldn't save his idol, he figured his presence might."

At last Yana looked up. The regality of her bearing had returned. Cindy despised what Yana Tosh had done; it was pure, selfish evil. But all the same; a tiny part of her couldn't help but admire the old battle-ax staying strong as she faced her punishment. "My son and Ben," Yana said finally, "are the only two people I've ever really loved, other than my husband. They've loved me too. They'd do anything to help me."

"You said you loved me too," Jay said. "Remember our car ride, Yana? What was that about?"

The former starlet's face gave away no emotion. "It's like that line in *The Godfather*: *'It's not personal. It's strictly business.'* I wanted to build rapport with you. Needed you on my side." She paused. "Although I really did like you, Jay. Still do."

"You tried to kill my best friend!" Cindy yelled. "And you did that right after I just lost my wife. I'm reeling here, grieving every minute of every day—and then you try to take away from me the only person who's keeping me alive. You are *evil*."

Yana nodded. "At least I didn't try to kill you. You should be flattered!"

"You're an evil, manipulative hag," Jay spat, his eyes filling with tears.

There was silence in the room for a moment.

"You are, of course, correct," Yana continued, unmoved by Jay's emotion. "About all of this. I've been selling my treasures off over the years, but I couldn't bear to have holes in my closet, reminding me of what I once had. I was selling them to pawn shops and flea market dealers—not getting the kind of prices Cindy and Jay or Dylan's company would get, of course. But then, I didn't need to. I had enough money for my needs, and I sold the pieces without the provenance."

"You really were able to do that?" Simon asked.

"Yes. The actual pieces were authentic, so it wasn't risky—they weren't forgeries. If someone didn't believe me, I simply didn't sell things to them. I'd explain how I'd gotten the pieces and then just say the documents were lost. Usually that worked."

"And then you had copies made so you could still have them in your collection."

She shrugged. "That's right. So when the time came, I could sell them again—fake costumes, real provenance. It had been so long since I sold the originals that no one would have ever known. Pieces move around—there's nothing to connect them to me. Until that conniving idiot Dylan Redman spotted that *Mirror Crack'd* painting. What a coincidence: my undoing is a tiny, insignificant painting—none of the legendary costumes I sold and had duplicated were questioned. A painting from a B movie was my mistake."

"When did you get worried about Dylan knowing?" Cindy asked.

"He told me he knew when he met with me privately to discuss the sale. He threatened to tell people I was selling fakes if I didn't give him and his horrid colleague the collection to sell—at a very steep commission. He was blackmailing me, and Yana Tosh does not get blackmailed. So I dumped a little of my special powder into his coffee and sent him on his way. What else could I have done, really?"

"And then you poisoned yourself as a diversion?"

She smiled. "I poisoned the cupcake that wretch Eydie brought because I wanted her to be blamed for everything. I really do hate that woman. Honestly, my biggest regret about getting caught is that this won't be blamed on her."

"Did anyone else know what you did?" Simon asked.

"I really have no idea," said Yana. "If they did, they probably convinced themselves otherwise to protect me. And isn't that your job to figure out, anyway, Detective?"

Simon looked at Warren. "Did you know about this?"

"No," Yana's son said, his voice firm. Then he sighed. "But I suppose in the back of my mind, I suspected there was something wrong. I just . . . well, she's my mom. I didn't want to see it."

"Did Ben?"

"I can't imagine he did," Warren said. "For Ben, my mother could do no wrong."

"Okay," Simon said, "that's all the information I need for now. Ms. Tosh, we'll be taking you to the station. I'm not looking to humiliate you or anything like that—but you are under arrest, and you are going straight to booking."

Yana looked up at Simon, her teeth gritted, displaying her first flash of anger. "Yana Tosh," she said, with all the pride she could muster under the circumstances, "decides her own fate. And I decided it twenty minutes ago. I slipped it into my tea—even if it was a Lipton—once I saw that Cindy and Jay had figured it all out."

Cindy lunged across the room, pushing the mug onto the floor and shattering it. But it was empty.

"I already drank it, Cindy," Yana said, laughing. "I'm not so dumb I'd tell you about it before it was done. Give me a little credit—I almost got away with murder, after all. If you'll give me another ten minutes, perhaps twenty, I will die, and you can do as you like with me after that."

Simon pressed the emergency button by Yana's bed, then picked up the room phone and started to dial the nurse's station. A sharp sound from Yana interrupted him. "Don't bother," she said. "I know more about poison than you do. There's no antidote for this. It's over. Don't make them come here and do a pointless examination. I'd rather not be poked and prodded in my final moments. Just let me go with some measure of dignity, yes? Not the dignity I once thought I would leave with, but still—something. Some measure of who I was."

"We're going to do everything we can to save you," Simon said bullishly. "We have to."

Yana ignored him. "It's a shame that you figured this out, Cindy and Jay. I like you two, I really do. I wanted to give you the consignment. We could have made a lot of money together, and no one would have known. It could have launched your business."

"You tried to kill me!" Jay yelled. His voice broke, so rich with emotion that even Simon looked over with a pained expression. "You delivered a poisoned letter to our home! Mary could've *died*! I could've died!"

"Oh, come off it," Yana said. "If you know me as well as you claim to, you know that it wasn't about you."

Jay continued to shout. Cindy had never seen him so upset. "It sure felt personal when the police were explaining that a letter addressed to me almost killed someone very close to me and Cindy. An innocent older woman."

Yana nodded. "I'm sorry for that, truly. I was desperate. And if it makes you feel any better, you are about to have your revenge by watching me die. I believe that's called a full circle ending."

Jay's face was still red with rage, but now, to Cindy's confusion, there was a hint of a smile on his lips. "I have a little confession to make," he said. He looked at Yana. "Once I figured out what you'd done to Dylan and tried to do to me, I knew you probably still had more pills on you. While you were in the bathroom, I took your purse and replaced your sodium fluoride pills with my caffeine pills. I knew you were a coward, and I wasn't going to let you have the easy way out."

"Wow," Cindy said. "Just . . . wow." Somehow, no matter how well she knew Jay, he could still manage to surprise her.

"Quick thinking," Simon marveled. Jay reached into his pocket and extracted an envelope. He tossed it to Simon, who made a nice catch. "Can you maybe not toss around evidence?"

"I knew you'd catch it," Jay said.

Simon smiled, even if reluctantly. "What is this you just threw at me?"

"Those are the pills I took out of Yana's purse. Test them. I'm sure they're sodium fluoride. That'll be your proof. You can probably even catch me making the switch on the hospital's security camera."

"I have to admit," Simon said, "I'm impressed."

Cindy was enjoying the flirtation between Jay and Simon. She felt something like pride, watching her ex-husband win over a hunk. That had to be a very particular kind of feeling—she wondered how many other people knew what that emotion was like.

"So, Yana, you're not going anywhere other than to the station with Detective Fletcher." Jay grinned. "And you'll be *wired* when you get there."

The former starlet gave a huge, dramatic sigh—but there was a twinkle in her eye, Cindy thought. A sense of fair play, maybe, and a respect for Jay having outwitted her last, desperate effort to escape justice. Simon approached her bed, offering his arm.

"Now that you mention it," Yana said, unflappable as ever, "I do feel rather energetic. Is this your secret, Jay? Why you're so damn productive?"

Jay shook his head. "I was energized by you, Yana. Your excitement for your collection rubbed off on me. I'm sorry it had to end like this."

Yana smiled at him but said nothing.

"We'll go out the back door," Simon said. "I won't let any reporters see you."

Yana looked confused. "You're not mad at me?"

Simon shook his head. "Not my job, ma'am," he said. "The judgment, the punishment, and all the rest? That's for a jury and judge to decide."

Yana fluffed her hair—the snow-white wig she took so much pride in—and straightened her shoulders. She stood on her own, refusing Simon's help, and checked her reflection in the mirror by the door. "We'll go out the front door," she said, her voice as powerful as ever. "Yana Tosh does not avoid her audience."

A week later, order was finally restored, and Cindy had never been so relieved. Yana Tosh had immediately pleaded guilty to Dylan Redman's murder and seemed unlikely to ever live outside a prison again. Warren Limon, with his mother a confessed felon, hired Cindy and Jay to conduct an appraisal of the collection. Based on their new knowledge of the presence of fakes, they hired a forensic textile expert to evaluate the age of the pieces. His conclusion, based on a sampling of only ten percent of the collection, which included all of the most valuable pieces, was that very little of Yana Tosh's original collection was left. A collection once estimated to be valued in the millions was worth, at most, fifty thousand dollars. Of course, the news coverage had brought in offers from for-profit, tourist-trap horror museums for some of the fake pieces—but Warren respected his mother too much, wanting her to be remembered as the star she'd once been.

The loss of the consignment of a lifetime was a bitter disappointment for Cindy and Jay, but it came with a substantial consolation prize. The national news coverage calling them the "Hooray for Hollywood Movie Memorabilia Sleuths" who'd cracked a case that stumped the police was the best launch they could have asked for. Their phones and inboxes were inundated with interest from people who had collections they wanted to sell—and others who had never even realized decor and costumes featured in movies were a thing, but now couldn't stop thinking about buying something.

In the end, the business they'd lost from the Yana Tosh collection being fake was more than offset by the business that came in from the publicity around the murder of Dylan Redman. The biggest loss for Cindy still felt like, as dumb as it sounded, her friendship with Yana. But she'd come to a certain understanding about it. Yana Tosh was an addict, and addicts could be driven to desperation, their basic character and decency undermined by that awful disease. Yana had written several long apology letters to her and Jay, and while Cindy could never be sure, they seemed heartfelt. She wondered if she'd ever go visit Yana in prison. Probably not, she decided—but then considered the idea again. Coldness toward Yana couldn't bring anyone back from the dead or make everything else right again, but warmth and forgiveness were the two values she cherished above all others. If that made her a patsy and a born mark, so be it. It was the only way she ever wanted to be.

Cindy was just getting ready to close the store for the day and head home to meet Jay when a familiar face peeked into the store: Lenae Randolph.

"Do you have a minute?" the gossip reporter asked. Her tone was the most timid Cindy had ever heard it, and almost washed away the resentment she had about Lenae's decision to sell her and Jay out in favor of a partnership with Eydie. Perhaps, she thought, it wasn't a pure generosity of spirit that had her in a forgiving mood right now. With the consignment gone anyway, there was little reason to hold a grudge.

"Sure," she said. "Let me guess. You still want to do that profile of me and Jay?"

Lenae was silent for a moment. "I'd be happy to. But first, I wanted to explain a few things to you about my situation."

They sat down, Lenae in the chair from the set of *Whatever Happened to Baby Jane?* and Cindy in another director's chair, this one from the set of *The Andy Williams Show.* Both had recently sold online, and Cindy would be shipping them out the next day.

"I didn't mean to betray you," Lenae said.

"But you did anyway," Cindy said.

She sighed. "This isn't easy for me. I'm not a person who's spent a lot of time apologizing for things."

Cindy smiled. "If it helps, I forgive you anyway."

Lenae sighed again, clearly relieved. "Thank you. I was desperate for money, Cindy, and Eydie made me an offer I couldn't turn down. She offered me twenty percent of the commission from the sale, if we landed it—hundreds of thousands of dollars. And I needed it badly. Plus she gave me a new car as a bonus just for agreeing to do the pitch."

Cindy was sympathetic at first, then confused. "How could you be that desperate for money? You're a big star."

"It's my granddaughter," she said. "The one whose son handles my social media. She's been running the business for me, and she's had me on a very short leash financially. I made all of these charitable commitments when things really started to take off with the website and the TV shows—but then, when the checks started coming, it was a pittance. A tiny fraction of what I'd thought it would be. At first I thought it was just because the business wasn't making as much as I'd expected, but then my great-grandson did some digging for me. His mother was keeping most of the revenue and not telling me."

"Oh, Lenae," Cindy said, "I'm so sorry."

"So, you see, I was desperate. Not for money for myself—I'm fine with the way I live, though I was happy to take the car upgrade when Eydie offered it to sweeten the pot. But I was into all of those things back in the '70s, and then . . . I realized how little any of it mattered. The most joy I get from money is when I give it to someone else. I want to be generous with the charities I care about. But now, I don't know what to do. It's my money, and I'm entitled to it."

Cindy pulled a pen out of her pocket but couldn't find a piece of paper. She went behind the counter to the register and pressed a key to make the receipt tape run a bit. Then she pulled it off and scribbled a phone number on it.

"I want you to call my former partner at my financial advisory firm," she said. "Tell her you're a friend of mine and that I said to take care of everything, no charge. She can go through all your information and make sure you're in the best setup. It might be as simple as an honest conversation with your granddaughter about what you're owed."

Lenae took the piece of paper and frowned. "I just hate the idea of conflict with my family, but it looks like I don't have a choice. I'd thought a little under-the-table money from Eydie would fix everything—I'd have enough to take care of the things I needed to take care of, and I wouldn't have to fight with my granddaughter. Lord, I sound like such an idiot. Lenae Randolph, tough-as-nails reporter, ready to spar with anyone except family. And I thought I had a solution to avoid it. But I guess there's no shortcut to anywhere worth going, is there?"

Cindy smiled as Lenae left—sad for her situation but in a way relieved that there was such a sympathetic explanation for what had seemed like a profound and personal betrayal. Then she thought of Eydie, a greedy, unscrupulous little piece of work if ever there was one—roping Lenae into a devious plot, flirting with Warren, all to try to get a consignment. Cindy tried not to indulge thoughts of revenge, but she loved that Eydie was back at her Cypress office, with absolutely no consignment to show for all her scheming. She hoped she'd never see the little tramp again. On the other hand, if she was going to stay in the memorabilia business . . . Eydie would be a competitor for a long time to come.

* * *

At eight o'clock sharp on Friday night, Cindy heard Simon pull into the driveway of the house. She'd been listening to Jay perseverate over the upcoming date for weeks, and now the day had finally arrived.

As Cindy had suspected, the "two Fridays from now" date had indeed put them free and clear of any outstanding homicide charges. He and Simon had spent dozens of texts going back and forth on possible restaurant choices. Jay had shown her each one and then gone over how to respond, like they were in junior high school again.

In the end, there was only one possibility for a first date that made sense to Jay: a date at home with Cindy and Bob Hope and Mae West. Cindy was honored. Jay told her that no matter how much Simon might come to mean to him, Simon would never be more than equal to Cindy in importance in Jay's life. Cindy felt the same way. If she ever did fall in love again, she knew it would never mean more to her than her relationships with Jay and Mary, and her memories of Esther. She liked that.

When Simon walked in, Jay was sitting at the dining room table with Cindy, Mae West on his lap. The cat purred softly, on the brink of falling asleep.

Simon smiled. "Do not," he said, "get up. Cats come first."

Jay laughed. "Good start." They sat around the dining room table, talking and drinking the sangria Jay had made. After about ten minutes, Mae West scurried off Jay's lap and over to the windowsill. She settled by the air conditioner, enjoying the change in moisture as her fur cooled off, staring down the occasional bird through the moonlit window.

When Jay got up to bring out the plates of seafood, prepared based on a book of recipes from the cast of *Murder, She Wrote*, Bob Hope joined them at the table. The dog was clearly hoping for a snack.

Mae West came back over from the window and curled up by Jay's feet, more interested in him than the food.

"That's a pretty special cat you have," Simon said, scooping some of the shrimp linguini onto his plate.

Jay nodded. "I don't know what I'd do without her."

"And I don't know what I would have done without you," Simon said. He paused awkwardly, like he was aware of what he'd said and wasn't sure he regretted it. "On the case, I mean. I like to think I would have gotten there eventually, but you and Cindy really did put it all together."

"Oh, you'd have figured it out," Jay said.

"In my defense, it was my first homicide case," Simon said.

"It was? You never told us that!" Cindy said.

Simon blushed. Cindy liked that. It was cute, seeing a gruff and macho detective like him embarrassed. "It's not exactly something you brag about to possible suspects." He made his voice unnaturally deep and spoke in a mocking tone. "Excuse me, sir. You're a suspect, but this is my first murder case, so you have absolutely nothing to worry about."

Jay laughed. "Well, you were wrong to suspect us, and we did have nothing to worry about. Also, there is a significant problem with your excuse that you couldn't solve it because it was your first murder case."

"Oh?" Simon said. "What's that?"

"It was our first murder case too," Jay said. "Cindy and I are a regular Rizzoli and Isles."

Simon smiled. "That's still an improvement from the Bonnie and Clyde I worried you two might be when we first met."

They drank and laughed and ate late into the night, taking turns getting up to choose a new record for the hi-fi in the living room. They started with the traditional dinner fare—Frank and Ella, Bing and Louis. But as the night wore on, Cindy watched as Jay cut loose and took a chance: He switched to Barry Manilow's "Copacabana." To her shock, that was when Simon really got into the music, singing along with the absurd lyrics like it was 1978 in the world's campiest disco.

"Oh, God," Cindy said. "You like Manilow too. If you end up spending a lot of time here, I'm going to have to enforce a moratorium on that man's music."

"There'll be two fans instead of one," Simon said, "so Jay will get to listen to him twice as often."

"That's not how this works!" Cindy said. "That's not how any of this works!"

"I'm in law enforcement," Simon said. "And I say that's the law." He and Jay high-fived.

"'Looks like we made it!'" Jay belted out, quoting another Manilow hit.

Cindy laughed. With all they'd been through together—marriage, a dream career, the end of that career and the end of the marriage, and then Hooray for Hollywood and Yana

Tosh—arguing with Jay about Barry Manilow had been one of the few constants.

It was a good omen, Cindy thought, how Simon seemed to fit almost seamlessly into their lives. It was nothing like what she and Jay had envisioned on their wedding day all those years ago. But in its own way, her life with Jay was better than anything she could have hoped for without Esther.

As if reading her mind, Jay looked her way.

"I wish Esther were here with us," he said.

Cindy was silent for a moment—overcome with feeling, that presence of endless love that had been in her heart since the first time she'd met Esther. "She is, Jay," she said. "And she says we're the best darn detective duo since Columbo and his dog."

"But which of us is which?"

Cindy grinned. She'd almost forgotten what it was like to smile so broadly. "Esther wouldn't say."

Author's Note about the World of Hollywood Memorabilia

I had this idea that I wanted to include an interview with a top dealer in Hollywood memorabilia at the back of this book—so that readers could learn a little about how it works and what's hot and what's not, from an expert instead of from a debut novelist looking stuff up on Wikipedia. I asked a few people in the antiques world who I should talk to, and everyone mentioned the same name: Joseph Maddalena, founder of Profiles in History, where he spent thirty-five years building the largest Hollywood memorabilia auction house in the world before becoming executive vice president at Heritage Auctions.

If Jay and Cindy were real, they'd be a lot like Maddalena.

When we spoke, the first thing he told me was that he'd read the description of my book on the publisher's website—and had thoughts about the plot.

"It's totally plausible," he said. "These people are crazy. You have some old lady with a collection no one's seen in Palm Springs, and get a couple dealers competing for it? Someone could hypothetically end up dead, absolutely. This memorabilia is an obsession. People covet it. It's not like any other collectibles category. There's a passion, an intensity that's different."

"Why?" I asked him.

"It's nostalgia," he said. "These objects give people a connection with these Hollywood stars. It's what movies do: they transport you somewhere, and then having the objects takes that to another level. If you have Dorothy's ruby slippers [which Maddalena once sold for more than two million dollars], what else do you need? It's the ultimate symbol of hope. That's the thing, to be able to have that moment. It's magic."

As Maddalena explains it, the hobby of Hollywood memorabilia collecting rose out of the ashes of the collapse of the studio system. With stars' salaries exploding once they were no longer the property of a single company, cash flows at the studios dried up. Twentieth Century Fox sold its backlot to Alcoa to raise money and then, in 1970, MGM sold the contents of its seven sound stages to a small auction house for just $1.5 million. That price included more than three hundred and fifty thousand costumes and countless props from the most iconic films in cinema history.

"From the ashes of the industry," Maddalena said, "our hobby creates itself. It started out with the ruby slippers. This guy, Kent Warner, was hired to help with the sale, but he just took the job because he wanted the ruby slippers. He found three pairs, stole one, and from then on it was decades of about a dozen conniving people, led by Debbie Reynolds, who were all backstabbing and stealing from each other to try to get stuff."

Memorabilia dealers are also detectives—constantly vetting authenticity and, even when pieces are definitely from *something*, figuring out what exactly they're from can be a years-long challenge.

A few years ago, an antiques picker came into Maddalena's office with a spaceship—about two feet tall, made from hand-tooled aluminum, with studio tags on it, probably from the 1950s.

"It's Flash Gordon's ship," the man said.

"I don't think it is," said Maddalena, but it looked familiar. So he pulled up a copy of one of the Flash Gordon movies and watched it. The spaceship wasn't from the film, but Maddalena bought it anyway, having no idea what it was, but suspecting it was something.

"I had this thing sitting on the floor in my office for four years. Then this guy comes in, takes one look at it, and says, 'That's from *Superman and the Mole Men*,'" a 1951 film starring George Reeves and Phyllis Coates. Maddalena watched the movie, and there it was.

"It went from being worth nothing to worth $50,000. All because some guy came in and knew what movie it was. That's the thing about this stuff I'm always amazed at: These movies are life to people, and they'll see some object and be transported, and they'll know exactly what it is."

As for what collectors are most excited about today: "What's driving the hobby is science fiction, fantasy, and horror: *Dracula, Frankenstein, The Mummy, Star Wars, Blade Runner, Indiana Jones*. Things that were twenty thousand to thirty thousand dollars seven or eight years ago are now two hundred thousand to three hundred thousand dollars. Stuff from *Gladiator* is also popular. A Russell Crowe Maximus costume is one hundred thousand to two hundred thousand dollars. It's the *Spartacus* of our time."

Good news for bargain-hunting value investors: the beginning of Hollywood has fallen badly out of favor. "W. C. Fields, Jean Harlow, Rudolf Valentino, Fatty Arbuckle, even Charlie Chaplin—there's very little demand. There was a time when you could get five thousand dollars for an eleven-by-fourteen custom print of Jean Harlow. That photograph now is five hundred dollars. Gene Autry, Hopalong Cassidy—worthless. War movies, westerns—nobody cares. Maybe there'll be a resurgence. Even Humphrey Bogart is fading into obscurity."

For an entry-level collector, vintage movie posters are a good place to start. Every Sunday, Heritage Auctions does an online poster sale, with prices starting at one dollar, and movies from the 1920s through today. A shooting script for *Butch Cassidy and the Sundance Kid*, used by an actor on the set, is also a bargain at three hundred to four hundred dollars.

And if you are looking to allocate more capital to it, Maddalena has good news.

"I'm selling things for six and seven figures all the time—really deep pockets, lots of people collecting. People kill for this stuff."

Acknowledgments

First a word about cozy writers: They're the kindest people I've ever encountered. They're as sweet as their books make them seem. In particular, I want to thank: Jenn McKinlay, Tamara Lush, Kate Carlisle, Dean James, Ellen Byron, Victoria Gilbert, Sherry Harris, Lisa Matthews, and JC Kenney. Your books delight me and each one I read makes me a little better at writing, and I look forward to reading many more.

For her expertise on poisons: Luci Hansson Zahray, aka The Poison Lady.

Kim Powers: The best first reader in the world, and an inspiringly nice person.

For getting this out there: John Michael Darga, David Kuhn, Toni Kirkpatrick, Rebecca Nelson, Dulce Botello, Madeline Rathle, Dana Kaye, Katelynn Dreyer, Hailey Dezort.

At the office: Steve Schurr, Matt Caltabiano, Cherri Wang, and Sam Millham.

And of course, Ryan: And I love you so . . .